S0-BDQ-311

EFFERVESCENT AND MILDLY ADDICTIVE—READING GRONOW IS LIKE DRINKING CHAMPAGNE

PREMIÈRES DANSEUSES AND THEIR ADMIRERS—THE GREEN ROOM OF THE OPERA HOUSE (KINGS THEATRE), 1822

EARL OF FIFE   MDLLE MERCANDOTTI   MDLLE NOBLET

THE LAST RECOLLECTIONS OF CAPTAIN GRONOW

In this volume of Gronow's reminiscences we meet Byron and Brummel, the Duke of Wellington, the outrageous Dan Mackinnon, the habitues of Almacks and the army of the Peninsula. There are amusing descriptions of life in Paris, French manners and French cooking ("It suits the French; but it would never do in England.") and Gronow gives a first hand account of the coup d'etat of 1851. He returns often to his favourite themes of the Napoleonic wars and Regency London and there is a full supporting cast, drawn from both the beau monde and the demi-monde, of emperors, actresses, dandies, lunatics, etc, including some "shocking bad hats".

Take a Gronow anecdote after lunch, two before dinner and not more than six or seven at bed-time.

The R.S. Surtees Society's edition combines in a single volume Gronow's "Celebrities of London and Paris" and "Last Recollections." It is based on the limited edition of 1889 and includes the 12 full-page coloured plates of that edition.

Price **£13.95** (including packing and postage) until 1st December, 1985. Thereafter the price will be £14.95.

Instructions for ordering are on page 323.

PLAIN

or

RINGLETS

Miss Rosa McDermott was on the make. She had two admirers. One was best pleased when her hair was dressed plain, the other preferred it in ringlets. So there were changes of style while Mamma made financial investigations—and there was an exciting moment when both Miss and Mamma had hopes of the Marquess of Marchhare.

The description of Brighton ("Roseberry Rocks") at the beginning of the railway age is most entertaining. (Surtees had been a frequent visitor since the 1820s and died there in 1864.) It includes a vivid account of a race meeting and the fleecing of a banker's foolish son.

There are three first rate hunting characters—Jock Haggish, probably drawn from the Duke of Buccleuch's huntsman Williamson, and Jovey Jessop and his Jug. Jovey Jessop was an excellent fellow and an excellent M.F.H. but he suffered from too much hospitality, mostly his own. He had a shock when he consulted a London specialist. So the Jug came to live with him to take the brunt of the drinking.

The R.S. Surtees Society's edition of *Plain or Ringlets?* which it is intended shall be available by the end of **March, 1986,** will reproduce in colour the 13 full-page hand-coloured plates from the first (1860) edition, printed from engravings on steel by **John Leech.** Sets of these plates will be available separately. The text will be a facsimile of the first edition, slightly enlarged, and will include 45 black and white illustrations, also by **John Leech.**

The cover will have the same pictorial stampings as the first edition. In size and format *Plain or Ringlets?* will be similar to the Society's earlier Surtees publications. **Molly Keane** has agreed to write an Introduction.

Pre-publication prices

For those who subscribe for *Plain or Ringlets?* **before 1st December, 1985:**

(a) **£10.75** for books which are collected and

(b) **£12.70** (including p. & p.) for books which are posted.

A list of those subscribing **before 1st December, 1985,** will be printed at the end of the book.

The post-publication price will be £14.95.

Subscribers collecting their books will be notified when they are available at J. A. Allen & Co., 1 Lower Grosvenor Place, Buckingham Palace Road, London S.W.1.

Instructions for ordering are on page 323.

EDITH ŒNONE SOMERVILLE AND MARTIN ROSS

Edith Œnone Somerville and Martin Ross were born more than a hundred years ago. Their genius was a joint heritage. In each of them a line went back to one of Ireland's wisest and most brilliant servants, Charles Kendal Bushe, Chief Justice of Ireland, known as "Silver tongued Bushe". Two distant halves of a gifted family met in these cousins, their brains complemented one the other. When two such intellects meet, and find a medium in which they can work together, a companionship as happy as any love affair must follow. The liberty of innocence was an aspect of the age they lived in.

Brilliant as Edith was, and a gifted painter, she could sometimes over-paint in words. The pure direction of phrase is occasionally complicated by too many currents of meaning. Martin's restraint filed humour down to a blade of wit. While she lived, and they worked together, there was never the lush word, or a descriptive phrase too many.

Brilliance can by-pass a generation; it is our priceless heritage that it shone out so gloriously in the writings of these cousins. Of all their writings, with the exception of that miraculous novel *The Real Charlotte*, the *Irish R.M.* has the most astringent quality; at other times we are toppled through disaster into a helpless revel of laughter.

Although their families were connected and had the same background of the landed Irish gentry, there was no ambience of familiarity in their childhood or early youth. Edith has written: "When we first met each other we were, as we thought, well stricken in years. That is to say, she was a little over twenty and I was four years older than she. Not absolutely in the earliest morning of life. . . ."

Literature, languages, music were the importances of a well-bred girl's education at that date. But it did not follow that the vast days of leisure, lolling wide for the daughters at home, were empty of interests and occupations. Vast as these leisured spaces look to us now, then they were filled with family obligations and duties that often kept the cousins apart, even when the joint work demanded their companionship.

Martin lived in the clutches and demands of the great family house, Ross, in Co. Galway, to which she and her mother had made a brave return after a difficult and enforced absenteeism. Edith's whole life was spent in the lusher, easier environment of Castle Townshend, in West Cork, where established families of Somervilles, Coghills and Chavasses lived in a happy and close society.

It is difficult now to envisage those times when a long day's hunting, shooting over miles of unpoached bog and mountain, or fishing when rivers were preserved inviolate, formed the very stuff and business of life. Equally, they were its pleasures. That the families of those days lived for pleasure only is not true. They carried heavy responsibilities towards their tenants and employees. More livelihoods than the landlord's were involved in the maintenance of those estates, now so few, and so dismembered.

An arid feeling of regret, and a great curiosity can possess one today, passing pillared entrance gates opening, or rather shutting, onto a raised, grass-grown track through fields, once a tree-grown avenue leading to a house, not the ghost of which is left.

Edith Somerville and Martin Ross were young when the dust on these drives was raised and tracks were worn by the wheels of dog carts, phaetons, wagonettes and side cars. (My mother would have said: "the car". Never side-car, somehow a non-u word.) I know a house where a man was employed for the sole duty of sweeping cattle and horse manure off the unfenced surfaces so that the ladies of the house might take their walks with clean boots, and carriages be free from spatterings as they bowled on their ways. One can nearly hear the lively sounds of fresh horses hacking on over-night to a strange stable and a distant meet of the hounds, to return, perhaps by moonlight, the different rhythm of their tired jog changing and quickening as they neared their own loose-box, deep in straw.

The books we love were written when these times were living and there was no thought of their mortality. In them we can realise the social relationships; the stratas of society; the differences in the language spoken by the upper and the middle classes—differences that exist no longer. More valuable is their understanding of the peasant people. They were their fellows in sport and their equals in wit. And for the language then spoken Edith and Martin had a perfect ear and memory. We must be grateful that they have immortalised that language—the native Irish speech, translated down the centuries since the Elizabethan English. The apt poetry of everyday talk is now sadly diminished by radio and television. But Somerville and Ross did not have to discover the atmosphere they wrote in. They were as much a part of it as was the air they breathed.

In the years before motor-cars families were rooted in their properties for long periods of time; and guests stayed for very long periods of time, as was natural when a journey from Galway to West Cork could take almost two days and many changes of trains to accomplish. Entertainment was dependent on the local sources available for boy to meet girl. So, in the summer months, it was lawn tennis on grass courts; boating and fishing on lakes when the trout rose to the Mayfly; sailing on dangerous coasts; much music, and shameless amateur singing; after dinner waltzing to the piano in the drawing-room; strict reading—our grandmothers were far more familiar with the classics than ourselves. Plays were staged, charades were frequent. Above all, there was conversation. A talent to amuse was beyond price. Perhaps it was from that seed that the *R.M.* derived.

Of all sports and pleasures, to the horse and the hound was owed the most absolute and unqualified support and allegiance. The education of younger sons was unhesitatingly sacrificed to the upkeep of the Family Pack. This accounted for the descending echelons of second and third cousinhoods. The classic example of this subgentry class, comparable only with Facey Romford, is Flurry Knox, every side of whose scintillating character is exploited with indulgent appreciation and affection in the *R.M.*

The other personality living on for ever is that of old Mrs. Knox of Aussolas: a scholar, classical in her allusions and sharp-witted past defeat in repartee who, in her youth (well endowed one supposes) had married a gentleman, unattractively named "Old Badger Knox", only to save the Hounds.

Less important characters receive the same scrupulous and inspired attention from their originators. A short story, "How I first met Dr. Hickey", has a Chekovian brevity, an economy of adjectives and a dry line in entertainment that exceeds many of the more robust epics of disaster, glorious as they are.

In their writing on Fox Hunting they are unequalled except by Surtees, and sometimes by that seldom-quoted sage of an earlier date, "Scrutator". Trollope is not in their class. Their intimate observation can share in the meanest dilemma of the chase: "The amateur Huntsman nervously uplifting his voice in falsetto encouragement, feeling much as if he was starting the solo of an anthem," has our total sympathy. But from such moments they can take us on to the heart of the matter;

through trial and disaster to a rhapsody on the most sublime exhilaration granted to the luckier of mankind. Perhaps, even because, he was an amateur in the Hunting Field Major Yeates can put into words that seizure of excitement which can translate even into ecstasy. . . .

"What followed was, I am told, a very fast fifteen minutes; for me, time was not; the empty fields rushed past uncounted, fences came and went in a flash, while the wind sang in my ears, and the dazzle of a morning sun was in my eyes. I saw the hounds occasionally, sometimes pouring over a green bank, as the charging breaker lifts and flings itself, sometimes driving across a field as the white tongues of foam slide racing over the sand; and always ahead of me was Flurry Knox, going as a man goes who knows his country, who knows his horse, whose heart is wholly and absolutely in the right place." Although they keep strictly within the bounds and the language proper to the account of such a run, it is as if a poet had got between the lines that describe it.

They skirt love like a skirting hound a covert. With the exception of that tragic Tolstoyan figure Francie in *The Real Charlotte* their heroines are curiously calm, sane and sober, and often dissolved in laughter: like themselves. Laughter, the inversion of the expected, is in the very bones of their writing; laughter with a bite of satire, as laughter was the touchstone in their collaboration which, Edith writes, was done conversationally: "One or other—not infrequently both simultaneously—would state a proposition. This would be argued, combatted, perhaps approved, or modified. It would be written down ... scratched out, scribbled in again, before finally transferred to decorous manuscript."

This seems a light-weight description of the clarity and closeness of their work. Possibly some of the success of this unparalleled collaboration was owing to the fact that the authors shared an identical background, enjoyed the same jokes and pleasures, the same delight in their country, the same critical appreciation of its discomforts and inconveniences. They were more than in love with a beautiful day, with the cry of hounds, or the absurd endearing ways of a little dog.

While the Flurrys, the Mrs. Cadogans, the Slippers have their personalities taken apart and displayed unsparingly for our astonished interest and delight, their own class and kind suffer equally under the scalpel of their understanding. The pleasant fools and stooges of all time, such as Bernard Shute, are set far apart from Major Yeates, who wears his own hair-shirt of discomfort and ridicule with a quiet and sober dignity. The greatest clowns are serious in their absurdities. In his splendid tolerance and understanding of the many uses and villainies to which he has been subject he stands inviolate in his own humour and tolerance. Though he suffers all things, he is no stooge, but the unsung hero of his Experiences.

It is the strength of their writing that in it they apportion neither praise nor blame but, with a genius withstanding time and surpassing fashion, they make us see and hear, laugh and live again in those days which, through their writing, are no longer nostalgic shadows from the past but as clear for us as when they wrote of the adventures, disasters, defeats and delights experienced by Major Sinclair Yeates. Beyond and above all they have given us the share we own in the wonderful fun these two very wonderful ladies knew how to enjoy and how to bequeath.

MOLLY KEANE

Dysert, Ardmore, Co. Waterford
  March 1983

IN MR. KNOX'S COUNTRY

"If ever you see hounds pointing this way, don't spare spurs
to get to the cliff before them!"

[Page 4.]

In Mr. Knox's Country

By

E. Œ. Somerville and Martin Ross

Authors of "Some Experiences of an Irish R.M.," "Further
Experiences of an Irish R.M.," "Some Irish Yesterdays,"
"All on the Irish Shore," "Dan Russel the Fox,"
"The Real Charlotte," etc. etc. etc.

With 8 Illustrations by E. Œ. Somerville

THE R.S. SURTEES SOCIETY

THE R.S. SURTEES SOCIETY

First published in this edition in 1985 by
The R.S. Surtees Society

Rockfield House
Nunney
Nr. Frome, Somerset

© This Edition and Compilation
The R.S. Surtees Society, 1985
ISBN 0 948560 00 2

Printed in Great Britain by
Redwood Press Limited
Melksham, Wiltshire

CONTENTS

LIST OF ILLUSTRATIONS

IN MR. KNOX'S COUNTRY

I

THE AUSSOLAS MARTIN CAT

Flurry Knox and I had driven some fourteen miles to a tryst with one David Courtney, of Fanaghy. But, at the appointed cross-roads, David Courtney was not. It was a gleaming morning in mid-May, when everything was young and tense and thin and fit to run for its life, like a Derby horse. Above us was such of the spacious bare country as we had not already climbed, with nothing on it taller than a thorn-bush from one end of it to the other. The hill-top blazed with yellow furze, and great silver balls of cloud looked over its edge. Nearly as white were the little white-washed houses that were tucked in and out of the grey rocks on the hill-side.

"It's up there somewhere he lives," said Flurry, turning his cart across the road; "which'll you do, hold the horse or go look for him?"

I said I would go to look for him. I mounted

the hill by a wandering bohireen resembling nothing so much as a series of bony elbows; a white-washed cottage presently confronted me, clinging, like a sea-anemone, to a rock. I knocked at the closed door, I tapped at a window held up by a great, speckled foreign shell, but without success. Climbing another elbow, I repeated the process at two successive houses, but without avail. All was as deserted as Pompeii, and, as at Pompeii, the live rock in the road was worn smooth by feet and scarred with wheel tracks.

An open doorway faced me; I stooped beneath its lintel and asked of seeming vacancy if there were "anyone inside." There was no reply. I advanced into a clean kitchen, with a well-swept earthen floor, and was suddenly aware of a human presence very close to me.

A youngish woman, with a heavy mop of dark hair, and brown eyes staring at the opposite wall, was sitting at the end of a settle behind the door. Every bit of her was trembling. She looked past me as if I did not exist. Feeling uncertain as to whether she or I were mad, I put to her my question as to where David Courtney lived, without much expectation of receiving an answer.

Still shaking from head to foot, and without turning her eyes, she replied:

Kitty the Shakes.

"A small piece to the north. The house on the bare rock."

The situation showed no symptom of expansion; I faltered thanks to her profile and returned to Flurry.

The house of David Courtney produced David Courtney's large and handsome wife, who told us that Himself was gone to a funeral, and all that was in the village was gone to it, but there was a couple of the boys below in the bog.

"What have they done with those cubs?" asked Flurry.

Mrs. Courtney shot at him a dark-blue side-glance, indulgent and amused, and, advancing to the edge of her rock terrace, made a trumpet of her hands and projected a long call down the valley.

"Mikeen! Con! Come hither!"

From a brown patch in the green below came a far-away response, and we presently saw two tall lads coming towards us, running up the hill as smoothly and easily as a couple of hounds. Their legs were bare and stained with bog-mould, they were young and light and radiant as the May weather.

I did not withhold my opinion of them from their proprietor.

"Why, then, I have six more as good as

3

them!" replied Mrs. Courtney, her hands on her hips.

We took the horse from the shafts and pushed him, deeply suspicious, into a darksome lair, in one corner of which glimmered a pale object, either pig or calf. When this was done we followed Mikeen and Con up through blossoming furze and blue-grey rock to the ridge of the hill, and there came face to face with the vast blue dazzle of the Atlantic, with a long line of cliffs standing it off, in snowy lather, as far as eye could follow them into the easterly haze.

" That's the cliff over-right you now," said one of the boys, pointing downwards, with a hand dark with bog-stuff, to a grey and green wedge thrust out into the blue. " It's there where she have her den. She have a pat' down for herself in it—it's hardly a bird could walk it—the five pups was following her, and two o' them rolled down into the strand, and our dogs held them. Ourselves was below in the cove gathering seaweed."

" Make a note of it now, Major," said Flurry, " and if ever you see hounds pointing this way, don't spare spurs to get to the cliff before them!"

" Why don't you get them out and blow up the place?"

" Is it get them out of that hole!" said one of

4

the boys. "If all the foxes in Europe was inside in it you couldn't get them out!"

"We mightn't want them either," said Flurry, his eye ranging the face of the cliff, and assimilating its uncompromising negations.

"Then there's plenty that would!" returned Mikeen, looking at us with an eye as blue and bright as the sea. "There was a man east here that cot a fox and her five young ones in the one night, and he got three half-crowns for every lad o' them!"

"He'd be turned out of hell for doing that," said Flurry, very severely.

We went back to the cottage on the rock, and the matter entered upon its more serious phase. I took no part in the negotiations, and employed myself in converse with Mrs. Courtney, who—it may not be out of place to recall—informed me, amongst other domestic details, that the farm wouldn't carry all the children she had, and that nowadays, when the ger'rls would be going to America, it's white nightdresses and flannelette nightdresses she should give them; and further, that she thought, if she lived to be as old as a goat, she'd never see them so tasty.

On the way home I asked Flurry what he was going to do with the two cubs, now immured in a market basket under the seat of the dog-cart.

Flurry was ambiguous and impenetrable; there were certain matters in which Flurry trusted nobody, knowing the darkness of his own heart and the inelasticity of other people's points of view.

"That woman, you know, that told you the way," he remarked, with palpable irrelevance, "'Kitty the Shakes,' they call her—they say she mightn't speak to anyone once in three months, and she shakes that way then. It's a pity that was the house you went into first."

"Why so?" said I.

"That's the why!" said Flurry.

It was during the week following this expedition that Philippa and I stayed for a few days at Aussolas, where Flurry and Mrs. Flurry were now more or less permanently in residence. The position of guest in old Mrs. Knox's house was one often fraught with more than the normal anxieties proper to guests. Her mood was like the weather, a matter incalculable and beyond control; it governed the day, and was the *leit motif* in the affairs of the household. I hope that it may be given to me to live until my mood also is as a dark tower full of armed men.

On the evening of our arrival my wife, whose

perception of danger is comparable only to that of the wild elephant, warned me that Mrs. Knox was rheumatic, and that I was on no account to condole with her. Later on the position revealed itself. Mrs. Knox's Dublin doctor had ordered her to Buxton with as little delay as possible; furthermore, she was to proceed to Brighton for the summer, possibly for the winter also. She had put Aussolas on a house agent's books, "out of spite," Flurry said sourly; "I suppose she thinks I'd pop the silver, or sell the feather beds."

It was a tribute to Mrs. Knox's character that her grandson treated her as a combatant in his own class, and did not for an instant consider himself bound to allow her weight for either age or sex.

At dinner that night Mrs. Knox was as favourable to me as usual; yet it was pointed out to me by Mrs. Flurry that she was wearing two shawls instead of one, always an indication to be noted as a portent of storm. At bridge she played a very sharp-edged game, in grimness scarcely mitigated by two well-brought-off revokes on the part of Philippa, who was playing with Flurry; a gross and unprincipled piece of chivalry on my wife's part that was justly resented by Mr. Knox.

Next morning the lady of the house was invisible, and Mullins, her maid, was heard to lament to an unknown sympathiser on the back stairs that the divil in the wild woods wouldn't content her.

In the grove at Aussolas, on a height behind the castle, romantically named Mount Ida, there is a half-circle of laurels that screens, with pleasing severity, an ancient bench and table of stone. The spot commands a fair and far prospect of Aussolas Lake, and, nearer at hand, it permitted a useful outlook upon the kitchen garden and its affairs. When old Mrs. Knox first led me thither to admire the view, she mentioned that it was a place to which she often repaired when the cook was on her trail with enquiries as to what the servants were to have for dinner.

Since our expedition to Fanaghy the glory of the weather had remained unshaken, and each day there was a shade of added warmth in the sunshine and a more caressing quality in the wind. Flurry and I went to Petty Sessions in the morning, and returned to find that Mrs. Knox was still in her room, and that our respective wives were awaiting us with a tea-basket in the classic shades of Mount Ida. Mrs. Knox had that mysterious quality of attraction given to some persons, and some dogs, of forming a social

vortex into which lesser beings inevitably swim ;
yet I cannot deny that her absence induced a
sneaking sensation of holiday. Had she been
there, for example, Mrs. Flurry would scarcely
have indicated, with a free gesture, the luxuriance
of the asparagus beds in the kitchen garden below,
nor promised to have a bundle of it cut for us
before we went home ; still less would she and
Philippa have smoked cigarettes, a practice considered by Mrs. Knox to be, in women, several
degrees worse than drinking.

To us there, through the green light of young
beech leaves and the upstriking azure glare of
myriads of bluebells, came the solid presence of
John Kane. It would be hard to define John
Kane's exact status at Aussolas ; Flurry had once
said that, whether it was the house, or the garden,
or the stables, whatever it'd be that you wanted
to do, John Kane'd be in it before you to hinder
you ; but that had been in a moment of excus-
able irritation, when John Kane had put a padlock
on the oat loft, and had given the key to Mrs.
Knox.

John Kane now ascended to us, and came to
a standstill, with his soft black hat in his hands ;
it was dusty, so were his boots, and the pockets
of his coat bulked large. Among the green
drifts and flakes of the pale young beech leaves

his bushy beard looked as red as a squirrel's tail.

"I have the commands here, Master Flurry," he began, "and it's to yourself I'd sooner give them. As for them ger'rls that's inside in the kitchen, they have every pup in the place in a thrain at the back door, and, if your tobacco went asthray, it's me that would be blemt."

"The commands"—*i.e.* some small parcels —were laid on the stone table, minor pockets yielded an assortment of small moneys that were each in turn counted and placed in heaps by their consort parcels.

"And as for the bottle, the misthress wrote down for me," said John Kane, his eye rounding up his audience like a sheep-dog, "I got me 'nough with the same bottle. But sure them's the stupidest people in Hennessy's! 'Twas to Hennessy himself I gave the misthress's paper, and he was there looking at it for a while. 'What have she in it?' says he to me. 'How would I know,' says I, 'me that have no learning?' He got the spy-glass to it then, and 'twas shortly till all was in the shop was gethered in it looking at it. 'Twould take an expairt to read it!' says one fella—— "

"True for him!" said Flurry.

"—— 'She have written it in Latin!' says

Hennessy. 'Faith she's able to write it that way, or anny other way for yee!' says I. 'Well, I'll tell ye now what ye'll do,' says Hennessy. 'There's a boy in the Medical Hall, and he's able to read all languages. Show it to him,' says he. I showed it then to the boy in the Medical Hall. Sure, the very minute he looked at it—'Elliman's Embrocation,' says he." John Kane waved his hand slightly to one side; his gestures had throughout been supple and restrained. "Sure them's the stupidest people in Hennessy's!"

My sympathies were with the house of Hennessy; I, too, had encountered Mrs. Knox's handwriting, and realised the high imaginative and deductive qualities needed in its interpreter. No individual word was decipherable, but, with a bold reader, groups could be made to conform to a scheme based on probabilities.

"You can tell the mistress what they were saying at Hennessy's about her," said Flurry.

"I will, your honour," replied John, accepting the turn in the conversation as easily as a skilful motorist changes gear. "I suppose you'll have a job for me at Tory Lodge when I get the sack from the misthress?"

"No, but they tell me I'm to be put on the Old Age Pension Committee," returned Flurry, "and I might get a chance to do something for you if you'd give over dyeing that beard you have."

"I'm sorry to say it's the Almighty is dyeing my beard for me, sir," replied John Kane, fingering a grey streak on his chin, "and I think He's after giving yourself a touch, too!" He glanced at the side of Flurry's head, and his eye travelled on to mine. There was an almost flagrant absence of triumph in it.

He put aside a beechen bough with his hand; "I'll leave the things on the hall table for you, sir," he said, choosing the perfect moment for departure, and passed out of sight. The bough swung into place behind him; it was like an exit in a pastoral play.

"She never told me about the embrocation," said Sally, leaning back against the mossed stones of the bench and looking up into the web of branches. "She never will admit that she's ill."

"Poor old Mrs. Knox!" said Philippa compassionately, "I thought she looked so ill last night when she was playing bridge. Such a tiny fragile thing, sitting wrapped up in that great old chair——"

Philippa is ineradicably romantic, yet my mind, too, dwelt upon the old autocrat lying there, ill and undefeated, in the heart of her ancient fortress.

"Fragile!" said Flurry, "you'd best not tell her that. With my grandmother no one's ill till they're dead, and no one's dead till they're buried!"

Away near the house the peacock uttered his defiant screech, a note of exclamation that seemed entirely appropriate to Aussolas; the turkey-cock in the yard accepted the challenge with effusion, and from further away the voice of Mrs. Knox's Kerry bull, equally instant in taking offence, ascended the gamut of wrath from growl to yell. Blended with these voices was another—a man's voice, in loud harangue, advancing down the long beech walk to the kitchen garden. As it approached, the wood-pigeons bolted in panic, with distracted clappings of wings, from the tall firs by the garden wall in which they were wont to sit arranging plans of campaign with regard to the fruit. We sat in tense silence. The latch of the garden gate clicked, and the voice said in stentorian tones:

"——My father 'e kept a splendid table!"

"I hear wheels!" breathed Sally Knox.

A hawthorn tree and a laburnum tree leaned over the garden gate, and from beneath their canopy of cream and pale gold there emerged the bath-chair of Mrs. Knox, with Mrs. Knox herself seated in it. It was propelled by Mullins

—even at that distance the indignation of Mullins was discernible—and it progressed up the central path. Beside it walked the personage whose father had kept a splendid table. Parenthetically it may be observed that he did credit to it.

"Glory be to Moses! Look at my grandmother!" said Flurry under his breath. "How fragile she is! Who the dickens has she got hold of?"

"He thinks she's deaf, anyhow," said Sally.

"That's where he makes the mistake!" returned Flurry.

"I don't see your glawss, Mrs. Knox," shouted the stout gentleman.

"That's very possible," replied the incisive and slightly cracked voice of Mrs. Knox, "because the little that is left of it is in the mortar on the wall, to keep thieves out, which it fails to do."

The pair passed on, and paused, still in high converse, at the asparagus beds ; Mullins, behind the bath-chair, wiped her indignant brow.

"You'll go home without the asparagus," whispered Flurry, "she has every stick of it counted by now!"

They moved on, heading for the further gate of the garden.

"I'll bet a sovereign he's come after the house!"

Flurry continued, following the *cortège* with a malevolent eye.

Later, when we returned to the house, we found a motor-bicycle, dusty and dwarfish, leaning against the hall door steps. Within was the sound of shouting. It was then half-past seven.

" Is it possible that she's keeping him for dinner ? " said Sally.

" Take care he's not staying for the night ! " said Flurry. " Look at the knapsack he has on the table ! "

" There's only one room he can possibly have," said Mrs. Flurry, with a strange and fixed gaze at her lord, " and that's the James the Second room. The others are cleared for the painters."

" Oh, that will be all right," replied her lord, easily.

When I came down to dinner I found the new arrival planted on his short, thick legs in front of the fireplace, still shouting at Mrs. Knox, who, notwithstanding the sinister presence of the two shawls of ill-omen, was listening with a propitious countenance. She looked very tired, and I committed the *gaucherie* of saying I was sorry to hear she had not been well.

" Oh, that was nothing ! " said Mrs. Knox, with a wave of her tiny, sunburnt, and be-diamonded hand. " I've shaken that off, ' like dewdrops from the lion's mane!' This is Mr. Tebbutts, from—er—England, Major Yeates."

Mr. Tebbutts, after a bewildered stare, presumably in search of the lion, proclaimed his gratification at meeting me, in a voice that might have been heard in the stable yard.

At dinner the position developed apace. The visitor was, it appeared, the representative of a patriarchal family, comprising samples of all the relationships mentioned in the table of affinities, and *fortissimo*, and at vast length, he laid down their personal histories and their various requirements. It was pretty to see how old Mrs. Knox, ill as she looked, and suffering as she undoubtedly was, mastered the bowling.

Did the Tebbutts ladies exact bathing for their young? The lake supplied it.

("It's all mud and swallow-holes!" said Flurry in an audible aside.)

Did the brothers demand trout fishing? the schoolboys rabbit shooting? the young ladies lawn tennis and society?—all were theirs, especially the latter. " My grandson and his wife will be within easy reach in their own house, Tory Lodge!"

The remark about the swallow-holes had not been lost upon the Lady of the Lake.

Mrs. Knox had her glass of port at dessert, an

act equivalent to snapping her rheumatic fingers in our faces, and withdrew, stiff but erect, and still on the best of terms with her prospective tenant. As I held the door open for her, she said to me :

" ' 'Twas whispered in heaven, 'twas muttered in hell.' "

By an amazing stroke of luck I was enabled to continue :

" ' And echo caught softly the sound as it fell ! ' " with a glance at Mr. Tebbutts that showed I was aware the quotation was directed at his missing aspirates.

As the door closed, the visitor turned to Flurry and said impressively :

" There's just one thing, Mr. Knox, I should like to mention, if you will allow me. Are the drains quite in order ? "

" God knows," said Flurry, pulling hard at a badly-lighted cigarette and throwing himself into a chair by the turf fire.

" Mrs. Knox's health has held out against them for about sixty years," I remarked.

" Well, as to that," replied Mr. Tebbutts, " I feel it is only right to mention that the dear old lady was very giddy with me in the garden this afternoon."

Flurry received this remarkable statement without emotion.

"Maybe she's taken a fancy to you!" he said brutally. "If it wasn't that it was whipped cream."

Mr. Tebbutts' bulging eyes sought mine in complete mystification; I turned to the fire, and to it revealed my emotions. Flurry was not at all amused.

"Well—er—I understood her maid to say she 'ad bin ailing," said the guest after a pause. "I'd have called it a kind of a megrim myself, and, as I say, I certainly perceived a sort of charnel-'ouse smell in the room I'm in. And look 'ere, Mr. Knox, 'ere's another thing. 'Ow about rats? You know what ladies are; there's one of my sisters-in-law, Mrs. William Tebbutts, who'd just scream the 'ouse down if she 'eard the 'alf of what was goin' on behind the panelling in my room this evening."

"Anyone that's afraid of rats had better keep out of Aussolas," said Flurry, getting up with a yawn.

"Mr. Tebbutts is in the James the Second room, isn't he?" said I, idly. "Isn't that the room with the powdering-closet off it?"

"It is," said Flurry. "Anything else you'd like to know?"

I recognised that someone had blundered, presumably myself, and made a move for the drawing-room.

Mrs. Knox had retired when we got there; my wife and Mrs. Flurry followed suit as soon as might be; and the guest said that, if the gentlemen had no objection, he thought he'd turn in too.

Flurry and I shut the windows—fresh air is a foible of the female sex—heaped turf on the fire, drew up chairs in front of it, and composed ourselves for that sweetest sleep of all, the sleep that has in it the bliss of abandonment, and is made almost passionate by the deep underlying knowledge that it can be but temporary.

How long we had slumbered I cannot say; it seemed but a moment when a door opened in our dreams, and the face of Mr. Tebbutts was developed before me in the air like the face of the Cheshire cat, only without the grin.

"Mr. Knox! Gentlemen!" he began, as if he were addressing a meeting. The thunder had left his voice; he stopped to take breath. He was in his shirt and trousers, and the laces of his boots trailed on the floor behind him. "I've 'ad a bit of a start upstairs. I was just winding up my watch at the dressing-table when I saw some kind of an animal gloide past the fireplace and across the room——"

"What was it like?" interrupted Flurry, sitting up in his chair.

"Well, Mr. Knox, it's 'ard to say what it was

like. It wasn't a cat, nor yet it wasn't what you could call a squirrel——"

Flurry got on to his feet.

"By the living Jingo!" he said, turning to me an awestruck countenance; "he's seen the Aussolas Martin Cat!"

I had never before heard of the Aussolas Martin Cat, and it is indisputable that a slight chill crept down my backbone.

Mr. Tebbutts' eyes bulged more than ever, and his lower lip fell.

"What way did it go?" said Flurry; "did it look at you?"

"It seemed to disappear in that recess by the door," faltered the seer of the vision; "it just vanished!"

"I don't know if it's for my grandmother or for me," said Flurry in a low voice, "but it's a death in the house anyway."

The colour in Mr. Tebbutts' face deepened to a glossy sealing-wax red.

"If one of you gents would come upstairs with me," he said, "I think I'll just get my traps together. I can be back at the 'otel in 'alf an 'our——"

Flurry and I accompanied Mr. Tebbutts to the James the Second room. Over Mrs. Knox's door there were panes of glass, and light came forth from them. (It is my belief that Mrs. Knox never goes to bed.) We trod softly as we passed it, and went along the uncarpeted boards of the Musicians' Gallery above the entrance hall.

There certainly was a peculiar odour in the James the Second room, and the adjective "charnel-'ouse" had not been misapplied.

I thought about a dead rat, and decided that the apparition had been one of the bandit tribe of tawny cats that inhabited the Aussolas stables. And yet legends of creatures that haunted old houses and followed old families came back to me; of one in particular, a tale of medieval France, wherein "a yellow furry animal" ran down the throat of a sleeping lady named Sagesse.

Mr. Tebbutts, by this time fully dressed, was swiftly bestowing a brush and comb in his knapsack. Perhaps he, too, had read the legend about Madame Sagesse. Flurry was silently, and with a perturbed countenance, examining the room; rapping at the panelling and peering up the cavernous chimney; I heard him sniff as he did so. Possibly he also held the dead-rat theory. He opened the flap in the door of the powdering-closet, and, striking a match, held it through the opening. I looked over his shoulder, and had a glimpse of black feathers on the floor, and a waft of a decidedly "charnel-'ouse" nature.

"Damn!" muttered Flurry to himself, and slammed down the flap.

"I think, sir," said Mr. Tebbutts, with his knapsack in his hand and his cap on his head, "I must ask you to let Mrs. Knox know that this 'ouse won't suit Mrs. William Tebbutts. You might just say I was called away rather sudden. Of course, you won't mention what I saw just now—I wouldn't wish to upset the pore old lady——"

We followed him from the room, and treading softly as before, traversed the gallery, and began to descend the slippery oak stairs. Flurry was still looking furtively about him, and the thought crossed my mind that in the most hard-headed Irishman there wanders a vein of superstition.

Before we had reached the first landing, the violent ringing of a handbell broke forth in the room with the light over the door, followed by a crash of fire-irons; then old Mrs. Knox's voice calling imperatively for Mullins.

There was a sound of rushing, slippered feet, a bumping of furniture; with a squall from Mullins the door flew open, and I was endowed with a never-to-be-forgotten vision of Mrs. Knox, swathed in hundreds of shawls, in the act of hurling the tongs at some unseen object.

Almost simultaneously there was a scurry of

claws on the oak floor above us, Mrs. Knox's door was slammed, and something whizzed past me. I am thankful to think that I possess, as a companion vision to that of Mrs. Knox, the face of Mr. Tebbutts with the candle light on it as he looked up from the foot of the stairs and saw the Aussolas Martin Cat in his track.

"Look out, Tebbutts!" yelled Flurry. "It's you he's after!"

Mr. Tebbutts here passed out of the incident into the night, and the Aussolas Martin Cat was swallowed up by a large hole in the surbase in the corner of the first landing.

"He'll come out in the wine-cellar," said Flurry, with the calm that was his in moments of crisis, "the way the cat did."

I pulled myself together.

"What's happened to the other Fanaghy cub?" I enquired with, I hope, equal calmness.

"He's gone to blazes," replied Flurry; "there isn't a wall in this house that hasn't a way in it. I knew I'd never have luck with them after you asking the way from Kitty the Shakes."

As is usual in my dealings with Flurry, the fault was mine.

While I reflected on this, the stillness of the night was studded in a long and diminishing line by the running pant of the motor-bicycle.

II

THE FINGER OF MRS. KNOX

A BEING stood in a dark corner under the gallery of the hall at Aussolas Castle; a being who had arrived noiselessly on bare feet, and now revealed its presence by hard breathing.

"Come in, Mary," commanded old Mrs. Knox without turning her head; "make up the fire."

"I will, ma'am," murmured the being, advancing with an apologetic eye upon me, and an undulating gait suggestive of a succession of incipient curtsies.

She was carrying an armful of logs, and, having stacked them on the fire in a heap calculated to set alight any chimney less roomy than the Severn Tunnel, she retired by way of the open hall door with the same deferential stealth with which she had entered.

"The hen-woman," explained Mrs. Knox casually, "the only person in this place who knows a dry log from a wet one."

Like all successful rulers, Mrs. Knox had the power of divining in her underlings their special gifts, and of wresting them to the sphere in which they shone, no matter what their normal functions might be. She herself pervaded all spheres.

"There's no pie but my grandmother has a finger in it," was Flurry Knox's epitome of these high qualities; a sour tribute from one freebooter to another.

"If the Mistress want a thing she mus' have it!" was the comment of John Kane, the gamekeeper, as he threw down the spade with which he was digging out a ferret, and armed himself with a holly-bush wherewith to sweep the drawing-room chimney.

As Mrs. Knox and I sat by the hen-woman's noble fire, and gossiped, the cook panted in with the tea-tray; the butler, it appeared, had gone out to shoot a rabbit for dinner. All these things pointed to the fact that Mrs. Knox's granddaughter-in-law, Mrs. Flurry, was not, at the moment, in residence at Aussolas. The Jungle was creeping in; Sally Knox, by virtue, I suppose, of her English mother, spasmodically endeavoured to keep it out, but with her departure the Wild triumphed.

It was an October afternoon, grey and still; the hall door stood open, as indeed it always did at Aussolas, and on the topmost of the broad limestone steps Mrs. Knox's white woolly dog sat, and magisterially regarded lake and wood

25

and lawn. The tawny bracken flowed like a sea to the palings that bounded the lawn; along its verge squatted the rabbits, motionless for the most part, sometimes languidly changing their ground, with hops like the dying efforts of a mechanical toy. The woolly dog had evidently learned in many fruitless charges the futility of frontal attack; a close and menacing supervision from the altitude of the steps was all that was consistent with dignity, but an occasional strong shudder betrayed his emotion. The open door framed also a pleasing view of my new car, standing in beautiful repose at the foot of the steps, splashed with the mud of a twenty-mile run from an outlying Petty Sessions Court; her presence added, for me, the touch of romance.

It was twilight in the back of the hall by the fireplace; the flames of the logs, branching like antlers, made a courteous and not too searching inquisition into dark corners, and lighted with a very suitable evasiveness Mrs. Knox's Witch of Endor profile. She wore her usual velvet bonnet; the rest of her attire recalled to my memory the summary of it by her kinswoman, Lady Knox, "A rag bag held together by diamond brooches." Yet, according to her wont, her personality was the only thing that counted; it reduced all externals to a proper insignificance.

The object of my visit had ostensibly been to see her grandson, but Flurry was away for the night.

"He's sleeping at Tory Lodge," said Mrs. Knox. "He's cubbing at Drumvoortneen, and he has to start early. He tried to torment me into allowing him to keep the hounds in the yard here this season, but I had the pleasure of telling him that old as I might be, I still retained possession of my hearing, my sense of smell, and, to a certain extent, of my wits."

"I should have thought," I said discreetly, "that Tory Lodge was more in the middle of his country."

"Undoubtedly," replied Flurry's grandmother; "but it is not in the middle of my straw, my meal, my buttermilk, my firewood, and anything else of mine that can be pilfered for the uses of a kennel!" She concluded with a chuckle that might have been uttered by a scald-crow.

I was pondering a diplomatic reply, when the quiet evening was rent by a shrill challenge from the woolly dog.

Thy sentinel am I!" he vociferated, barking himself backwards into the hall, in proper strategic retreat upon his base.

A slow foot ascended the steps, and the twilight in the hall deepened as a man's figure appeared in the doorway; a middle-aged man, with his hat in one hand, and in the other a thick stick, with which he was making respectfully intimidating demonstrations to the woolly dog.

"Who are you?" called out Mrs. Knox from her big chair.

"I'm Casey, your ladyship," replied the visitor in a deplorable voice, "from Killoge."

"Cornelius Casey?" queried Mrs. Knox.

"No, but his son, your honour ma'am, Stephen Casey, one of the tenants."

"Well, come in, Stephen," said Mrs. Knox affably, supplementing her spectacles with a gold-rimmed single eye-glass, and looking at him with interest. "I knew your father well in old times, when he used to stop the earths in Killoge Wood for the Colonel. They tell me that's all cut down now?"

"There's not the boiling of a kettle left in it afther Goggin, my lady!" said Casey eagerly. Mrs. Knox cut him short.

"Many a good hunt the Colonel had out of Killoge, and I too, for the matter of that!" she added, turning to me; "my cousin Bessie Hamilton and I were the only huntresses in the country in those days, and people thought us shocking tomboys, I believe. Now, what with driving motors and riding astride, the gentlemen are all ladies, and the ladies are gentlemen!'

With another scald-crow chuckle she turned to Casey. "Did your father ever tell you of the great hunt out of Killoge into the Fanaghy cliffs?"

"He did, your ladyship, he did!" responded Casey, with a touch of life in his lamentable voice. "Often he told me that it knocked fire from his eyes to see yourself facing in at the Killoge river."

"I was riding Bijou, the grandmother of old Trinket, in that run," said Mrs. Knox, leaning back in her chair, with a smile that had something of the light of other days in it.

I remembered the story that Colonel Knox had run away with her after a hunt, and wondered if that had been the occasion when she had knocked fire from the eyes of Cornelius Casey.

Her thin old hand drooped in momentary languor over the arm of her chair ; and the woolly dog thrust his nose under it, with a beady eye fixed upon the hot cakes.

"Here!" said Mrs. Knox, sitting up, and throwing a buttery bun on the floor. "Be off with you! Well, Casey," she went on, "what is it you want with me?"

"Great trouble I got, Mrs. Knox, your honour ma'am," replied Casey from the door-mat, "great trouble entirely." He came a step or two nearer. He had a long, clean-shaved face, with mournful eyes, like a sick bloodhound, and the enviable, countryman's thatch of thick, strong hair, with scarcely a touch of grey in it.

"That Goggin, that has the shop at Killoge Cross, has me processed. I'm pairsecuted with him; and the few little bastes I has, and me donkey and all—" his voice thinned to a whimper, "he's to drive them to-morrow———"

"I suppose that's Goggin, the Gombeen?" said Mrs. Knox; "how were you fool enough to get into dealings with him?"

The statement of Casey's wrongs occupied quite ten minutes, and was generous in detail. His land was bad, ever and always. The grass that was in it was as bare as that you could pick pins in it. He had no pushing land at all for cattle. Didn't he buy a heifer at Scabawn fair and the praisings she got was beyant all raves, and he had her one month, and kinder company he never had, and she giving seven pints at every meal, and wasn't that the divil's own produce? One month, indeed, was all he had her till she got a dropsy, and the dropsy supported her for a while, and when it left her she faded away. And didn't his wife lose all her hens in one week? "They fell dead on her, like hailstones!" He ceased, and a tear wandered down the channels in his long cheek.

"How much do you owe Goggin?" asked Mrs. Knox sharply.

What Casey owed to Goggin had, as might have been expected, but a remote relation to the sum that Goggin was now endeavouring to extract from Casey. At the heart of the transaction was a shop account, complicated by loans of single pounds (and in my mind's eye I could see, and with my mind's nose I could smell, the dirty crumpled notes). It was further entangled by per-contra accounts of cribs of turf, scores of eggs, and a day's work now and again. I had, from the judgment seat, listened to many such recitals, so, apparently, had Mrs. Knox, judging by the ease with which she straightened Casey's devious narrative at critical points, and shepherded him to his facts, like a cunning old collie steering a sheep to its pen. The conclusion of the matter was that Goggin was, on the morrow, to take possession of Casey's remaining stock, consisting of three calves, a donkey, and a couple of goats, in liquidation of a debt of £15, and that he, Stephen Casey, knew that Mrs. Knox would never be satisfied to see one of her own tenants wronged.

"I have no tenants," replied Mrs. Knox tartly; "the Government is your landlord now, and I wish you joy of each other!"

"Then I wish to God it was yourself we had

in it again!" lamented Stephen Casey; "it was better for us when the gentry was managing their own business. They'd *give* patience, and they'd *have* patience."

"Well, that will do now," said Mrs. Knox; "go round to the servants' hall and have your tea. I'll see what I can do."

There was silence while Stephen Casey withdrew. As the sound of his hobnailed tread died away the woolly dog advanced very stiffly to the hall door, and, with his eyes fixed on the departing visitor, licked his lips hungrily.

"When those rascals in Parliament took our land from us," said Mrs. Knox, flinging a sod of turf on to the huge fire with practised aim, "we thought we should have some peace, now we're both beggared and bothered!" She turned upon me a countenance like that of an ancient and spectacled falcon. "Major Yeates! You have often offered me a drive in your motor-car. Will you take me to Killoge to-morrow morning?"

It was a brisk and windy morning, with the sharpness of 9 A.M. in it, when Mullins, Mrs. Knox's tirewoman, met me at the hall door of Aussolas with her arms full of shawls, and a countenance dark with doom and wrath. She informed me that it was a shame for me to be enticing the Mistress out of her bed at this hour of the morning, and that she would get her death out of it. I was repudiating this soft impeachment (which had indeed some flavour of the Restoration drama about it), when the companion of my flight appeared.

"How would anyone know the minute—" continued Mullins, addressing the universe, "that this what's-this-I'll-call-it wouldn't turn into a bog-hole?" She put this conundrum while fiercely swaddling her mistress in cloak upon cloak. I attempted no reply, and Mrs. Knox, winking both eyes at me over the rim of the topmost shawl, was hoisted into the back of the car; as we glided away I had, at all events, the consolation of knowing that, in the event of an accident, Mrs. Knox in her cloaks would float from the car as softly and bulkily as a bumble bee.

As we ran out of the gates on to the high road I remembered that my passenger's age was variously reckoned at from ninety to a hundred, and thought it well to ask her if fifteen miles an hour would be too fast for pleasure.

"You can't go too fast to please me," replied Mrs. Knox, through the meshes of a Shetland shawl. "When I was a girl I rode a fourteen-hand pony to the fourteenth milestone on the Cork road in a minute under the hour! I think you should be able to double that!"

I replied to this challenge with twenty miles an hour, which, with a head wind and a bad road, I considered to be fast enough for any old lady. As a matter of fact it was too fast for her costume. We had run some eight or nine miles before, looking back, I noticed that a change of some sort had occurred.

"Oh, the red one blew away long ago!" screamed Mrs. Knox against the wind; "it doesn't matter, I shall get it back—I'll ask Father Scanlan to speak about it at Mass next Sunday. There's a veil gone too—how frantic Mullins will be!"

A skirl of laughter came from the recesses of the remaining shawls.

We were running now on a level road under the lee of a long line of hills; a strip of plantation, gay with the yellows and greens of autumn, clung to a steep slope ahead of us, and, at the top of it, some ragged pines looked like blots against the sky. As we neared it, a faint and long-drawn call came from the height; presently among the tree-trunks we saw hounds, like creatures in a tapestry hunting scene, working up and up through the brown undergrowth. I slackened speed.

"'Pon my honour, we've hit off the Hunt!" exclaimed Mrs. Knox.

As she spoke there was a responsive yelp from a tract of briars in the lower part of the wood;

two or three couples jostled downwards to their comrade, and a full chorus, led by the soprano squeals of the Hunt terrier, arose and streamed along the wood above the road. I came to a full stop, and, just in front of us, a rabbit emerged very quietly from the fence of the wood, crept along in the ditch, and disappeared in a hole in the bank. The hounds still uttered the classic pæans of the Chase; hoofs clattered in a steep lane on the hill-side, and Flurry Knox charged on to the road a little ahead of us.

"Forrad, forrad, forrad!" he shouted as he came.

"Rabbit, rabbit, rabbit!" cackled his grand-mother at him in malevolent imitation.

I let the car go, and as we flew past him he asked me, sideways out of a very red face, what the devil I was doing there. It was evident that Mrs. Knox's observation had been accepted in the spirit in which it was offered.

"That will do my young gentleman no harm!" said Mrs. Knox complacently, as we became a speck in the distance.

It was about ten o'clock when we ran down a valley between steep hills to Killoge cross-roads. The hill-sides were set thick with tree stumps, like the crowded headstones of a cemetery, with coarse grass and briars filling the spaces between them. Here and there a slender, orphaned ash sapling, spared because despised, stood among the havoc, and showed with its handful of yellow leaves what the autumn colours might once have been here. A starkly new, cemented public-house, with " J. Goggin " on the name board, stood at the fork of the roads. Doubtless into it had flowed the blood-money of the wood; it repre-sented the alternative offered to the community by Mr. Goggin. I slowed up and looked about me.

" I suppose this is—or was—Killoge Wood?" I said to my passenger.

Mrs. Knox was staring through her spectacles at the devastated hill-side.

" Ichabod, Ichabod!" she murmured, and leaned back in her place.

A man got up from a heap of stones by the roadside and came slowly towards the car.

" Well, Stephen," began Mrs. Knox irritably, " what about the cattle? He looks as if he were walking behind his own coffin!" she continued in a loud aside to me.

Stephen Casey removed his hat, and with it indicated a group composed of three calves—and nothing can look as dejected as an ill-fed, under-bred calf—two goats, and a donkey, attended by a boy with a stick, and a couple of cur dogs.

" Himself and the sheriff's man is after driving

them, my lady," replied their proprietor, and proceeded to envelop the name of Goggin in a flowing mantle of curses.

" There, that will do for the present," said Mrs. Knox peremptorily, as Casey, with tears streaming down his face, paused to catch his wind. "Where's Goggin ? "

"The two of them is inside in the shop," answered the miserable Casey, still weeping copiously.

I drove over to the public-house, thinking that if Casey could not put up a better fight than this it would be difficult to do much for him. The door of the pub was already filled by the large and decent figure of Mr. Goggin, who advanced to meet us, taking off his hat reverentially ; I remembered at once his pale and pimpled face, his pink nose, his shabby grey and yellow beard. He had been before me in a matter of selling drink on Sunday, and had sailed out of court in stainless triumph, on sworn evidence that he was merely extending hospitality to some friends that had come to make a match for a niece of his own, and were tired after walking the land and putting a price on the cattle.

"Well, Goggin," said Mrs. Knox, waving towards the hill-side a tiny hand in a mouldy old black kid glove, "you've done a great work here!

You've destroyed in six months what it took the Colonel and the Lord Almighty eighty years to make. That's something to be proud of!"

Goggin, again, and with even deeper reverence, removed his hat, and murmured something about being a poor man.

"It was your own grandfather that planted those trees for the Colonel," continued Mrs. Knox, diving, as it were, into an ancient armoury and snatching a rusty weapon from the wall.

"That's the case, ma'am," replied Mr. Goggin solemnly. "The Lord have mercy on his soul!"

"You'll be wanting mercy on your own soul in the next world, if you meet the Colonel there!" said Mrs. Knox unhesitatingly.

"I mightn't have the honour of meeting the Colonel there, ma'am!" tittered Goggin sycophantically.

"You might not indeed," responded Mrs. Knox, "but you might find your grandfather making up a good fire for you with the logs out of Killoge Wood!"

"Ha, ha! That's good, faith!" said a fat voice from the porter-flavoured depths of the pub. I recognised among other half-seen faces the round cheeks and bristling moustache of little M'Sweeny, the sheriff's officer, at Goggin's elbow.

"And what's this I hear about Stephen

38

Casey?" went on Mrs. Knox, in shrill and trenchant tones, delivering her real attack now that she had breached the wall. "You lent him five pounds two years ago, and now you're driving all his stock off! What do you call that, I'd thank you to tell me?"

In the discussion that followed I could almost have been sorry for Goggin, so entirely over-weighted was he by Mrs. Knox's traditional prestige, by my official position, by knowledge of the unseen audience in the pub, and by the inherent rottenness of his case. Nevertheless, the defence put forward by him was a very creditable work of art. The whole affair had its foundation in a foolish philanthropy, the outcome of generous instincts exploited to their utmost, only, indeed, kept within bounds by Mr. Goggin's own financial embarrassments. These he primarily referred back to the excessive price extorted from him by Mrs. Knox's agent for the purchase of his land under the Act; and secondarily to the bad debts with which Stephen Casey and other customers had loaded him in their dealings with his little shop. There were moments when I almost had to accept Mr. Goggin's point of view, so well-ordered and so mildly stated were his facts. But Mrs. Knox's convictions were beyond and above any possibility of being shaken by mere evidence; she has often said to me that if all justice magistrates were deaf there would be more done. She herself was not in the least deaf, but she knew Mr. Goggin, which did as well.

"Fifteen pounds worth of stock to pay a debt that was never more than £7! What do you call that, Major Yeates?"

She darted the question at me.

I had, some little time before, felt my last moment of sympathy with Goggin expire, and I replied with considerable heat that, if Mrs. Knox would forgive my saying so, I called it damned usury.

From this point the Affaire Casey went out swiftly on an ebb tide. It was insinuated by someone, M'Sweeny, I think, that an instalment of five pounds might be accepted, and the eyes of Goggin turned, tentatively, to Mrs. Knox. It has always been said of that venerable warrior that if there were a job to be done for a friend she would work her fingers to the bone, but she would never put them in her pocket. I observed that the eye of Goggin, having failed in its quest of hers, was concentrating itself upon me. The two walls of a corner seemed to rise mysteriously on either side of me; I suddenly, and without premeditation, found myself promising to be responsible for the five pounds.

Before the glow of this impulse had time to be succeeded by its too familiar reaction, the broken, yet persistent cry of hounds came to my ear. It advanced swiftly, coming, seemingly, from higher levels, into the desolated spaces that had once been Killoge Wood. From the inner depths of Mrs. Knox's wrappings the face of the woolly dog amazingly presented itself; from the companion depths of the public-house an equally unexpected party of *convives* burst forth and stood at gaze. Mrs. Knox tried to stand up, was borne down by the sheer weight of rugs and the woolly dog, glared at me for a tense moment, and hissed, "They're coming this way! Try to get a view!"

Before the words had passed her lips someone in the group at the door vociferated, "Look at him above! Look at him!"

I looked "above," but could see nothing. Not so the rest of the group.

"Now! look at him going west the rock! Now! He's passing the little holly-tree—he's over the fence——"

I bore, as I have so often borne, the exasperation of, as it were, hearing instead of seeing a cinematograph, but I saw no reason why I should submit to the presence of Mr. M'Sweeny, who had sociably sprung into the motor beside me in order to obtain a better view.

"Look at him over the wall!" howled the cinematograph. "Look at the size he is! Isn't he the divil of a sheep!"

It was at this moment that I first caught sight of the fox, about fifty yards on the farther side of Casey's assortment of live stock and their guardian cur dogs, gliding over the wall like a cat, and slipping away up the road. At this point Mr. M'Sweeny, finding the disadvantage of his want of stature, bounded on to the seat beside me and uttered a long yell.

"Hi! At him! Tiger, good dog! Hi! Rosy!"

I cannot now say whether I smote M'Sweeny in the legs before he jumped, or if I merely accelerated the act; he appeared to be running before he touched the ground, and he probably took it as a send-off, administered in irrepressible fellow-feeling.

Tiger and Rosy were already laying themselves out down the road, and their yelps streamed back from them like the sparks from an engine. The party at the door was suddenly in full flight after them with a swiftness and unanimity that again recalled the cinematograph. They caught away with them Stephen Casey and his animals; and I had an enlivening glimpse of the donkey at the top of the hunt, braying as it went; of Goggin trying in vain to stem the companion flight of the calves. The bend of the road hid them all from us; the thumping of heavy feet, the sobbing bray of the donkey, passed rapidly into remoteness, and Mrs. Knox and I were left with nothing remaining to us of the situation save the well-defined footmarks of M'Sweeny on the seat beside me (indelible, as I afterwards discovered).

"Get on, Major Yeates!" screamed Mrs. Knox, above the barking of the woolly dog. "We must see it out!"

I started the car, and just before we in our turn rounded the corner I looked back, and saw the leading hounds coming down the hill-side. I slackened and saw them drop into the road and there remain, mystified, no doubt, by the astonishing variety of scents, from goat to gombeen man, that presented themselves. Of Flurry and his followers there was no sign.

"Get on, get on," reiterated Mrs. Knox, divining, no doubt, my feelings; "we shall do no more harm than the rest!"

I gave the car her head, knowing that whatever I did Flurry would have my blood. In less than two minutes we were all but into Stephen Casey's goats, who, being yoked together in body but not in spirit, required the full width of the road for their argument. We passed Stephen Casey and the gombeen man cornering the disputed calves in the sympathetic accord that such an operation demands. As we neared M'Sweeny, who brought up the rear, the body of the hunt, still headed by the donkey, swept into a field on the left of the road. The fox, as might have been expected, had passed from the ken of the cur dogs, and these, intoxicated by the incitements of their owners, now flung themselves, with the adaptability of their kind, into the pursuit of the donkey.

I stopped and looked back. The leading hounds were galloping behind the car; I recognised at their heads Rattler and Roman, the puppies I had walked, and for a moment was touched by this mark of affection. The gratification was brief. They passed me without a glance, and with anticipatory cries of joy flung themselves into the field and joined in the chase of the donkey.

"They'll kill him!" exclaimed Mrs. Knox, restraining with difficulty the woolly dog; "what good is Flurry that he can't keep with his hounds!"

Galloping hoofs on the road behind us clattered a reply, accompanied by what I can only describe as imprecations on the horn, and Flurry hurtled by and swung his horse into the field over a low bank with all the dramatic fury of the hero rushing to the rescue of the leading lady. It recalled the incidents that in the palmy days of the Hippodrome gloriously ended in a plunge into deep water, amid a salvo of firearms.

In Flurry's wake came the rest of the pack, and with them Dr. Jerome Hickey. "A great morning's cubbing!" he called out, snatching off his old velvet cap. "Thirty minutes with an old fox, and now a nice burst with a jackass!"

For the next three or four minutes shrieks, like nothing so much as forked lightning, lacerated the air, as the guilty hounds began to receive that which was their due. It seemed possible that my turn would come next; I looked about to see what the chances were of turning the car and withdrawing as soon as might be, and decided to move on down the road in search of facilities. We had proceeded perhaps a hundred yards without improving the situation, when my eye was caught by something moving swiftly through the furze-bushes that clothed a little hill on the right of the road. It was brownish red, it slid into the deep furze that crested the hill, and was gone.

Here was a heaven-sent peace-offering!

"Tally-ho!" I bellowed, rising in my place and waving my cap high in air. "Tally-ho, over!"

The forked lightning ceased.

"What way is he?" came an answering bellow from Flurry.

"This way, over the hill!"

The hounds were already coming to the holloa. I achieved some very creditable falsetto screeches; I leaped from the car, and cheered and capped them over the fence; I shouted precise directions to the Master and Whip, who were now, with the clamours proper to their calling, steeplechasing into the road and out of it again, followed by two or three of the Field, including the new District Inspector of the Royal Irish Constabulary (recently come from Meath with a high reputation as a goer). They scrambled and struggled up the hill-side, through rocks and furze (in connection with which I heard the new D.I. making some strenuous comments to his Meath hunter), the hounds streamed and screamed over the ridge of the hill, the riders shoved their puffing horses after them, topped it, and dropped behind it. The furzy skyline and the pleasant blue and white sky above it remained serene and silent.

I returned to the car, and my passenger, who, as I now realised, had remained very still during these excitements.

"That was a bit of luck!" I said happily, inflated by the sense of personal merit that is the portion of one who has viewed a fox away. As I spoke I became aware of something fixed in Mrs.

46

Knox's expression, something rigid, as though she were repressing emotion ; a fear flashed through my mind that she was overtired, and that the cry of the hounds had brought back to her the days when she too had known what a first burst away with a fox out of Killoge Wood had felt like.

" Major Yeates," she said sepulchrally, and yet with some inward thrill in her voice, " I think the sooner we start for home the better."

I could not turn the car, but, rather than lose time, I ran it backwards towards the cross-roads ; it was a branch of the art in which I had not become proficient, and as, with my head over my shoulder, I dodged the ditches, I found myself continually encountering Mrs. Knox's eye, and was startled by something in it that was both jubilant and compassionate. I also surprised her in the act of wiping her eyes. I wondered if she were becoming hysterical, and yearned for Mullins as the policeman (no doubt) yearns for the mother of the lost child.

On the road near the public-house we came upon M'Sweeny, Goggin, and Casey, obviously awaiting us. I stopped the car, not without reluctance.

" That will be all right, Goggin," said Mrs. Knox airily ; " we're in a hurry to get home now."

The three protagonists looked at one another dubiously, and simultaneously cleared their throats.

" I beg your pardon, Mrs. Knox, ma'am," began Mr. Goggin very delicately. " Mr M'Sweeny would be thankful to speak a word to you before you go."

" Well, let him speak and be quick about it," returned Mrs. Knox, who seemed to have recovered remarkably from her moment of emotion.

" You must excuse me, Major Yeates," said Mr. M'Sweeny, chivalrously selecting me as the person to whom to present the business end of the transaction, " but I'm afraid I must trouble you about that little matter of the five pounds that we arranged a while ago—I couldn't go back without it was settled——"

Mr. Goggin coughed, and looked at his boots ; Stephen Casey sighed heavily.

At the same moment I thought I heard the horn.

" I'm afraid I haven't got it with me," I said, pulling out a handful of silver and a half-sovereign. " I suppose eighteen and sixpence wouldn't be any use to you ? "

Mr. M'Sweeny smiled deprecatingly, as at a passing jest, and again I heard the horn, several harsh and prolonged notes.

Mrs. Knox leaned forward and poked me in the back with some violence.

" Goggin will lend it to you," she said, with the splendid simplicity of a great mind.

"I heard scald-crow laughter behind me in the shawls."

It must be recorded of Goggin that he accepted this singular inversion of the position like a gentleman. We moved on to his house and he went in with an excellent show of alacrity to fetch the money wherewith I was to stop his own mouth. It was while we were waiting that a small wet collie, reddish-brown in colour, came flying across the road, and darted in at the open door of the house. Its tongue was hanging out, it was panting heavily.

"I seen her going over the hill, and the hounds after her; I thought she wouldn't go three sthretches before they'd have her cot," said M'Sweeny pleasantly. "But I declare she gave them a nice chase. When she seen the Doctor beating the hounds, that's the time she ran."

I turned feebly in my place and looked at Mrs. Knox.

"It was a very natural mistake," she said, again wiping her eyes; "I myself was taken in for a moment—but only for a moment!" she added, with abominable glee.

I gave her but one glance, laden with reproach, and turned to M'Sweeny.

"You'll get the five pounds from Goggin," I said, starting the car.

As we ran out of Killoge, at something near thirty miles an hour, I heard scald-crow laughter behind me in the shawls.

49

III

THE FRIEND OF HER YOUTH

IT has come to this with me, I am not the
country-house visitor that I once was. It is a
sign of age, I suppose, and of growing unamia-
bility ; so, at any rate, my wife tells me. For
my part, I think it indicates a power of discrimi-
nating between the things that are good enough,
and the infinitely more numerous things that are
the reverse.

"Do you mean to say this isn't good enough?"
said Philippa, putting down the novel that, at
11 A.M., she was shamelessly reading, and indi-
cating our surroundings with a swing of her open
parasol.

It was a perfect morning in August. She and
I were seated in incredible leisure, in comfortable
basket chairs, on a space of sward that sank in
pleasant curves to the verge of the summer sea.
We looked across three miles of burnished water
to the Castle Manus hills, that showed mistily
through grey veils of heat ; in the middle distance
a 40-ton cutter yacht drowsed at anchor ; at the
end of the sward a strand, theatrical in the perfec-

tion of its pale sand and dark rocks, laid itself out to attract the bather.

"I think it is very good," I replied, "but it won't last. At any minute old Derryclare will come and compel me to go out trawling, or mending nets, or cutting up bait, or mucking out the dinghey——"

"You may be thankful if he lets you off with that!" said Philippa, flitting from her first position and taking up one in advance of mine.

Following the direction of her eyes, I perceived, as it were at the back of the stage, two mysterious, shrouded figures pursuing a swift course towards the house through a shrubbery of immense hydrangea bushes. Their heads resembled monster black door-handles, round their shoulders hung flounces of black muslin; in gauntleted hands they bore trays loaded with "sections" of honey; even at a distance of fifty yards we could see their attendant *cortége* of indignant bees.

"Taken thirty pounds this morning!" shouted the leading door-handle, speeding towards the house. "Splendid heather honey!"

"You ought to show some interest," said my wife malignly. "Go in and look at it. He's your host!"

"Not if he were all the hosts of Midian!" I said, but I felt shaken.

I rose from my chair.

" I'm going to the motor-house," I said firmly.

"Very well, I shall bathe," replied Philippa.

" I suppose you are aware that your old friend, Mr. Chichester, is at present in possession of the bathing cove," I returned, "and it might be as well to ascertain the opinion of your hostess on the subject of mixed bathing."

" Did you observe that Lord Derryclare was wearing your new motor-gloves ? " said Philippa as I moved away.

I magnanimously left the last word with her.

The Derryclares were in the habit of hurling themselves, at intervals, out of civilisation, and into the wilderness, with much the same zest with which those who live in the wilderness hurl themselves into civilisation.   In the wilderness, twenty miles from a railway station, they had built them a nest, and there led that variety of the simple life that is founded on good servants, old clothes, and a total indifference to weather.   Wandering friends on motor tours swooped occasionally out of space; married daughters, with intervals between visits to be filled in, arrived without warning, towing reluctant husbands (who had been there before).   Lost men, implicated with Royal Commissions and Congested Districts, were washed in at intervals ; Lady Derryclare said she never asked anyone ; people came.

It is true that she had asked us, but the invitation had been given on our wedding-day, and had been put away with our duplicate wedding presents ; we had now disinterred it, because I had bought a motor, and was still in the stage of enthusiasm when the amateur driver will beat up visits for his wife to pay. I do not know how Chichester got there ; he, like Lady Derryclare, dated from the benighted period before Philippa knew me, and I may admit that, in common with most husbands, I am not attracted by the male friends of my wife's youth. If Chichester had been the type she fancied, was I merely a Super-Chichester ?

Chichester was an elderly young man, worn smooth by much visiting in country houses, and thoroughly competent in the avocations proper to his career. He knew the best " stands " at half the shoots in Ireland, and could tell to half a crown the value set upon each by the keeper ; if you gave him a map he could put a pudgy finger upon the good cooks as promptly as an archbishop upon his cathedral towns ; he played a useful and remunerative game of bridge ; to see his eye, critical, yet alight with healthful voracity, travelling down the array of dishes on the side-table at breakfast, and arranging unhesitatingly the order in which they were to be attacked, was a lesson to the heedless who blunt the fine edge of appetite with porridge.

He faced me at lunch, plump and pink and shining after his bathe ; he was clean-shaved (the only reliable remedy for a greying moustache, as I did not fail to point out to Philippa) ; it increased his resemblance to a well-fed and *passé* schoolboy. Old Derryclare, whose foible it was to believe that he never had any luncheon, was standing at the sideboard, devouring informally a slice of bread and honey. One of his eyes was bunged up by bee-stings, and the end of his large nose shone red from the same cause.

"Bill," he said, addressing his eldest son, "don't you forget to take those sections on board this afternoon."

"No fear!" responded Bill, helping himself to a beaker of barley-water with hands that bore indelible traces of tar and motor grease.

Bill was a vigorous youth, of the type that I have heard my friend Slipper describe as "a hardy young splinter"; he was supposed to be preparing for a diplomatic career, and in the meantime was apparently qualifying for the engine-room of a tramp steamer (of which, it may be added, his father would have made a most admirable skipper).

"Great stuff, honey, with a rice-pudding,"

went on Bill. "Mrs. Yeates, do you know I can make a topping rice-pudding?"

I noticed that Chichester, who was seated next to Philippa, suddenly ceased to chew.

"I can do you a very high-class omelette, too," continued Bill, bashing a brutal spoon into the fragile elegance of something that looked as if it were made of snow and spun glass. "I'm not so certain about my mutton-chops and beefsteak, but I've had the knives sharpened, anyhow!"

Chichester turned his head away, as from a jest too clownish to be worthy of attention. His cheek was large, and had a tender, beefy flush in it.

"In *my* house," he said to Philippa, "I never allow the knives to be sharpened. If meat requires a sharp knife it is not fit to eat."

"No, of course not!" replied Philippa, with nauseating hypocrisy.

"The principle on which my wife buys meat," I said to the table at large, "is to say to the butcher, 'I want the best meat in your shop; but don't show it to me!'"

"Mrs. Yeates is quite right," said Chichester seriously; "you should be able to trust your butcher."

The door flew open, and Lady Derryclare strode in, wrestling as she came with the strings of a painting apron, whose office had been no sinecure. She was tall and grey-haired, and was just sufficiently engrossed in her own pursuits to be an attractive hostess.

" It was perfectly lovely out there on the *Sheila*," she said, handing the apron to the butler, who removed it from the room with respectful disapproval. " If only she hadn't swung with the tide! I found my sketch had more and more in it every moment—turning into a panorama, in fact! Yachts would be perfect if they had long solid legs and stood on concrete."

I said that I thought a small island would do as well.

Lady Derryclare disputed this, and argued that an island would involve a garden, whereas the charm of a yacht was that one hideous bunch of flowers on the cabin table was all that was expected of it, and that kind people ashore always gave it vegetables.

I said that these things did not concern me, as I usually neither opened my eyes or touched food while yachting. I said this very firmly, being not without fear that I might yet find myself hustled into becoming one of the party that was to go aboard the *Sheila* that very night. They were to start on the top of the tide, that is to say, at 4 A.M. the following morning, to sail round the coast to a bay some thirty miles away, renowned for its pollack-fishing, and there to fish. Pollack-fishing, as a sport, does not appeal to me ; according to my experience, it consists in hauling up coarse fish out of deep water by means of a hook baited with red flannel. It might appear poor-spirited, even effeminate, but nothing short of a press-gang should get me on board the *Sheila* that night.

"Every expedition requires its martyr," said Lady Derryclare, helping herself to some of the best cold salmon it has been my lot to encounter, "it makes it so much pleasanter for the others ; some one they can despise and say funny things about."

"The situation may produce its martyr," I said.

Lady Derryclare glanced quickly at me, and then at Chichester, who was now expounding to Philippa the method, peculiar to himself, by which he secured mountain mutton of the essential age.

At nine-thirty that night I sat with my hostess and my wife, engaged in a domestic game of Poker-patience. Shaded lights and a softly burning turf fire shed a mellow radiance ; an exquisite completeness was added by a silken rustle of misty rain against the south window.

"Do you think they'll start in this weather?" said Philippa sympathetically.

"Seventy-five, and one full house, ten, that's eighty-five," said Lady Derryclare abstractedly. "Start? you may be quite sure they'll start! Then we three shall have an empty house. That ought to count at least twenty!"

Lady Derryclare was far too good a hostess not to appreciate the charms of solitude; that Philippa and I should be looked upon as solitude was soothing to the heart of the guest, the heart that, however good the hostess, inevitably conceals some measure of apprehension.

"Has Mr. Chichester been on board the *Sheila?*" I enquired, with elaborate unconcern.

"*Never!*" said Lady Derryclare melodramatically.

"I believe he has done some yachting?" I continued.

"A five-hundred-ton steam yacht to the West Indies!" replied Lady Derryclare. "Bathrooms and a *chef*——"

There was a thumping of heavy feet outside the door, and the yacht party entered, headed by Lord Derryclare with a lighted lantern. They were clad in oilskins and sou'-westers; Bill had a string of onions in one hand and a sponge-bag in the other; Chichester carried a large gold-mounted umbrella.

"You look as if you were acting a charade," said Lady Derryclare, shuffling the cards for the next game, the game that would take place when the pleasure-seekers had gone forth into the rain. "The word is Fare-well, I understand?"

It occurred to me that to fare well was the last thing that Chichester was likely to do; and, furthermore, that the same thing had occurred to him.

"'Fare thee well, my own Mary Anne!'" sang Lord Derryclare, in a voice like a bassoon, and much out of tune. "It's a dirty night, but the glass is rising, and" (here he relapsed again into song) "'We are bound for the sea, Mary Anne! We are bound for the sea!'"

"Then we're to meet you on Friday?" said Philippa, addressing herself to Chichester in palpable and egregious consolation.

"Dear lady," replied Chichester tartly, "in the South of Ireland it is quite absurd to make plans. One is the plaything of the climate!"

"All aboard," said Lord Derryclare, with a swing of his lantern.

As they left the room the eye of Bill met mine, not without understanding.

"Now D's perfectly happy," remarked Lady Derryclare, sorting her suits; "but I'm not quite so sure about the Super-Cargo."

The game progressed pleasantly, and we heard the rain enwrap the house softly, as with a mantle.

The next three days were spent in inglorious peace, not to say sloth. On one of them, which was wet, I cleared off outstanding letters and browsed among new books and innumerable magazines: on the others, which were fine, I ran the ladies in the car back into the hills, and pottered after grouse with a venerable red setter, while Lady Derryclare painted, and Philippa made tea. When not otherwise employed, I thanked heaven that I was not on board the *Sheila*.

On Thursday night came a telegram from the yacht:

"Ronnie's flotilla in; luncheon party to-morrow; come early.—BILL."

At nine o'clock the next morning we were on the road; there was a light northerly breeze, enough to dry the roads and to clear the sky of all save a few silver feathers of cloud; the heather was in bloom on the hills, the bogs were bronze and green, the mountains behind them were as blue as grapes; best of all, the car was running like a saint, floating up the minor hills, pounding unfalteringly up the big ones. She and I were still in the honeymoon stage, and her most normal virtues were to me miraculous; even my two ladies, though, like their sex, grossly utilitarian, and incapable, as I did not fail to assure them, of appreciating the poesy of mechanism, were complimentary.

In that part of Ireland in which my lot is cast signposts do not exist. The residents, very reasonably, consider them to be superfluous, even ridiculous, in view of the fact that every one knows the way, and as for strangers, "haven't they tongues in their heads as well as another?" It all tends to conversation and an increased knowledge of human nature. Therefore it was that when we had descended from the hills, and found ourselves near the head of Dunerris Bay, at a junction of three roads, any one of which might have been ours, our only course was to pause there and await enlightenment.

It came, plentifully, borne by an outside car, and bestowed by no less than four beautifully dressed young ladies. I alighted and approached the outside car, and was instructed by the driver as to the route, an intricate one, to Eyries Harbour. The young ladies offered supplementary suggestions; they were mysteriously acquainted with the fact that the *Sheila* was our destination, and were also authorities on the movements of that section of the British Navy that was known to the family of Sub-Lieutenant the Hon. Ronald Cunningham as " Ronnie's Flotilla."

" We met the yacht gentlemen at tea on Mr. Cunningham's torpedo-boat yesterday afternoon," volunteered the prettiest of the young ladies, with a droop of her eyelashes.

The party then laughed, and looked at each other, as those do who have together heard the chimes at midnight.

" Why, we're going to lunch with them to-day at the hotel at Ecclestown !   And with you, too ! " broke in another, with a sudden squeal of laughter.

I said that the prospect left nothing to be desired.

" Mr. Chichester invited us yesterday ! " put in a third from the other side of the car.

" I don't think it's pollack he'll order for luncheon," said the fourth of the party from under the driver's elbow, a flapper, with a slow, hoarse voice, and a heavy cold in her head.

" Shut up, Katty, you brat ! " said the eldest, with lightning utterance.

The quartette again dissolved into laughter. I said " Au revoir," and withdrew to report progress to my deeply interested passengers.

As the outside car disappeared from view at a

corner, the Flapper waved a large pocket-handkerchief to me.

"You seem to have done wonderfully well in the time," said Lady Derryclare kindly.

For half an hour or more we ran west along the southern shore of the great bay ; Ecclestown, where Chichester's luncheon-party was to take place, was faintly visible on the further side. So sparkling was the sea, so benign the breeze, that even I looked forward without anxiety, almost with enjoyment, to the sail across the bay.

There is a bland and peaceful suggestion about the word village that is wholly inapplicable to the village of Eyries, a collection of dismal, slated cabins, grouped round a public-house, like a company of shabby little hens round a shabby and bedraggled cock. The road that had conveyed us to this place of entertainment committed suicide on a weedy beach below, its last moments much embittered by chaotic heaps of timber, stones, and gravel. A paternal Board was building a pier, and "mountains of gold was flying into it, but the divil a much would ever come out of it."

This I was told by the publican as I bestowed the car in an outhouse in his yard, wherein, he assured me, "neither chick nor child would find it."

The *Sheila* was anchored near the mouth of the harbour; there was a cheerful air of expectancy about her, and her big mainsail was hoisted; her punt, propelled by Bill, was already tripping towards us over the little waves; the air was salt, and clean, and appetising. Bill appeared to be in robust health; he had taken on a good many extra tones of sunburn, and it was difficult, on a cursory inspection, to decide where his neck ended and his brown flannel shirt began.

"—— Oh, a topping time!" he said, as we moved out over the green, clear water, through which glimmered to us the broken pots and pans of Eyries that lay below. "Any amount of fish going. We've had to give away no end."

"I should like to hear what you've been giving Mr. Chichester to eat?" said Lady Derryclare suavely.

"Well, there was the leg of mutton that we took with us; he ate that pretty well; and a sort of a hash next day, fair to middling."

"And after that?" said his mother, with polite interest.

"Well, after that," said Bill, leaning his elbows on his sculls and ticking off the items on his fingers, "we had boiled pollack, and fried pollack, and pollack *réchauffé aux fines herbes*—onions, you know——"

Bill broke off artistically, and I recalled to myself a saying of an American sage, "Those that go down to the sea in ships see the works of the Lord, but those that go down to the sea in cutters see hell."

"He went ashore yesterday," said Bill, resuming his narrative and the sculls, "and came aboard with a pig's face and a pot of jam that he got at the pub, and I say!—that pig's face!— Phew! My aunt!"

"'Look in my face; my name is Might-have-been,'" quoted Lady Derryclare.

Philippa shuddered aloud.

"But he's going to come level to-day," went on Bill; "he's standing us all lunch at the Ecclestown Hotel, Ronnie's skipper and all. He spent a good half-hour writing out a menu, and Ronnie took it over last night. We had tea on board Ronnie's ship, you know."

We said we knew all about the tea-party and the guests.

"Oh, you do, do you?" said Bill; "then you know a good deal! Chichester can tell you a bit more about the dark one if you like to ask him!"

"He seems to have outgrown his fancy for fair people," I said.

Philippa put her nose in the air.

"He's gorgeously dressed for the occasion," continued Bill.

"More than you are!" said his mother.

"Oh, my one don't care. No more does Ronnie's. What they enjoyed was the engine-room."

"It seems to me," said Lady Derryclare to Philippa, "that we are rather superfluous to this entertainment."

Chichester stood at the gangway and helped the ladies on to the narrow, hog-backed deck of the *Sheila*. He was indeed beautifully dressed, but to the critical eye it seemed that the spotless grey flannel suit hung a shade easier, and that the line of his cheek was less freshly rounded. His nose had warmed to a healthful scarlet, but his eye was cold, and distinctly bleak. He was silent, not, it was obvious to me, because he had nothing to say, but because he might have more to say than would be convenient. In all senses save the literal one he suggested the simple phrase, "Fed up." I felt for him. As I saw the grim deck-bosses on which we might have to sit, and the dark mouth of the cabin in which we might have to eat, and tripped over a rope, and grasped at the boom, which yielded instead of supporting me, I thought with a lover's ardour of the superiority—whether as means of progression or as toy

—of the little car, tucked away in the Eyries publican's back-yard, where neither chick nor child would find her.

"You ought to have come with us, Yeates," said Derryclare, emerging from the companion-hatch with a fishing-line in his hand. "Great sport! we got a hundred and fifty yesterday— beats trout-fishing! Doesn't it, Chichester?"

Chichester smiled sarcastically and looked at his watch.

"Quite right," said his lordship, twisting his huge hairy paw, and consulting the nickel time-keeper on his wrist. "Time to be off—mustn't keep our young ladies waiting. We'll slip across in no time with this nice breeze. Regular ladies' day. Now then, Bill! get that fores'l on her— we'll up anchor and be off!"

There are few places in creation where the onlooker can find himself more painfully and perpetually *de trop* than on the deck of a small yacht. I followed the ladies to the saloon. Chichester remained on deck. As I carefully descended the companion-ladder I saw him look-ing again at his watch, and from it across the bay to the hazy white specks, some four miles away, in one of which assiduous waiters were even now, it might be, setting forth the repast that was to indemnify him for three days of pollack.

"P'ff; I wonder if they ever open the windows," said Lady Derryclare, fitting herself skilfully into the revolving chair at the end of the cabin table. "Do sit down—these starting operations are always lengthy."

I took my seat, that is to say, I began to sit down in the air, well outside the flap of the table, and gradually inserted myself underneath it. The bunch of flowers, foretold by Lady Derryclare, confronted us, packed suffocatingly into its vase, and even the least astute of the party (I allude to myself) was able unhesitatingly to place it as an attention from the fair ones of the outside car. Behind my shoulders, a species of trough filled the interval between the back of the seat and the sloping side of the yacht; in it lay old tweed caps, old sixpenny magazines, field-glasses, cans of tobacco, and a well-worn box of "Patience" cards. Above and behind it a rack made of netting was darkly charged with signal-flags, fishing-rods, and minor offal.

"Think of them all, smoking here on a wet night," said Lady Derryclare with abhorrence; "with the windows shut and no shade on the lamp! Let nothing tempt any of you to open the pantry door; we might see the pig's face. Unfortunate George Chichester!"

"I shouldn't pity him too much," said I. "I

expect he wouldn't take five pounds for his appetite this moment!"

The rhythmic creak of the windlass told that the anchor was coming up. It continued for some moments, and then stopped abruptly.

"Now then, all together!" said Lord Derryclare's voice.

A pause, punctuated by heavy grunts of effort—then Bill's voice.

"What the blazes is holding it? Come on, Chichester, and put your back into it!"

Chichester's back, ample as it would seem, had no appreciable effect on the situation.

"You ought to go and help them, Sinclair," said my wife, with that readiness to offer a vicarious sacrifice that is so characteristic of wives.

I said I would wait till I was asked. I had not to wait long.

I took my turn at the warm handle-bar of the windlass, and grunted and strove as strenuously as my predecessors. The sun poured down in undesired geniality, the mainsail lurched and flapped; the boom tugged at its tether; the water jabbered and gurgled past the bows.

"I think we're in the *consommé!*" remarked Bill, putting his hands in his pockets.

"Here," said Lord Derryclare, with a very red face; "confound her! we'll sail her off it!"

Chichester sat down in a deck-chair as remote as possible from his kind, and once again consulted his watch. Bill took the tiller; ropes were hauled, slacked, made fast; the boom awoke to devastating life; the *Sheila* swung, tilted over to the breeze, and made a rush for freedom. The rush ended in a jerk, the anchor remained immovable, and the process was repeated in the opposite direction, with a vigour that restored Chichester abruptly to the bosom of society—in point of fact, my bosom. He said nothing, or at least nothing to signify, as I assisted him to rise, but I felt as if I were handling a live shell.

During the succeeding quarter of an hour the *Sheila*, so it seemed to my untutored mind, continued to sail in tangents towards all the points of the compass, and at the end of each tangent was brought up with an uncompromising negative from the anchor. By that time my invariable yacht-headache was established, and all the other men in the ship were advancing, at a varying rate of progress, into a frame of mind that precluded human intercourse, and was entirely removed from perceiving any humour in the situation.

Through all these affairs the sound of conversation ascended steadily through the main-hatch. Lady Derryclare and my wife were playing Patience in the cabin, and were at the same time discussing intricate matters in connection with District Nurses, with that strange power of doing one thing and talking about another that I have often noticed in women. It was at about this period that the small, rat-like head of Bill's kitchen-maid, Jimmy, appeared at the fore-hatch (accompanied by a reek of such potency that I immediately assigned it to the pig's face), and made the suggestion about the Congested Diver. That the Diver, however congested, was a public official, engaged at the moment in laying the foundations of the Eyries Pier, did not, this being Ireland, complicate the situation. The punt, with Bill, hot and taciturn, in the stern, sprang forth on her errand, smashing and bouncing through the sharpened edges of the little waves. As I faced that dainty and appetising breeze, I felt the first pang of the same hunger that was, I knew, already gnawing Chichester like a wolf.

"We must have fouled some old moorings," said Derryclare, coming up from the cabin, with a large slice of bread and honey in his hand, and an equanimity somewhat restored by a working solution of the problem. " Damn nuisance, but it can't be helped. Better get something to eat, Chichester; you won't get to Ecclestown before three o'clock at the best."

"No, thank you," said Chichester, without raising his eyes from the four-day-old paper that he was affecting to read.

I strolled discreetly away, and again looked down through the skylight into the cabin. The ladies were no longer there, and, in defiance of all nautical regulations, a spirit-lamp with a kettle upon it was burning on the table, a sufficient indication to a person of my experience that Philippa and Lady Derryclare had abandoned hope of the Ecclestown lunch and were making tea. The prospect of something to eat, of any description, was not unpleasing ; in the meantime I took the field-glasses, and went forward to follow, pessimistically, the progress of the punt in its search for the Diver.

There was no one on the pier. Bill landed, went up the beach, and was lost to sight in the yard of the public-house.

"It must be he's at his dinner," said Jimmy at my elbow, descrying these movements with a vision that appeared to be equal to mine plus the field-glasses. There was an interval, during which I transferred my attention to Ecclestown ; its white hotel basked in sunshine, settled and balmy, as of the land of Beulah. Its comfortable aspect suggested roast chicken, tingling glasses of beer, even of champagne. A torpedo-boat, with a thread of smoke coming quietly from its foremost funnel, lay in front of the hotel. It seemed as though it were enjoying an after-luncheon cigarette.

"They're coming out now!" said Jimmy, with excitement; "it must be they were within in the house looking at the motor."

I turned the field-glasses on Eyries; a fair proportion of its population was emerging from the yard of the public-house, and the length to which their scientific interest had carried them formed a pleasing subject for meditation.

"There's the ha'past-one mail-car coming in," said Jimmy; "it's likely he'll wait for the letters now."

The mirage of the Ecclestown lunch here melted away, as far as I was concerned, and with a resignation perfected in many Petty Sessions courts, I turned my appetite to humbler issues. To those who have breakfasted at eight, and have motored over thirty miles of moorland, tea and sardines at two o'clock are a mere affair of outposts, that leave the heart of the position untouched. Yet a temporary glow of achievement may be attained by their means, and the news brought back by Bill, coupled with a fresh loaf, that the Diver was coming at once, flattered the hope that the game was

still alive. Bill had also brought a telegram for
Chichester.

"Who has the nerve to tell Mr. Chichester that
there's something to eat here?" said Lady Derryclare, minutely examining the butter.

"Philippa is obviously indicated," I said malignly. "She is the Friend of his Youth!"

"You're all odious," said Philippa, sliding from
beneath the flap of the table with the light of the
lion-tamer in her eye.

What transpired between her and the lion we
shall never know. She returned almost immediately, with a heightened colour, and the irrelevant
information that the Diver had come on board.
The news had the lifting power of a high
explosive. We burst from the cabin and went
on deck as one man, with the exception of my
wife, who, with a forethought that did her credit,
turned back to improvise a cosy for the teapot.

The Diver was a large person, of few words,
with a lowering brow and a heavy moustache.
He did not minimise the greatness of his con-
descension in coming aboard the yacht; he listened gloomily to the explanations of Lord Derryclare. At the conclusion of the narrative he
moved in silence to the bows and surveyed the
situation. His boat, containing the apparatus of
his trade, was alongside; a stalwart underling,

clad in a brown jersey, sat in the bows; in the stern was enthroned the helmet, goggling upon us like a decapitated motorist. It imparted a thrill that I had not experienced since I read Jules Verne at school.

"Here, Jeremiah," said the Diver.

The satellite came on deck with the single sinuous movement of a salmon.

The Diver motioned him to the windlass. "We'll take a turn at this first," he said.

They took each a handle, they bent to their task, and the anchor rose at their summons like a hot knife out of butter.

Every man present, with the exception of the Diver and the satellite, made the simple declaration that he was damned, and it was in the period of paralysis following on this that a fresh ingredient was added to the situation.

A giant voice filled the air, and in a windy bellow came the words :

"Nice lot you are!"

We faced about and saw "Ronnie's torpedoboat" executing a sweeping curve in the mouth of Eyries Harbour.

"Couldn't wait any longer!" proceeded the voice of the Megaphone. "We've got to pick up the others outside. Thanks awfully for luncheon! Top-hole!"

T.B. No. 1000 completed the curve and headed for the open sea with a white mane of water rising above her bows. There was something else white fluttering at the stern. I put up the field-glasses, and with their aid perceived upon the deck a party of four ladies, one of whom was waving a large pocket handkerchief. The glasses were here taken out of my hand by Chichester, but not before I had identified the Flapper.

What Chichester said of Ronnie was heard only by me, and possibly by Jimmy, who did not count. I think it may have saved his life, being akin to opening a vein. That I was the sole recipient of these confidences was perhaps due to the fact that the *Sheila*, so swiftly and amazingly untethered, here began to fall away to leeward, with all the wilful helplessness of her kind, and instant and general confusion was the result. There were a few moments during which ropes, spars, and human beings pursued me wherever I went. Then I heard Lord Derryclare's voice—" Let go that anchor again!"

The sliding rattle of the chain followed, the anchor plunged ; the *status quo* was re-established.

Chichester went ashore with the Diver to catch the outgoing mail-car. The telegram that had arrived with Bill was brought into action flagrantly, and was as flagrantly accepted. (It was found, subsequently, on his cabin floor, and was to the effect that the cartridges had been forwarded as directed.) The farewells were made, the parting regrets very creditably accomplished, and we stood on the deck and saw him go, with his suit-case, his rods, his gun-case, heaped imposingly in the bow, his rug, and his coats, the greater and the less, piled beside him in the stern.

The wind had freshened; the Diver and Jeremiah drove the boat into it with a will, and the heavy oars struck spray off the crests of the waves. We saw Chichester draw forth the greater coat, and stand up and put it on. The boat lurched, and he sat down abruptly, only to start to his feet again as if he had been stung by a wasp. He thrust his hand into the pocket, and Philippa clutched my arm.

"Could it have been into the pocket of *his* coat that I put the teapot——?" she breathed.

IV

HARRINGTON'S

Breakfast was over; Philippa was feeding the dogs. Philippa's cousin, Captain Andrew Larpent, R.E., was looking out of the window with that air of unemployment that touches the conscience of a host like a spur. Andrew did not smoke, a serious matter in a male guest, which means that there are, for him, no moments of lethargy, and that, when he idles, his idleness stands stark in the foreground against a clear sky, a reproach and a menace to his entertainers.

It was a cold day about the middle of September, and there was an unrest among the trees that commemorated a night of storm ; the gravel was wet, the lawn-tennis ground was strewn with sycamore leaves.

" I suppose you'll say I'm drunk," said Andrew, " but the fact remains that I see two Natives coming up the drive."

In the green tunnel that was the avenue at Shreelane were two dark figures ; both were dressed in frock-coats, of which the tails fluttered meagrely in the wind ; their faces were black ;

with the half-hearted blackness of a leg in a black silk stocking; one of them wore a tall hat.

"This is what comes of leaving Calcutta without paying your bills," I suggested; "or perhaps it's a Missionary Deputation——"

The Natives advanced into the middle distance.

"It's the Sweep!" exclaimed Philippa. "It's my beloved Cantillon!"

She flung open the window.

"Oh, Cantillon!" she cried, invoking the gentleman in the top-hat as if he were an idol, "I've been longing to see you!"

The leading Native halted beneath the window and curtseyed.

"I partly guessed it, my Lady!" he replied modestly, and curtseyed again.

"Then why didn't you come before?" screamed Philippa, suppressing with difficulty the indignation of the dogs.

"I had the toothache, my Lady, and a howlt in my poll," returned the sweep, in dignified narrative. "I may say my hands was crackin' with the stren'th of pain, and these four days back there was the rumour of passpiration all over me, with respex to ye——"

"I'll see you in the kitchen," said Philippa, shutting the window abruptly. "My poor friends," she continued, "this means a cold luncheon for you, and a still colder reception for me from Mrs. Cadogan, but if I let Cantillon escape me now, I may never see him again—which is unthinkable ! "

I presume that white is the complimentary colour of a sweep. In half an hour after the arrival of Mr. Cantillon the sitting-rooms were snowed over with sheets, covering alike floor and furniture, while he and his disciple moved from room to room on tiptoe, with ostentatious humility, leaving a round black spoor upon the snow. My writing-table was inaccessible, so also was the piano, which could usually be trusted to keep Andrew quiet for an hour of the morning. Perhaps it would be more accurate to say it kept him occupied. Captain Larpent had not been many years in the service of his country, yet it was already told of him that "From Birr to Bareilly," undeterred by hardships, his intrepid piano had accompanied him, and that house-rents fell to zero within a half-mile radius of his vicinity. Daily the walls of Shreelane shook to the thunder of his practising ; nightly his duets with my wife roared like a torrent over my sleeping head. Sometimes, also, he sang, chiefly in German (a language I do not understand), and with what seemed to me superfluous energy. But this, I am told, means "temperament."

Haunting as a waltz refrain the flavour of soot stole through the menu at dinner; it was whispered in the soup, it was muttered in the savoury, and in the coffee it abandoned subterfuge and shouted down all opposition. Next morning, at breakfast, Philippa asked if the car wanted exercise, because it seemed to her a day marked out by Providence for calling on the Chicken Farmers. We might start early, take sandwiches, show Andrew something of the country—the programme was impulsively sketched in, but none the less I divined that an indignant household had demanded a day of atonement in which to obliterate the memory of the sweep.

It was, as well as I remember, in the preceding spring that the Chicken Farmers had come before the swallow dared, and had taken—in addition to the winds of March—a small farm about midway in the wilderness between us and the Derryclares. They were two young women who had recently been commended to our special attention by Lady Derryclare; they were, she said, Pioneers, and were going to make their fortunes, and would incidentally set an example to the district. Philippa had met them on the Derryclares' yacht.

"One of them is very pretty," she explained to Andrew, "and the other is a doctor."

" I wonder which of them does most damage ? " said Andrew. " I think I'll stay at home."

None the less he came.

It was not until the car was at the door that I found we were to be favoured with the society of my eldest son, Anthony, in consequence of the facts that (1) the day before had been his ninth birthday, (2) that he had not cried when he met the sweep in the passage, and (3) that for lack of the kitchen fire he had had no birthday cake. Minx, also, was one of us, but as she came as a stowaway, this did not transpire till later, when explanations were superfluous.

It was at the moment of departure that I perceived a donkey-cart, modestly screening itself behind the evergreens on the way to the yard, and one of Flurry Knox's men approached me with Mr. Knox's compliments, and would I lend him the loan of the long ladder ? Some two years ago, in a moment of weakness, I had provided myself with a ladder wherewith to attain to the eaveshoots of Shreelane, since when I had found myself in the undesired position of public benefactor. How life without a long ladder had hitherto been possible for my neighbours I was at a loss to imagine, and as I was also at a loss for any valid excuse for refusing to lend it, the ladder enjoyed a butterfly existence of country-house visiting. Its visits to Mr. Knox had been especially lengthy and debilitating. It is, as Mrs. Cadogan is wont to say, the last straw that puts the hump on the camel. The blood suddenly mounted to my brain, and with it came inspiration.

"You can tell Mr. Knox that the eaveshoots of this house are leaking like sieves, and I want the ladder myself."

In the glow of satisfaction kindled by the delivery of this message I started the caravan. The western breeze fanned my brow agreeably, the car purred her satisfaction with our new and only stretch of steam-rolled road, and Anthony was still in the condition of Being Good (a condition, nevertheless, by no means to be relied on, and quite distinct from Goodness).

We ran west, we ran north; we skirted grey and sounding bays of the Atlantic; we climbed high among heathery, stone-besprinkled moors; we lunched by the roadside in the lee of a rick of turf, and Anthony, by this time emerging from the condition of Being Good, broke the Thermos, and flashed his birthday electric torch in Minx's face until she very properly bit him, and Philippa slurred over the incident with impartial chocolate, and said it was time to start.

The region in which the Chicken Farmers had

established themselves suggested the nurture of
snipe and sea-gulls rather than chickens. It was
an indeterminate patchwork of stony knobs of hill
and pockets of bog, among which the road humped
and sagged, accepting pessimistically the facts of
nature. Hardy, noisy hill-streams scurried beside
it, or over it, as seemed good to them; finally a
sharp turn, a high horizon of sea, and a steep
down-hill grade, ending on the shore of a small,
round lake. There was a little pink box of a
house on its farther side, with a few bunches of
trees round it, and among them a pigmy village
of prim wooden huts.

"That's the place," said Philippa, who had
been there with Lady Derryclare. "And those
are the last cry in hen-houses. Now remember,
both of you, one of them is a doctor, Scotch, and
a theosophist, or something mysterious of that
sort; and the pretty one was engaged to a
gunner and it was broken off—why, I don't
know—drink, I fancy, or mad—so you had
better be careful——"

"I shall be guarded in my condolences," I
said, turning in at the little gate, with the
sensation of being forcibly fed.

"As far as one can gather," said Andrew,
"there remains no topic in heaven or earth
that——"

"Music and poultry," said Philippa in a breath, as I drew up at the hall door.

Andrew rang the bell, and a flock of white ducks hurried up from among the trees and gathered round him with loud cries of welcome. There was no other reply to his summons, and at the second essay the bell-wire came out by the roots with generous completeness.

"The ladies is gone to th' oxtion!" cried a voice from among the hen-coops, and the ducks lifted up their voices in ardent reply.

"Where is the auction?" Philippa called, when a comparative silence had fallen.

"In Harrington's, beyond at the Mines!" replied the oracle, on a well-sustained high G.

"Put the cards on the hall table," said Philippa, "we might go back that way."

Several things combine in the spell that an auction casts upon my wife, as upon many others of her sex; the gamble, the competition, the lure of the second-hand, the thrill of possible treasure-trove. We proceeded along the coast road towards the mines, and I could hear Philippa expounding to her first-born the nature and functions of auctions, even as the maternal carnivore instructs her young in the art of slaughter. The road with which we were now dealing ran, or, it would be more accurate to say, walked, across the stony laps of the hills. The cliffs were on our right; the sea was still flustered after the storm, like a dog that has fought and is ready to fight again. We toiled over the shoulder of a headland, and there caught sight of "Harrington's."

On a green plateau, high above the sea, were a couple of iron sheds and a small squat tower; landward of them was a square and hideous house, of the type that springs up, as if inevitably, in the neighbourhood of mines, which are, in themselves, among the most hideous works of man. One of the sheds had but half a roof; a truck lay on its side in a pool of water; defeat was written starkly over all.

"Copper, and precious little of it," I explained to Andrew; "and they got some gold too—just enough to go to their heads, and ruin them."

"Did they put it in their mouths—where you have it, Father?" enquired Anthony, who was hanging on my words and on the back of my seat.

"Suppose you shut yours," I replied, with the brutality that is the only effective defence against the frontal attacks of the young.

We found the yard at Harrington's thronged with a shabby company of carts, cars, and traps of many varieties; donkey-carts had made their own of the road outside, even the small circle of gravel in front of the hall door was bordered by bicycles ; apparently an auction was a fashionable function in the region of the Lug-na-Coppal copper-mines. Dingy backs bulged from the open door of the hall, and over their heads as we arrived floated the voice of the auctioneer, demanding in tragic incredulity if people thought his conscience would permit him to let an aneroid barometer go for half-a-crown. Without a word Philippa inserted herself between the backs, followed by her son, and was lost to view.

"Thank you, madam!" said the voice, with a new note of cheer in it. "Five shillings I am bid! Any advance on five shillings?"

"That's a good weather-glass!" hissed a farmer's daughter with a plumed hat, to a friend with a black shawl over her head. "An' I coming into the house to-day I gave it a puck, and it knocked a lep out o' the needle. It's in grand working order."

"I'm told it was the last thing in the house poor Mr. Harrington left a hand on, the day he made away with himself, the Lord save us!" remarked a large matron, casually, to Andrew and me.

"I thought the Coroner's Jury found that he

fell down the shaft?" I returned, accepting the conversational opening in the spirit in which it was offered.

The matron winked at me with a mixture of compassion and confederacy.

"Ah, the poor fellow was insured, and the jury were decent men, they wouldn't wish to have anything said that'd put the wife out of the money."

"The right men in the right place, evidently," said Andrew, who rather fancies his dry humour. "But apart from the climate and the architecture, was there any reason for suicide?"

"I'm told he was a little annoyed," said an enormous old farmer, delicately.

"It was the weather preyed on him," said the matron. "There was a vessel was coming round to him with coal and all sorts, weather-bound she was, in Kinsale, and in the latther end she met a rock, and she went down in a lump, and his own brother that was in her was drownded."

"There were grounds for annoyance, I admit," said Andrew.

The big farmer, who had, perhaps, been one of the jury, remarked non-committally that he wouldn't say much for the weather we were getting now, and there was one of them planets was after the moon always.

We moved on to the yard, in which prospective buyers were prowling among wheelbarrows, coils of rope, ladders, and the various rubbish proper to such scenes, and Andrew discoursed of the accessories that would be needed for the repair of my eaveshoots, with the large-mindedness of the Government official who has his own spurs and another man's horse. He was in the act of assuring me that I should save half a man's wages by having a second long ladder, when some one in the house began to play on a piano, with knowledge and vigour. The effect on Captain Larpent was as when a hound, outside a covert, hears the voice of a comrade within. The room from which the music came was on the ground floor, the back door was open, and Andrew walked in.

"That is one of those young ladies who have come here to make their fortunes with poultry," observed a melancholy-looking clergyman at my elbow, "Miss Longmuir, I expect; she is the musician. Her friend, Dr. Catherine Fraser, is here also. Wonderful young ladies—no wish for society. I begged them to come and live near my church—I offered them a spare corner of the churchyard for their hen-coops—all of no avail."

I said that they seemed hard to please.

"Very, very," assented the clergyman ; "yet I assure you there is nothing cynical about them. They are merely recloozes."

He sighed, on what seemed to be general grounds, and moved away.

I followed Andrew into the house and found myself in the kitchen. The unspeakable dreariness of an auction was upon it. Pagodas of various crockeries stood high on the tables, and on benches round the walls sat, rook-like, an assembly of hooded countrywomen. A man with a dingy pale face was standing in front of the cold fireplace, addressing the company. On my arrival he removed his hat with stately grace, and with an effort I recognised Cantillon the sweep, in mufti—that is to say, minus some of his usual top-dressing of soot.

"It's what I was saying, Major Yeates," he resumed. " I'm sweeping those chimneys thirty years, and five managers I seen in this house, and there wasn't one o' them that got the price of their ticket to Cork out o' that mine. This poor man was as well-liked as anyone in the world, but there was a covey of blagyards in it that'd rob St. Pether, let alone poor Mr. Harrington !"

The company assented with a groan of general application, and the ensuing pause was filled by the piano in the next room, large and heavy chords, suggestive of the hand of Andrew.

"God! Mrs. Harrington was a fine woman!" croaked one of the rooks on the bench.

"She was, and very stylish," answered another. "Oh, surely she was a crown!"

"And very plain," put in a third, taking up the encomium like a part in a fugue, "as plain as the grass on the hills!"

I moved on, and met my wife in a crowd at the door of the dining-room, and in an atmosphere which I prefer not to characterise.

"I've got the barometer!" she said breathlessly. "No one bid for it, and I got it for five shillings! A lovely old one. It's been in the house for at least fifty years, handed on from one manager to another."

"It doesn't seem to have brought them luck," I said. "What have you done with Anthony? Lost him, I hope!"

"There have been moments when I could have spared him," Philippa admitted, "especially when it came to his bidding against me, from the heart of the crowd, for a brass tea-kettle, and running the price up to the skies before I discovered him. Then I found him upstairs, auctioning a nauseous old tail of false hair, amidst the yells of country girls; and finally he tried to drop

out of the staircase window—ten feet at least—
with a stolen basket of tools round his neck. I
just saw his hands on the edge of the window-
sill."

"I think it's time to go home," I said grimly.

"Darling, *not* till I've bought the copper coal-
scuttle. Come and look at it!"

I followed her, uttering the impotent growls of
a husband. As we approached the drawing-room
the music broke forth again, this time in power.
Three broad countrywomen, in black hooded
cloaks and brown kid gloves, were seated on a
sofa; two deeply-engrossed backs at the piano
accounted for the music. There is no denying
the fact that a piano duet has some inescapable
association with the schoolroom, no matter how
dashing the execution, how superior the per-
formers.

"Poor old 'Semiramide'!" whispered Philippa;
"I played that overture when I was twelve!"
Over her shoulder I had a view of Andrew's
sleek black poll and brown neck, and an impression of fluffy hair, and a slight and shapely back
in a Norfolk jacket.

"He seems to have done very well in the
time," I said. " That's the pretty one, isn't it?"

I here became aware that the hall was filling with people, and that Mr. Armstrong, the

auctioneer, with his attendant swarm of buyers, was at my elbow.

"That's a sweet instrument," he said dispassionately, "and, I may say, magnificently played. Come, ladies and gentlemen, we'll not interrupt the concert. It might be as good for me to take the yard next, before the rain comes."

He led away his swarm, like a queen bee; "Semiramide" stormed on; some people strayed into the room and began to examine the furniture. The afternoon had grown overcast and threatening, and I noticed that a tall man in dark clothes and a yachting cap had stationed himself near the treble's right hand. He was standing between her and the light, rather rudely, it seemed to me, but the players did not appear to notice.

"That was rather a free and easy fellow," I said to Philippa, as we were borne along to the back door by the tide of auction.

"Who? Do you mean Mr. Armstrong?" said Philippa. "I'm rather fond of him——"

"No, the tall chap in the yachting cap."

"I didn't notice him—" began Philippa, but at this moment we were shot into the yard by pressure from behind. Mr. Armstrong took his stand on a packing-case, the people hived in round him, and I saw my wife no more.

Coils of fencing wire and sheets of corrugated

iron were proffered, and left the audience cold ; a faint interest was roused when the auctioneer's clerk held up one of a party of zinc pails for inspection.

"You'd count the stars through that one!" said a woman beside me.

"You can buy it for a telescope, ma'am!" said Mr. Armstrong swiftly.

"Well, well, hasn't he a very fine delivery!" said my neighbour, regarding Mr. Armstrong as if he were a landscape.

"Hannah," said the woman on my other hand, in a deep and reproachful contralto, speaking as if I did not exist, "did ye let the kitchen chairs go from you?"

"There wasn't one o' them but had a leg astray," apologised Hannah—"they got great hardship. When Harrington 'd have a drop taken he'd throw them here and there."

"Ladies! Ladies!" reproved Mr. Armstrong. "Is this an oxtion or is it a conversassiony? John! show that ladder."

"A big lot of use a forty-foot ladder 'd be to the people round this place!" said a superior young farmer in a new suit of clothes ; "there isn't a house here, unless it's my father's, would have any occasion for it."

Hannah dug me hard in the ribs with her elbow and put out her tongue.

"Five shillings I am bid for a forty-foot ladder!" said Mr. Armstrong to the Heavens; "I'd get a better price at a jumble sale!"

"Look at the poker they have in it by the way of a rung!" continued the young farmer. "I wouldn't be bothered buying things at oxtions; if it was only gettin' marr'ed you were you'd like a new woman!"

"Seven and six!"

To my own astonishment I heard my voice saying this.

"Seven and six I am bid," said the auctioneer, seizing me with his eye. "Ten shillings may I say? Thank you, sir——"

The clergyman had entered the lists against me.

I advanced against him by half-crowns; the audience looked on as at a battle of giants. At twenty-five shillings I knew that he was weakening; at thirty shillings the ladder was mine.

I backed out of the crowd with the victor's laurels on my brow, and, as I did so, a speck of rain hit me in the eye. The sea was looking cold and angry, and the horizon to windward was as thick as a hedge. It was obviously time to go, and I proceeded in the direction of the car.

As I left the yard a remarkable little animal, which for a single wild instant I took for a fox or a badger, came running up the road. It was reddish brown, with white cheeks and a white throat; it advanced hesitatingly and circled round me with agitated and apologetic whimpers.

"Minx!" I said incredulously.

The fox or badger flung itself on its side and waved a forepaw at me.

"It's hunting rabbits below on the cliffs she was," said a boy in a white flannel jacket, who was sitting on the wall.

"Oh, there you are," said Philippa's voice behind me; "I wanted to remind you to remember the aneroid. It's on the dining-room table. I'm feeling rather unhappy about that child," she went on, "I can't find him anywhere."

"*I'll* go in and find him," I said, with a father's ferocity.

"I hope he's there," said Philippa uncomfortably. "Good gracious! Is that Minx?"

I left the boy to explain, and made for the house, getting through the crowd in the doorway by the use of tongue and elbows, and making my way upstairs, strode hastily through the dark and repellent bedrooms of "Harrington's." Anthony was not there.

In the dining-room I heard Andrew's voice. I went in and found him sitting at the dinner-table with two ladies, one of whom was holding his hand and examining it attentively.

She had pale eyelashes, and pale golden hair, very firmly and repressively arranged; she was big and fresh and countrified looking, and her eyes were water-green. She looked like an Icelander or a Finn, but I recognised her as the second Chicken Farmer, Dr. Fraser.

"I was looking for Anthony," I said, withholding with difficulty an apology for intrusion. "We've got to get away, Andrew——"

"I was having my fortune told," said Andrew, looking foolish.

"I saw your little boy going across the field there, about half an hour ago," said Dr. Fraser, looking up at me with eyes of immediate understanding. "The white terrier was with him."

"Towards the cliffs?" I said, feeling glad that Philippa was not there.

"No, to the right—towards the tower." She went to the window. "There was some one with him," she added quickly. "There he is now—that man in a yachting cap, by the tower——"

"I don't see anyone," I said, refixing my eyeglass.

Miss Fraser continued to stare out of the window. "You're short-sighted," she said, without looking at me. "Perhaps if the window were open——"

Before I could help her she had opened it, and the west wind rushed in, with big drops in it.

"I must be blind," I said, "I can see no one."

"Nor can I—now," she said, drawing back from the window.

She sat down at the table as if her knees had given way, and her strong white hand fell slackly on Philippa's purchase, the old aneroid barometer, and rested there. The other girl looked at her anxiously.

"Hold up, Cathie!" she said, as one speaks to a horse when it stumbles.

Her friend's eyes were fixed, and empty of expression, and the fresh pervading pink of her face had paled.

"Perhaps we had better go and look for that kid," said Andrew, getting up, and I knew that he too was aware of something uncomfortable in the atmosphere. Before we could get out of the room, Dr. "Cathie" spoke.

"I see tram-lines," she said gropingly, "and water—I wonder if he's asleep——"

She sighed. Andrew and I, standing aghast, saw her colour begin to return.

Her friend's eye indicated to us the door. We closed it behind us, and shoved our way through the hall.

"I say!" said Andrew, as we got outside, "I thought she was going to chuck a fit, or have hysterics, or something. Didn't you?"

I did not answer. Cantillon, the sweep, was hurrying towards me with tidings in his face.

"Mrs. Yeates is after going to the cliff looking for the young gentleman—but sure what I was saying——"

I did not wait to hear what Cantillon's observations had been, because I had caught sight of Philippa, away in a field near the edge of the cliffs. She was running, and the boy with the white flannel jacket was in front of her. It seemed ridiculous to hurry, when I knew that Anthony had been accompanied by a large man in a yachting cap (in itself a guarantee of competency).

None the less, I ran, with the wind and the heavy raindrops in my face, across country, not round by the road, and ran the faster for seeing my wife and her companion sinking out of sight over the edge of the cliff, as by an oblique path. My way took me past the tower; there was a little plateau there, with a drooping wire fence round it, and I had a glimpse of the square black mouth of the disused shaft.

"Near the tower," the girl had said; but she had also said there was a man with him.

I ran on, but fear had sprung out of the shaft and came with me.

A hard-trodden path led from the tower to the cliff; it fell steeper and steeper, till, at a hairpin turn, it became rocky steps, slanting in sharp-cut zigzags down the face of the cliff. On the right hand the rocks leaned out above my head, yellow and grey and dripping, and tufted with sea pinks; on the left there was nothing except the wind. A couple of hundred feet below the sea growled and bellowed, plunging among broken rocks. I did not give room to the thought of Anthony's light body, tossed about there.

At a corner far below I had a glimpse of Philippa and the boy in the white jacket; he was leading her down—holding her hand—my poor Philippa, whose nightmare is height, who has *vertige* on a step-ladder. She must have had a sure word that Anthony had gone down this dizzy path before her. A mass of rock rose up between us, and they were gone, and in that gusty and treacherous wind it was impossible to make better speed.

The damnable iteration of the steps continued till my knees shook and my brain was half numb. They ceased at last at the mouth of a tunnel, half-way down the vertical face of the cliff; there was a platform outside it, over the edge of which two rusty rails projected into space above a narrow cove, where yellow foam, far below, churned and blew upwards in heavy flakes. Philippa and her guide had vanished. I felt for my match-box, and plunged into the dark and dripping tunnel.

I pushed ahead, at such speed as is possible for a six-foot man in a five-foot passage, splashing in the stream that gurgled between the tram-rails, and stumbling over the sleepers. Soon the last touches of daylight glinted in the water, they died, and it was pitch dark. I struck a match, sheltering it with my cap from the drips of the roof, and shouted, and stood still, listening. There was no sound, except the muffled roar of the sea outside; the match kindled broad sparkles of copper ore in the rock, but other response there was none.

Match by match I got ahead, shouting at intervals, stooping, groping, clutching at the greasy baulks of timber that supported the roof and sides, till a cold draught blew out my match. My next revealed a cross-gallery, with a broken truck blocking one entrance. There remained two ways to choose between. It was certain that the tram-rails must lead to the shaft, but which way had Philippa gone? And Anthony —I stood in maddening blackness; some darkness is a negative thing, this seemed an active, malevolent pressure. I counted my matches, and shouted, and still my voice came back to me, baffled, and without a hope in it. There were not half a dozen matches left.

A faint, paddling sound became audible above the drippings from the roof; I struck another of my matches, and something low and brown came panting into the circle of light. It was Minx, coming to me along the gallery of the tram-rails. She paused just short of the cross-ways, staring as though I were a stranger, and again a circling wind blew out my match. A fresh light showed her, still motionless; her back was up, not in the ordinary ridge, but in patches here and there; she was looking at something behind me; she made her mouth as round as a shilling, held up her white throat, and howled, thinly and carefully, as if she were keening. I cannot deny that I stiffened as I stood, and that second being that inhabits us, the being that is awake when we are asleep (and is always afraid), took charge for a moment; the other partner, who is, I try to think, my real self, pulled himself together with a certain amount of bad language, thrust Minx aside, and went ahead along the gallery of the tram-lines.

It needed only a dozen steps, and what Minx

had or had not seen became a negligible matter. A white light, that turned the flame of my match to orange, began to irradiate the tunnel like moonrise, defining theatrically the profiles of rock, and the sagging props and beams. It came from an electric lamp, Anthony's electric lamp, standing on a heap of shale. The boy in the flannel jacket was holding a lighted candle-end in his fingers, and bending low over Philippa, who was kneeling between the tram-lines in the muddy water, holding Anthony in her arms. He was motionless and limp, and I felt that sickening drop of the heart that comes when the thing that seems too bad to think of becomes in an instant the thing that is.

"Tram-lines and water—" said a level voice in my brain. "I wonder if he is asleep——"

I wondered too.

Philippa looked up, with eyes that accepted me without comment.

"Only stunned, I think," she said hoarsely. "He opened his eyes an instant ago."

"The timber fell on him," said the country boy. "Look where he have the old prop knocked. 'Twas little but he was dead."

Anthony stirred uneasily.

"Oh, mother, you're holding me too tight!" he said fractiously.

From somewhere ahead vague noises came, rumblings, scrapings, bangings like falling stones—

"It must be they're putting a ladder down in the shaft," said the boy.

Anthony had broken his collar-bone. So Dr. Fraser said; she tied him up with her knitted scarf by the light of the electric torch; I carried him up the ladder, and have an ineffaceable memory of the lavender glare of daylight that met us, and of the welcome that was in the everyday rain and the wet grass. In the relief of the upper air I even bore with serenity the didactics of Andrew, who assured me that he had seen from the first that the shaft was the centre of the position, though he had never been in the slightest degree uneasy, because Dr. Fraser had seen some one with Anthony.

Dr. Fraser said nothing; no more did I.

"See now," said Cantillon the sweep, who, in common with the rest of the auction, was standing round the car to view our departure, "it pinched me like death when they told me the Major had that laddher bought!"

Being at the time sufficiently occupied in preparing to get away, I did not enquire why Cantillon should have taken the matter so much to heart.

"But after all," he proceeded, having secured the attention of his audience by an effective opening, "wasn't it the mercy of God them chaps Mr. Knox has at the kennels had it lent to the Mahonys, and them that's here took it from the Mahonys in a hurry the time Mr. Harrington died! And through all it was the Major's ladder."

Andrew had the ill-breeding to laugh.

"Sure it'd be no blame for a gentleman not to know the like of it," said Cantillon with severity. "Faith, I mightn't know it meself only for the old poker I stuck in it one time at Mr. Knox's when a rung broke under me——"

It is a valuable property of the motor-car that it can, at a moment's notice, fill an inconvenient interval with loud noises. I set the engine going and jumped into the car.

Something, covered by a rug, cracked and squashed under my foot. It was the aneroid.

When we reached a point in the road where it skirts the cliff I stopped the car, and flung the aneroid, like a quoit, over the edge, through the wind and the rain, into oblivion.

V

THE MAROAN PONY

It had taken ten minutes to work the car over the bridge at Poundlick, so intricate was the crowd of people and carts, so blind and deaf to any concerns save their own; a crowd that offered sometimes the resistance of the feather bed, sometimes that of the dead wall, an intractable mass, competent to reduce the traffic of Piccadilly to chaos, and the august Piccadilly police to the point of rushing to the nearest lunatic asylum, and saying, "Let us in! We are mad!"

The town of Poundlick is built at so accommodating a tilt that it is possible to stand on the bridge at its foot, and observe the life of its single street displayed like a poster on the hillside; even to compare the degrees of custom enjoyed by its public-houses, and to estimate the number of cur dogs to the square yard of pavement. I speak of an ordinary day. But this hot twentieth of September was far from being ordinary.

The Poundlick Races are, I believe, an ancient

and annual function, but, being fifteen miles from anywhere, I had hitherto been content to gauge their attractions by their aftermath of cases in the Petty Sessions Court next following the fixture. There is, however, no creature more the sport of circumstances than a married man with a recent motor ; my attendance, and that of the car, at the Poundlick Races had been arranged to the last sandwich before I had time to collect objections (and this method, after all, saves some wear and tear).

The races are held on the banks of the Arrigadheel River, within hail of the town, and are reached—as everything in Ireland is reached—by a short cut. We—that is to say, my wife, her cousin, Captain Andrew Larpent, R.E., and I—were gathered into the jovial crowd that straggled, and hustled, and discoursed over the marshy meadows of the river, and ploughed through the brown mud in the gaps without a check in pace or conversation. The Committee had indeed " knocked " walls, and breached banks, but had not further interfered with the course of nature, and we filed at length on to the course across a tributary of the river, paying a penny each for the facilities offered by a narrow and bounding plank and the muddy elbow of a young man who stood in mid-stream ; an amenity accepted with suitable yells by the ladies (of whom at least ninety per cent. remarked "O God!" in transit).

The fact that there are but four sound and level fields within a ten-mile radius of Poundlick had simplified the labours of the Committee in the selection of a course. Rocky hills rose steeply on two sides of the favoured spot, the Arrigadheel laid down the law as to its boundaries, and within these limitations an oval course had been laid out by the simple expedient of breaking gaps in the banks. The single jump-race on the pro-gramme was arranged for by filling the gaps with bundles of furze, and there was also a water-jump, more or less forced upon the Committee by the intervention of a ditch pertaining to one of the fences. A section of the ditch had been widened and dammed, and the shallow trough of pea-soup that resulted had been raised from the rank of a puddle by a thin decoration of cut furze-bushes.

The races had not begun, but many horses were galloping about and over the course, whether engaged in unofficial competitions or in adding a final bloom to their training, I am unable to say. We wandered deviously among groups of country people, anchored in conversation, or moving, still in conversation, as irresistibly as a bog-slide. Whether we barged into them, or they into us, was a matter of as complete indifference to them as it would have been to a drove of their own bony cattle.

"These are the sort of people I love," said Philippa, her eyes ranging over the tented field and its throngs, and its little red and green flags flapping in the sunshine. "Real Primitives, like a chorus in *Acis and Galatea!*"

She straightened her hat with a gasp, as a couple of weighty female primitives went through us and passed on. (In all circumstances and fashions, my wife wears a large hat, and thereby adds enormously to the difficulties of life.) Among the stalls of apples and biscuits, and adjacent to the drink tent, a roulette table occurred, at which the public were invited to stake on various items of the arms of the United Kingdom. The public had accepted the invitation in considerable numbers, and I did not fail to point out to Philippa the sophisticated ease with which Acis flung his penny upon "Harp," while Galatea, planking twopence upon the Prince of Wales' plumes, declared that the last races she was at she got the price of her ticket on "Feather."

We passed on, awaking elusive hopes in the bosoms of two neglected bookmakers, who had at intervals bellowed listlessly to the elements, and now eagerly offered me Rambling Katty at two to one.

"Boys, hurry! There's a man dead, north!"

shrieked a boy, leaping from the top of a bank. "Come north till we see him!"

A rush of boys went over us; the roulette table was deserted in a flash, and its proprietor and the bookmakers exchanged glances expressive of the despicable frivolity of the rustics of Poundlick.

"We ought to try to find Dr. Fraser," said Philippa, hurrying in the wake of the stampede.

"I did not know that the Chicken Farmers were to be among the attractions," I said to Andrew, realising, not for the first time, that I am but an infant crying in the night where matters of the higher diplomacy are toward.

Andrew made no reply, as is the simple method of some men when they do not propose to give themselves away, and we proceeded in the direction of the catastrophe.

The dead man was even less dead than I had expected. He was leaning against a fence, explaining to Dr. Catherine Fraser that he felt all the noise of all the wars of all the worlds within in his head.

Dr. Fraser, who was holding his wrist, while her friend, Miss Longmuir, kept the small boys at bay, replied that she would like a more precise description. The sufferer, whose colour was returning, varied the metaphor, and said that the sound was for all the world like the quacking of ducks.

"Lyney's a tough dog!"

"You'd better go home and keep quiet," said Dr. Fraser, accepting the symptom with professional gravity.

I asked my next door neighbour how the accident had occurred.

"Danny Lyons here was practising this young mare of Herlihy's for Lyney Garrett, that's to ride her in the first race," said my neighbour, a serious man with bushy black whiskers, like an old-fashioned French waiter, "and sure she's as loose as a hare, and when she saw the flag before her on the fence, she went into the sky, and Danny dhruv in the spur to keep the balance, and with that then the sterrup broke."

"It's little blagyarding she'd have if it was Lyney was riding her!" said some one else.

"Ah, Lyney's a tough dog," said my neighbour; "in the Ring of Ireland there isn't a nicer rider."

"There might be men as good as him in Poundlick!" said an ugly little black-muzzled fellow, suddenly and offensively, "and horses too! As good as any *he'll* throw his leg over!"

Dr. Fraser's patient stood up abruptly.

"Oh, oh, oh!" said the man with the bushy whiskers, placing himself in front of the invalid. "Let you be said by the lady, Danny, and go home! Have behaviour now, Peter Lynch!"

The matter hung for a moment; a bell began

to ring in the middle of the course, and the onlookers flung the situation from them like a squeezed lemon, and swept *en masse* towards the summons, bearing with them the invalid.

"Off the stage I have never seen people clear out so fast," remarked Andrew. "Now that we've seen Dr. Fraser's Lightning Cure, I suppose we may as well go too."

His eyes, by a singular coincidence, met those of Miss Longmuir, which were very pretty eyes, dark and soft.

"I must go and hunt up our pony," she said, with a very businesslike air; "we've entered her for the third race, you know."

She put back her hair as it blew across her forehead, and the gold in it glinted in the sun.

"How sporting of you!" we heard Andrew say, as they walked away together.

My wife and Dr. Fraser and I turned as one man, and went in the opposite direction.

We steered for an island of furze and grey boulders that had been flung into the valley like a vedette from the fortified hill-side, and was placed, considerately, at the apex of the oval course. Half a dozen men were already grouped upon the boulders, like cormorants. We clambered to a higher *étage*, and there spread forth ourselves and our belongings upon the warm slabs. The sun was hot, yet not too hot, the smell of trodden turf was pleasant in the air, the river sparkled and gurgled beside us; the chimneys of Poundlick sent up languid spires of blue smoke; its yellow and pink and white houses became poetic in the September haze. The first delicate pangs of hunger were stealing upon us, and I felt reasonably certain that nothing necessary to our welfare had been forgotten. I lit a cigarette and pulled my cap over my eyes, and listened to a lark, spiring, like the smoke, into the blue, while my wife clattered in the luncheon basket. It was a moment of entire well-being, overshadowed only by the prospect of having to take an interest in the racing.

I said as much to Dr. Fraser, who was dismembering a cold chicken with almost awful surgical dexterity.

"You must wake up for our race," she said. "I'll call you in time."

"Must I? I hope you're going to ride."

"Heaven forfend!" replied Dr. Fraser. "Nothing more spirited than a weight-carrying bicycle! I'm not in the least horsey. Meg was dying to ride, but as we bought the pony from the great Lyney, and he had won any number of races on her, he was distinctly indicated."

"Quite right too," I said, with dowager-like propriety. "And I should wish it to be clearly understood that if, at the last moment, your friend Mr. Lyney should be too drunk to ride, I will not take his place."

"He doesn't drink," said Dr. Fraser, who has an unsympathetic way of keeping to the point. "He's been a great friend of mine ever since I mended a broken finger for him."

There was a stir among the cormorants on the lower tier of boulders, a shot was fired at the far end of the course, every one began to shout, and an irregularly shaped mass was detached from the crowd, and resolved itself into a group of seven horses, pounding towards us at a lumbering canter. One of the riders had a green jacket, the others were in shirt sleeves, with coloured scarves over their shoulders; all were bare-headed. As they neared the first jump, I found myself on my feet on my boulder, with two unknown men hanging on to me to steady themselves.

"That's no throuble to them!" shouted one of my *attachés*, as each horse in turn galloped over or through the barrier of furze in the gap.

"Which is Lyney Garrett?" I asked.

"That's him on the chestnut mare—the jock that have the dhress on him." He pointed to the wearer of the green jacket.

"Ah ha! Lyney's the boy! Look at him now, how he'll stoop and leave the horse to go for herself! He'll easy the horse, and he'll easy himself!"

"That Rambling Katty he's riding's a nice loose mare—she has a good fly in her," said another.

"Lyney's built for it. If there's any sort of a spring in a horse at all, he'll make him do it."

"He'd make a donkey plough!" flung in another enthusiast.

As they neared the flags at the turn of the oval—and an uncommonly sharp turn it was— the pace improved, each man trying to get the inside station; I could already see, written on the countenance of a large young grey horse, his determination to pursue an undeviating course of his own.

"Now, Lyney! Spare him in the angle!" shouted my neighbour, hanging on to my sleeve and rocking perilously.

Lyney, a square-shouldered young man, pale and long-jawed, bored determinedly on to the first flag, hit it with his right knee, wrenched Rambling Katty round the second flag, and got away for the water-jump three lengths ahead of anyone else.

"Look at that for ye—how he goes round the corner on one leg!" roared his supporter. "He'd not stop for the Lord Leftenant!"

The remaining riders fought their way round the flags, with strange tangents and interlacing curves; all, that is to say, save the grey horse, who held on unswervingly and made straight for the river. The spectators, seated on the low bank at its edge, left their seats with singular unanimity. The majority fled, a little boy turned a somersault backwards into the water, but three or four hardier spirits tore off their coats, swung them like flails in front of the grey, and threw their caps in his face, with a wealth of objurgation that I have rarely heard equalled.

" The speed was in him and he couldn't turn," explained one of my neighbours, at the top of his voice, as the grey, yielding to public opinion, returned to the course and resumed the race.

" That horse is no good," said a dapper young priest, who had joined our crowd on the rock. " Look at his great flat feet! You'd bake a cake on each of them!"

" Well, that's the case indeed, Father," replied a grizzled old farmer, " but he's a fine cool horse, and a great farming horse for ever. Be gance! He'd plough the rocks!"

" Well, he'll get a nice view of the race, anyway," said the young priest, " he has it all before him."

" They don't seem to be getting any delay with the water-jump," said some one else regretfully.

" Ah, what's in it but the full of a few tin cans!" said my adherent.

"Well, for all, it knocked a good lep out o' Rambling Katty: she went mountains over it!"

"Look south! Look south! They're coming on again, and only five o' them in it——"

The cheering was hotter this time, and it was entirely characteristic that it was the riders who were shouted for and not the horses.

"They'll win now this turn—there's three o' them very thick, that's a nice tidy race," said the old farmer.

"Good boy, Kenny! Go on, Kenny!" bellowed some one on a lower ledge.

"Who's second, coming up to the flag now?" panted Philippa, who was hanging on to the collar of my coat and trying to see over my shoulder.

"That's Jimmy Kenny," responded the man below, turning a black-muzzled face up towards us, his light eyes gleaming between their black lashes in the sunshine, like aquamarines. I recognised Peter Lynch, whom we had met earlier in the day.

"It's young Kenny out of the shop," explained the old farmer to me; "he rides very nate."

No one was found to endorse his opinion. The horses came on, sweating and blowing, the riders, by this time very red in the face, already taking to their whips. By some intricate process of jostling, young Kenny got the inside place at the first flag.

"Now is he nate! What was I saying!" exulted the old farmer.

"Lyney! Lyney!" roared the faithful gallery, as the leaders hustled round the second flag and went away up the course.

"Up, Kenny!" replied the raucous tenor of Peter Lynch in solitary defiance.

Last of all, the grey horse, who would plough the rocks, came on indomitably, and made, as before, a bee-line for the river. Here, however, he was confronted by a demonstration hurriedly arranged by his friends, who advanced upon him waving tall furze-bushes, with which they beat him in the face. The grey horse changed his mind with such celerity that he burst his girths; some one caught him by the head, while his rider hung precariously upon his neck; some one else dragged off the saddle, replanted his jockey upon his broad bare back, and speeded him on his way by bringing the saddle down upon his hind-quarters with an all-embracing thump.

"It's only the age he wants," said a partisan. "If they'd keep him up to the practice, he'd be a sweeper yet!"

Tumult at the end of the course, and a pistol-shot, here announced that the race was over.

"Lyney have it!" shouted some men, standing on the fence by the water-jump.

"What happened Kenny?" bawled Peter Lynch.

"He was passing the flag and he got clung in the pole, and the next man knocked him down out of the pole!" shouted back the Field Telegraph.

"Oh pity!" said the old farmer.

"He didn't get fair play!" vociferated Peter Lynch, glowering up at the adherents of Lyney with a very green light in his eye.

The young priest made a slight and repressive gesture with his hand. "That'll do now, Peter," he said, and turned to the old farmer. "Well, Rambling Katty's a hardy bit of stuff," he went on, brushing the rock-lichen from his black coat.

"She is that, Father," responded my late adherent, who, to my considerable relief, had now ceased to adhere. "And nothing in her but a fistful of bran!"

"She's the dryest horse that came in," said the young priest, descending actively from the rock.

With the knowledge that the Committee would allow an hour at least for the effects of a race to pass off before launching another, we climbed to the summit of the island, and began upon the luncheon basket; and, as vultures drop from the blue empyrean, so did Andrew and Miss Longmuir arrive from nowhere and settle upon the sandwiches.

" Oh, I can't eat our own game, can I ? " said the latter, with a slight shudder, as I placed the chicken before her. " No—really—not even for your sake ! " She regarded me very pleasingly, but I notice that it is only since my hair began to turn grey over my ears that these things are openly said to me. " I had to feed four dozen of the brutes before we started this morning, and I shall have to do it all over again when we get home ! "

" I don't know how you stand it, I should let 'em starve," said Andrew, his eyes travelling from her white forehead to her brown hands. " *I* don't consider it is work for ladies."

" You can come and help the ladies if you like," said Miss Longmuir, glancing at him as she drove her white teeth into a sandwich.

" Do you mean that ? " said Andrew in a low voice.

" She's blown him to pieces before he's left the covert," I said to myself, and immediately withdrew into blameless conversation with my wife and Dr. Fraser.

We had gone pretty well down through the luncheon basket, and had arrived at a second and even more balmy—being well-fed—period of peace, before it occurred to Miss Longmuir to look at her watch, and to spoil the best cigarette of the day with agitations concerning the non-appearance of her pony. I suggested that she and Captain Larpent should go in search of it, and for a brief interval the disturbing element was eliminated. It returned, with added agitation, in a quarter of an hour.

"Cathie! I can't find Nancy anywhere! We've been all round the course," cried Miss Longmuir from below. "And John Sullivan is nowhere to be found either, and I can't get near Lyney, he's riding in the Trotting Race."

"You'll find the pony is somewhere about all right," I said, with the optimism of combined indolence and indifference.

"That seems probable," said Andrew, "but the point is, she's somewhere where we're not."

"The point is, she ought to be here," said Miss Longmuir, with a very bright colour in her cheeks as she looked up at us.

"Heavens! They're very angry!" I murmured to Dr. Fraser.

"Well, what do you want us to do?" enquired Dr. Fraser lethargically.

"You might take some faint shadow of interest in the fact that Nancy is lost," replied Miss Longmuir.

"I think we'd better organise a search-party," said Philippa (who does not smoke).

We rose stiffly, descended from our sun-warmed boulders, and took up the White Man's Burden.

A sweeping movement was inaugurated, whose objects were to find the pony or her attendant, John Sullivan, or Lyney.

"Should you know the pony if you saw her?" I said confidentially to Dr. Fraser, as she and I set forth together.

"We've not had it very long," she replied dubiously. "Luckily it's an easy colour. John Sullivan calls it maroan—a sort of mixture of roan and maroon."

We advanced from field to field, driving like twin darning-needles through the groups of people, but neither John Sullivan nor the maroan pony transpired.

"Come on, come on! The Stepping Match is starting!" shouted some one.

Dr. Fraser and I were caught in the tightening mesh of the crowd, as in the intricacies of a trammel net; an irregular thumping of hoofs, and a row of bare and bobbing heads, passing above the heads of the crowd, indicated that the Stepping Match was under way. Lyney's dour face and green jacket were in the lead, and, as before, had he been Diana of the Ephesians, he could not have been more passionately called upon. As it was obviously useless for us to do so at this juncture, we climbed on to a bank near the winning post, and watched the race. Lyney was riding a long-backed yellow animal with a face as cross as his own, and a step as fast as the tick of a watch.

"Anny other man than Lyney wouldn't carry that old pony round," said one man.

"She has a score o' years surely, but she's as wicked as a bee," said another.

"Lyney's very knacky; he couldn't be bate," said the first man.

"Well, well, look at Jimmy Kenny and his father, and the two o' them riding!" went on the commentator. "Faith, I'd give the father the sway. Jimmy's riding uneven. When the nag is rising, he's falling."

"Sure he has his two elbows into his ears! Go on, Lyney boy!"

The horses pounded past, splashing through the shallow flood of the water-jump, and trampling over such furze-bushes as had withstood the vicissitudes of the steeplechase. They passed from our view, and Dr. Fraser and I agreed that we should be justified in staying where we were till the finish. Three times they passed us, enveloped in a travelling roar of encouragements, and with each passing the supporters of Lyney and Kenny bayed and howled more emulously. The competitors, now, to all practical intent, reduced to the Kennys, *père et fils*, and Lyney, again disappeared on their last round, and the volleys of incitement became a dropping fire of criticism.

"Kenny's mare is the one, the others is too crippled."

"She'll not bate Lyney! Divil blast the bate she have in her! she's too dropped and too narra!"

"What horse is first?"

"I d'know; only one, I think."

"Look at young Kenny coming up on the father now!"

"Ah, there's more in the owld fella, never fear him!"

"Come on, Lyney! Come on, Kenny! Lyney! Lyney!"

Lyney won. The bee-like wickedness of the yellow mare apparently served her as well as youth, and despite the fact that she was but little over fourteen hands and was carrying twelve stone, she finished a dozen lengths in front. The interest of the race was at once transferred to the struggle for second place between the Kennys.

"Come on, Tom! Come on, Jimmy! Begor' the father have it!" yelled the crowd, as Kenny *père*, flourishing his whip over his grey head, finished half a length in front of his son.

"Them two tight wheels at the corner, 'twas there he squeezed the advantage on the son."

" No, but the father had a drop taken, 'twas
that that gave him the heart."

Dr. Fraser and I got off our fence and steered
for Lyney.

He was in the act of throwing the reins on
the pony's neck and himself off her back as we
arrived.

" Here! " he said to the owner, " take your
old skin! "—he tossed his whip on to the
ground—" and your old whip too! "

The owner took the " old skin " by her drooping and dripping head, and picked up the whip,
in reverential submission, and the ring of admirers evidently accepted this mood of the hero
as entirely befitting his dignity.

Dr. Fraser advanced through them with the
effortless impressiveness of a big woman, and
made her enquiries about the pony. Lyney
dropped the hero manner.

" I don't at all doubt but John Sullivan's gone
up to Lynch's for her, Doctor; you needn't be
uneasy at all," he said, with a respect that must
have greatly enhanced our position in the eyes
of the crowd. " I told him he shouldn't bring
her too soon for fear she'd sour on us. We
have an hour yet."

Soothed by this assurance we moved on, and
even, in this moment of unexpected leisure,
dallied with the roulette table. I had, in fact,

lost ninepence, when the remainder of the search-party bore down upon us at speed.

"The pony is *not* here!" said Miss Longmuir, regarding our outspread coppers with an eye of burning indignation, "and Sullivan's brother doesn't know where he is—says he went up to the town two hours ago. I'm going up to look for him, but of course if you'd rather stay and play roulette—" Her voice shook. I need hardly say that we went.

On our arrival at the town of Poundlick we found it to be exclusively inhabited by grand-mothers. Lynch's public-house was garrisoned by a very competent member of the force, who emerged from the kitchen with an infant in her arms, and another attached to her clothing. She knew nothing of the pony, she knew nothing of John Sullivan. There was certainly a young lad that came in, and he having drink taken, and wherever he got it, it wasn't in this house, and what did he do but to commence jumping the counter, you'd think he'd jump the house. She paused, and I murmured to Dr. Fraser that she was like a Holbein, and Dr. Fraser replied that she did not believe one word she said, which was rather my own idea, only more so. It appeared that her son Peter had, an hour ago, expelled the young lad from the house (lest its fair fame should be sullied), and as for Peter, the dear knew where he was, she didn't see him since.

Miss Longmuir and Andrew here left the shop, very purposefully ; we pursued, and saw them open the gate of Lynch's yard and stride in. The yard was a small one, littered with cases of bottles, and congested by the outside cars and carts of race-goers ; such level spaces as it possessed had been dug out of the side of the hill, and slatternly stables and outhouses were perched on the different levels. Through a low-browed doorway might be seen the horses of race-goers, standing "ready dight," like the steeds of Branksome Hall, with heads hanging, in resigned depression, before empty ranks and mangers. But of the maroan pony there was no sign.

Fierce as terriers on a rat-hunt, Miss Longmuir and Andrew dashed in and out of the dark sheds and outhouses, till there remained unexplored but one hovel, whose open door revealed only semi-darkness, edged with fern-litter. None the less, the leading terrier determined to make good the ground. A sharp yelp told of a find, and Miss Longmuir emerged, holding aloft a new check horse-sheet, with the initials "M. L." large upon it.

"They must have taken her down to the race-course, after all—" I began.

"Thoughtless of them to take her without her

saddle or bridle," said Andrew bitingly. "Here they are behind the door!"

The silence that followed this discovery was broken by Philippa.

"I hear some one snoring!" she said in a conspirator's whisper. "Do come away. I'm sure it's a drunken man."

"Quite so," said Andrew, who had been pursuing his researches. "Allow me to introduce Mr. John Sullivan."

In the dark corner behind the door lay a stout youth, comfortably extended, with his flushed face half hidden in the dry and tawny bracken, and his open mouth framing long and quiet snores. He was obviously at peace with all the world.

Some heartless assaults on the part of Captain Larpent had no appreciable result, so inveterate was the peace, so potent the means by which it had been invoked. The ladies had retired during the interview, and, as we rejoined them in the yard, we all became aware of muffled and thunderous sounds near at hand; they were suggestive of a ponderous and chaotic clog-dance, and proceeded from an outhouse, built against the bank that formed the upper side of the yard, with its gable askew to the other buildings.

"'Lots of things is coor'us,' as Anthony said when I told him about Jonah and the Whale," remarked Philippa, who, throughout, had not taken the affair as seriously as it deserved. " I suppose the party that John Sullivan was at is going on up there."

Miss Longmuir darted round the gable of the house, a wild and summoning cry followed, the call of the terrier who has run his rat to ground.

We found her at the foot of a low flight of irregular stone steps (in telling the story I have formed the habit of saying that there were ten of them) that led to a doorway in a loft. In the doorway, with a cabbage leaf in her mouth, was the maroan pony, looking down at us with an expression of mild surprise.

We all said unanimously, and with equal futility, " How—on—earth——? "

After which Andrew, who dislikes miracles, arranged that she had, of course, got into the loft from the back, where the ground was high. Unfortunately the theory did not work, an inspection of the loft revealing nothing but four walls, a large store of dried bracken, and a donkey-panier filled with cabbages.

" These mountainy ponies climb like monkeys," said Philippa, with her inevitable effort to shelter the discomfited, as Andrew returned with the ruins of his theory, " she must have walked up the steps ! "

Miss Longmuir, snatching out her watch, said

she didn't care how the pony got there, the point
was to get her down as quickly as possible. " If
people would only *do* something and not talk ! "
she added, under her breath.

" If she walked up she can walk down," said
Andrew firmly.

He mounted the steps and took the pony
by the halter. The pony immediately backed
thunderously out of sight, taking Andrew with
her. Miss Longmuir flew up the steps to his
assistance, and unseen sarabands pummelled the
floor of the loft.

" Go up and help them, you great lazy thing ! "
said Philippa to me.

" There's no room for any one else," I protested.

Here the combatants reappeared in the doorway, gradually, with endearments on one side,
and suspicious snortings on the other. The steps
were broad and not too intimidating ; the pony
advanced almost to the sill, repented in haste,
and in her retreat flung Andrew against the
panier of cabbages. A donkey's panier is made
to resist shocks ; in this case it apparently gave
more than it took ; Andrew said nothing, but he
dragged the basket over the sill and hurled it
down the steps with considerable emotion. I
joined the party in the loft, and Philippa collected
the cabbages, and laid them in rows upon the
steps as if it were a harvest festival, in the hope

of luring the pony to the descent. The lure was rejected with indignation, and I proceeded to offer a few plain truths. That the floor would come down before the mare did. That it would take six men, and planks, and cartloads of straw, to get her out. Finally, that her race was due to start in twenty minutes.

"We're done," said Miss Longmuir tragically, addressing Philippa and Dr. Fraser from the top of the steps, as if they were a stage mob. "These brutes have beaten us! Don't you remember that Lyney's father said, 'Let ye keep out from them lads in Poundlick'? And after all our trouble, and the training, and everything—" She turned abruptly away from the door.

Dr. Fraser stood still, with her hand to her forehead, as though she were trying to remember something. Then she too came up into the loft. The pony had now backed into the pile of bracken; Andrew, whose back teeth were evidently set tight, was tugging at her halter, and she was responding by throwing her nose in the air and showing the whites of her eyes.

"Meg," said Dr. Fraser, at the doorway, " I've remembered something that I was once told—" She peered into the darkness of the loft. " May I try?" she said, advancing quietly to the pony's head.

"By all means," said Andrew, as chillingly as

was possible for a man who was very red in the face and was draped with cobwebs.

Looking back now to the affair, I cannot remember that Dr. Fraser did anything in the least remarkable. She took hold of the halter with one hand and with the other patted the pony's neck, high up, near the ears. She also spoke to it, the sort of things anyone might say. For the life of me I could not see that she did more than anyone else had done, but Nancy lowered her head and put her ears forward.

Dr. Fraser gave the halter a gentle pull, and said, " Come on, old girl! " and the pony started forward with a little run.

At the doorway she stopped. We held our breaths. Dr. Fraser patted her again and placidly descended the first step; the maroan pony placed a trembling foot upon the threshold, steadied herself, poked her nose forward, and dropped her forefeet on to the second step.

" She'll come down on top of her! " said Andrew, starting forward.

" Don't touch her! " exclaimed Miss Longmuir, grasping his arm.

With the tense caution of an old dog, the pony let herself down from step to step, planting her little hoofs cunningly on the rough-set stones, bracing herself with the skill learned on the rocky staircases of her native hills. Dr. Fraser kept a step in advance of her. Thus, with slow clattering, and in deep gravity, they joined Philippa in the yard.

Five people cannot advantageously collaborate in putting a saddle and bridle on a pony, but we tried, and in the grim hustle that resulted no one asked questions or made comments. Amongst us the thing was done, and there were still seven minutes in hand when Andrew shot out of the yard on her back. Hard on her heels followed Philippa and Miss Longmuir, with scarcely inferior velocity. I returned to the remaining member of the party and found that she had seated herself on the steps.

She said she was tired, and she looked it.

" I daresay getting that beast down the steps was rather a strain ? " I said, spreading the pony's rug for her to sit on.

"Oh, that was nothing. Please don't wait for me."

I said in my best ironic manner that doctors were of course impervious to fatigue, and indeed superior to all human ills.

She laughed. " I admit that I was rather nervous that the thing wouldn't work, or would break down half-way."

"What thing?" I demanded. " The pony?"

" No. The secret. It *is* a secret, you know. My grandfather gave Rarey thirty pounds for it.

I've never had much to say to horses, but I have started a jibbing hansom horse in Oxford Street with it." She laughed again, apologetically.

"You needn't believe it unless you like. I must say I was afraid it mightn't include a flight of steps!" She paused and put back her abundant fair hair. "How hot it was up in that loft! I wonder if you could get me a glass of water?"

I told her that I was old enough to believe anything, but added that after what she had told me I would get a second glass of water, with sal volatile in it, for myself.

The Holbein grandmother was standing at the back door of the house, with the baby still on her arm. She and the baby fetched the glass of water. She said wasn't the pony a Fright for ever after the way he came down them steps, but why wouldn't the lady take him out through the other door into the field above?

I made no reply, but while Dr. Fraser was drinking the water, I went up into the loft, and cleared away the bracken that had been piled in front of the "door into the field above." I opened the door, and walked out into the field, and viewed the small hoof-prints that led to the door of the loft.

I returned to Dr. Fraser, and very gently broke the news to her.

· · · · · · ·

Of course Lyney and the maroan pony won the race. Had this not been a foregone conclusion it is possible that John Sullivan might have scored less heavily in the matter of free drinks.

As I was conducting my exhausted but triumphant party off the course, the Poundlick Sergeant of Police met me and asked me if I would sign a few summonses for him, as he was after taking some parties into custody for fighting.

"Drunk, I suppose?"

The Sergeant admitted it, and said the dispute had arisen between the Kennys and the Lynches on the one side, and the partisans of Lyney Garrett on the other, out of "circumstances connected with the last race." The Sergeant's eye rested for an instant, with what may be described as a respectful twinkle, upon Miss Longmuir.

"It was mostly heavy offers and small blows, Major," he concluded.

"Look here, Sergeant," I said oracularly, "take them all to the water-jump. Build up the furze in front of it. Make them jump it. Anyone that gets over it may be considered sober. Anyone that falls in will be sober enough when he gets out."

I have not, in my judicial career, delivered a judgment that gave more satisfaction to the public.

VI

MAJOR APOLLO RIGGS

Part I

THE leave of Captain Andrew Larpent, R.E., was expiring, dying hard, "in rings of strenuous flight," (and my motor) on the road between Shreelane and Licknavar, which is the home of the Chicken Farmers. Philippa, who regards a flirtation with an enthusiasm that is as disinterested as it is inexplicable, assured me that the state of affairs was perfectly unmistakable. She further said that the male determination to deny and ignore these things was partly sympathetic secretiveness, partly the affectation of despising gossip, and mainly stupidity. She took a long breath after all this, and, seeing Andrew approaching along the garden path in apparently romantic meditation, enjoined me to be nice to the poor thing, and departed.

The sun was bright, with the shallow brightness of early October, and the Virginian creeper made a conflagration on the weather-slated end of the house. The poor thing deposited himself beside me on the garden seat. I noticed that his eye rested upon a white chicken with a brilliant scarlet comb; it was one of several, purchased from the Chicken Farmers. I would not for worlds have admitted it to Philippa, but there was undoubtedly sentiment in the glance.

"I hear they're having beastly weather at the Curragh," he said, leaning back and looking gloomily up into the melting blue sky. "Stunning that red stuff looks on the house!" He surveyed it, and sighed; then, suddenly, sentiment faded from his glance. "D'you know, old boy, that chimney up there is well out of the perpendicular. It'll be down about your ears some day."

I replied that it had maintained that angle for the seven years of my tenancy.

"It won't do it much longer," returned my guest. "Look at that crack in the plaster!"

"Which crack?" I said coldly. (Mr. Flurry Knox is my landlord, and it is my misfortune to have a repairing lease.)

"Take your choice," said Andrew, scanning the chimneys with the alert and pitiful eye of the Royal Engineer. "My money's on the northern one, under the jackdaw."

"Oh, confound you and the jackdaws!" I said pettishly. "The chimney draws all right."

But the matter did not end there. Before luncheon, Andrew and I had made a tour of the roof, and he had demonstrated unanswerably, and with appalling examples from barracks that he had repaired in Central India, and built in Wei-hai-Wei, that nothing but habit and family feeling induced any one of the chimney stacks to stand up.

At luncheon he told Philippa that he hoped she would insure the children before the next westerly gale. Philippa replied by asking if he, or anyone else, had ever heard of a chimney falling, unless it had been struck by lightning, in which case it wouldn't matter if it were straight or crooked ; and though this was manifestly worthless as an argument, neither Andrew nor I could remember an instance in support of our case. That the case had now become mine as well as Andrew's was the logical result of illogical opposition, and at Philippa's door I deposit the responsibility for a winter of as varied discomforts as it has been our lot to endure.

The matter matured rapidly. In the mellow moment that comes with coffee and cigarettes, I began, almost pleasurably, to lay out the campaign.

"I can't see any point in wasting money on a contractor," said Andrew airily. "Any of your local masons could do it if I explained the job to him. A fortnight ought to see it through."

It was at this point that I should have sat heavily upon Andrew. I was not without ex-

"Walkin' Aisy."

perience of the local mason and his fortnights;
what could Andrew know of such? I had a brief
and warning vision of Captain Larpent, seated at
an office table adorned with sheets of perfect
ground-plans and elevations, issuing instructions
to a tensely intelligent Sapper Sergeant. I saw
the Sergeant, supreme in scientific skill (and invariably sober), passing on the orders to a scarcely
less skilled company of prompt subordinates—but
my "worser angel" obliterated it. And that very
afternoon, on our way to Aussolas, we chanced
to meet upon the road the local mason himself,
William Shanahan, better known to fame as
"Walkin' Aisy." He was progressing at a rate
of speed that accorded with his sub-title, and, as
I approached him, a line of half-forgotten verse
came back :

"Entreat her not, her eyes are full of dreams."

Nevertheless, I stopped the car.

In answer to enquiries, he mused, with his
apostolic countenance bent upon the ground ;
after a period of profound meditation, he asked
me why wouldn't I get one of the big fellas out
from the town? I have never known Walkin'
Aisy to accept a job without suggesting that
some one else could do it better than he (in which
he was probably quite right). This may have

been humility, due to the fact that his father had been that despised thing, "a dry-wall builder"; it may have been from coquetry, but I am inclined to think it was due to a mixture of other-worldliness and sloth.

On pressure he said that he had still a small pieceen of work to finish, but he might be able to come down to-morrow to travel the roof and see what would be wanting to us, and on Monday week, with the help of God, he would come in it. His blue eyes wavered towards the horizon. The interview closed.

"'Fair and young were they when in hope they began that long journey,'" cooed Philippa, as we moved away. The quotation did not, as I well knew, refer to our visit to the Knoxes.

At Aussolas I aired my project to my landlord. Flurry is not a person to whom it is agreeable to air a project.

"Rebuild the chimneys, is it? Oh, with all my heart. Is there anything the matter with them?"

Andrew explained the imminence of our peril, and Flurry listened to him with his inscrutable eye on me.

"Well, it'll be some fun for you during the winter, Major, but be careful when you're cutting the ivy!"

I was betrayed into asking why.

"Because there's only it and the weather-slating keeping the walls standing."

"If I may presume to contradict one so much younger than myself," said old Mrs. Knox, "Shreelane is as well built a house as there is in the county." Her voice was, as ever, reminiscent of a bygone century and society; it was also keen-edged, as became a weapon of many wars, ancient and modern. She turned to me. "In the storm of '39 I remember that my father said that if Shreelane fell not a house in Ireland would stand. Every one in the house spent that night in the kitchen."

"May be that was nothing new to them," suggested Flurry.

Mrs. Knox regarded her grandson steadfastly and continued her story. It has already been noted that when he and she were of the same company they considered no other antagonist worthy of their steel.

"It was my great-grandfather who built Shreelane in honour of his marriage," she went on. "He married a Riggs of Castle Riggs, a cousin of the celebrated Major Apollo—and thereby hangs a tale!" She blinked her eyes like an old rat, and looked round at each of us in turn. I felt as if I were being regarded through a telescope, from the standpoint of a distant century.

"They knew how to build in those days," she began again. "The basement story of Shreelane is all vaulted."

"I daresay the kitchen would make a nice vault," said Flurry.

His grandmother looked hard at him, and was silent, which seemed to me a rather remarkable occurrence.

On the following day, Andrew and Walkin' Aisy "travelled the roof," and I accompanied them—that is to say, I sat on the warm lead, with my back against the sunny side of a chimney, and smoked torpidly, while Andrew preached, firmly and distinctly, from the top of a ladder. Walkin' Aisy stood at the foot of the ladder, submissive, with folded hands, and upturned bearded face, looking like an elderly saint in the lower corner of a stained-glass window. At the conclusion of the lecture he said that surely the chimneys might fall any minute, but, for all, they might stand a hundred years; a criticism almost stupefying in its width of outlook.

The following day Captain Larpent departed to the Curragh, and, as is often the way of human beings with regard to their guests, we partly breathed more freely, and partly regretted him. On the whole it was restful.

A fortnight passed, and I had almost forgotten

about the chimneys; I was in the act of making an early start for an absence of a couple of days at the farther side of my district, when I encountered Walkin' Aisy at the hall door.

"I'm here since six o'clock this morning, but I had no one to tend me," he began.

I was familiar with this plaint, and proffered him the yard boy.

"The young fella's too wake," replied Walkin' Aisy, in his slow and dreamy voice, "and they takes him from me." His mild eyes rested upon me in saddened reverie. "And there should be morthar mixed," he resumed slowly, "and there's not a pick of gravel in the yard."

I said, as I pulled on my gloves, that he could have Johnny Brien from the garden to minister to him, and that there was no hurry about the mortar.

"Well, it's what I was saying to the gardener," returned Walkin' Aisy very slowly, "I have no business coming here at all till those chimneys is taken down. The sahmint that's on them is very strong. It's what the gardener said, that quarrymen would be wanting."

"Why the devil didn't you say this at first?" I demanded, not without heat. "You and Captain Larpent told me that the old cement had no more hold than the sugar on a cake."

"Well, the Captain knows best," replied Walkin'
Aisy gently, " we should do what he says."

"Well, get the chimneys down; I don't care
who does it."

I drove away, and from the turn of the drive
saw Walkin' Aisy, in motionless trance, looking
after the car as if it were a chariot of fire.

The well-known routine followed; the long
and airless day in the Court-house, the roar of
battle of the rival solicitors, the wearisome iteration of drunks and trespasses, the intricacies of
family feuds ; the stodgy and solitary dinner at
the hotel, followed by the evening in the arid
smoking-room, the stale politics of its habitués, the
stagnant pessimism of the proprietor, the same
thing over again next day and the day after.

It was not until the afternoon of the third day
that I found myself serenely gliding homeward,
with the wind behind me, and before me the
prospect of that idleness that, like the only thirst
worth having, has been earned. I was in the
straight for the hall door, when I saw my wife
dart from the house, gesticulating, and waving
her handkerchief as if to check my approach.
She was followed, at no great interval, by an
avalanche of rubble and bricks from the roof, that
fell like a portent from heaven, and joined itself
to a considerable heap by the steps.

"You never know when it's coming!" she cried breathlessly. "I've been watching for you. It's impossible to make them hear from below, and I can't find any of the men—they're all on the roof."

The restoration had begun, but that fact might not have occurred to a stranger. Next day, and for many days—six weeks, to be exact—the house shook as from the blows of a battering-ram, in response to the efforts of the quarrymen to remove from the chimneys the cement that had no more hold on them than the sugar on a cake, and at frequent and uncertain intervals various debris rumbled down the roof and fell heavily below. There were days when it fell in front of the house, there were days when it fell in the flower garden ; where it fell, there it lay, because there was no one to take it away ; all were absorbed in tending Walkin' Aisy, and the murmurs of their inexhaustible conversation came to us down the chimneys like the hoarse cooing of wood pigeons. There were also days when by reason of storms and rain nothing was done, and black and evil floods descended into the rooms down the ruins of the chimneys, and through the slates, broken by the feet of the quarrymen. At Christmas the kitchen chimney alone remained in action, and we ate our Christmas dinner in fur coats and a

fireless dining-room. Philippa refrained from
any allusion to the quotation from Longfellow
that she had made after that first interview with
Walkin' Aisy. She even denied herself the
gratification of adding its context :

" Faded and old were they when in disappoint-
ment it ended," but I knew that she was thinking it.

PART II

It was somewhere towards the end of March
that one chimney stack re-entered the list of
combatants, trim in new cement, and crowned
with tall and hideous chimney-pots. They all
smoked, a thing that had never occurred before,
but Walkin' Aisy said that the chimneys were
cold, and that they wouldn't do it when they'd
come to themselves ; and (this was a little later
on) that any chimney would smoke in an east
wind. It was true that a period of east wind
and drought had set in. The pump in the yard
went dry ; carts had to be sent half a mile for
water, and it was reported to me that the
masons had as much water put astray, mixing
mortar and all sorts, as would drown a herring.

Other unpleasant things occurred. The house-
maid gave half-an-hour's warning, and married
one of the quarrymen, and Mrs. Cadogan then

revealed that it wasn't once nor twice during the winter that she had given that particular quarryman the full of the poker, to put him out from under her feet when she'd be dishing up the dinner. Shreelane was twice drawn blank by Flurry Knox's hounds, and their master said that as long as I had every idle blackguard in the country tending Walkin' Aisy, and making short cuts through the covert, how would I have foxes there? I ignored the conundrum, and hoped that the quarryman's yellow dog would remain where I had last seen him, in the ashpit, till Flurry had left the premises.

It was some little time after this that Captain Larpent advanced upon us on a week's leave from the Curragh; he wrote to say that I evidently wanted a Clerk of the Works, and that he would see if he couldn't get a move on Shanahan. I was away when he arrived, and on my return Philippa met me in the hall.

"Meg Longmuir is here!" she said, not without a touch of defiance. "Doctor Catherine had to go to Scotland, so I asked Meg here for a few days. She'll play duets with Andrew. She's up on the roof with him now."

"Better have a string band up there at once," I said, "and open it as a public recreation ground."

"And the Flurry Knoxes and Bernard Shute

are coming to dinner," continued my wife, ignoring this *jeu d'esprit;* "the smoking-room chimney is all right, and we can have the oil stove and some music in the drawing-room."

With this agreeable prospect in store, we sat down to dinner. We were too many for general conversation, and the table was round, which is unfavourable for *tête-à-têtes.* Yet it was not round enough to frustrate Miss Meg Longmuir's peculiar gift for duets, and I was presently aware that she was unwarrantably devoting herself to Bernard Shute, leaving Captain Larpent derelict, and that the latter was, after the manner of derelicts, becoming a danger to navigation, and was laying down laws and arguing about them acridly with Mr. Knox. I realised too late that there should have been champagne. Whisky and soda is all very well, but it will not warm wet blankets.

Meg Longmuir, however, was doing remarkably well without either; she wore something intricate that was either green or blue or both, and glittered. I recognised it as the panoply of war, and knew that the tomahawk was concealed in its folds. So also was Andrew's scalp; I don't know why I felt some pleasure in remembering that it had a bald patch on it.

After the ladies had gone, Bernard, to whose head Miss Longmuir had mounted as effectively as if she had been the missing champagne, re-joined the lesser world of men by asking Flurry why he had shut up the season so early, and suggested a by-day, if only for the sake of giving the horses something to do.

Flurry put the end of his cigarette into his finger-glass, and lit another at the flaming tongue of my tame Chinese dragon.

"I didn't know you had one that would carry a lady?" he said.

"Oh rot!" said Bernard helplessly.

"I haven't one that will carry myself," went on Flurry. "There's five lame legs among three of them this minute. Anyway the hounds are in sulphur."

The discussion progressed with the prolixity proper to such themes; I think it was Andrew who suggested the paper-chase. He had, he said, ridden in paper-chases in Egypt, and he gave us details of the stark mud walls and fathomless water-courses that were common-places of these events. We were left with the impression that none of us had ever seen obstacles so intimidating, and, more than that, if we had seen them we should have gone home in tears.

"I think we'd better make a hare of *you*," said Flurry, fixing expressionless eyes upon Captain Larpent. "It mightn't be hard."

The double edge of this suggestion was lost upon Andrew, who accepted it as a tribute, but said he was afraid he didn't know the country well enough.

" That's your Egyptian darkness," said Flurry with unexpected erudition.

Andrew glanced sideways and suspiciously at him over the bridge of his sunburnt nose, and said rather defiantly that if he could get hold of a decent horse he wouldn't mind having a try.

" I suppose you ride about 11.6 ? " asked Flurry, after a moment or two of silence. His manner had softened ; I thought I knew what was coming. " I've a little horse that I was thinking of parting . . ." he began.

A yell, sharp and sudden as a flash of lightning, was uttered outside the door, followed by a sliding crash of crockery, and more yells. We plunged into the hall, and saw Julia, the elderly parlourmaid, struggling on the floor amid ruins of coffee cups and their adjuncts.

" The rat ! He went in under me foot ! " she shrieked. " He's in under me this minute ! "

Here the rat emerged from the ruins. Simultaneously the drawing-room door burst open, and the streaming shrieks of Minx and her son and daughter were added to those of the still prostrate Julia.

The chase swept down the passage to the kitchen stairs, the pack augmented by Bob, the red setter, and closely followed by the dinner party. A rat is a poor performer on a staircase, and, at the door leading into the turf-house, the dogs seemed to be on top of him. The bolt-hole under the door, that his own teeth had prepared, gave him an instant of advantage; Flurry had the door open in a second, someone snatched the passage lamp from the wall, but it was obviously six to four on the rat.

The turf-house was a large space at the very root of the house, vaulted and mysterious, bearing Shreelane on its back like the tortoise that supports the world. Barrels draped with cobwebs stood along one wall, but the rat was not behind them, and Minx and her family drove like hawks into a corner, in which, beneath a chaotic heap of broken furniture and household debris, the rat had gone to ground. We followed, treading softly in the turf-mould of unnumbered winters. We tore out the furniture, which yielded itself in fragments; the delirium of the terriers mounting with each crash, and being, if possible, enhanced by the well-meant but intolerable efforts of the red setter to assist them. Finally we worked down to an old door, lying on its face on something that raised it a few inches from the ground.

"Now! Mind yourselves!" said Flurry, heaving up the door and flinging it back against the wall.

The rat bolted gallantly, and darted into an old box, of singular shape, that lay, half open, among the debris, and there, in a storm of tattered paper, met his fate. Minx jumped out of the box very deliberately, with the rat across her jaws, and a scarlet bite in her white muzzle. With frozen calm, and a menacing eye directed at the red setter, she laid it on the turf mould, and stiffly withdrew. Her son and daughter advanced in turn, smelt it respectfully and retired. There was no swagger; all complied with the ritual of fox-terrier form laid down for such occasions.

I was then for the first time aware that the ladies, in all the glitter and glory of their evening dresses, had each mounted herself upon a barrel; in the theatrical gloom of the vaulted turf-house, they suggested the resurrection of Ali Baba's Forty Thieves.

"Look where he had his nest in among the old letters!" said Flurry to Philippa, as she descended from her barrel to felicitate Minx and to condole with the rat. "That box came out of the rumble of an old coach, the Lord knows when!"

"There's some sort of a ring in the floor

here," said Andrew, who was rooting with a rusty crowbar in the turf-mould where the door had lain. "Bring the light, someone——"

The lamp revealed a large iron ring which was fixed in a flat stone; we scraped away the turf-mould and found that the stone was fastened down with an iron bar, passing through a staple at either end, and padlocked.

"As long as I'm in this place," said Flurry, "I never saw this outfit before."

"There's a seal over the keyhole," said Andrew, turning over the padlock.

"That means it was not intended it should be opened," said Meg Longmuir quickly.

I looked round, and, bad as the light was, I thought her face looked pale.

Andrew did not answer her. He poised the crowbar scientifically, and drove it at the padlock. It broke at the second blow, releasing the bar.

"No trouble about that!" he said, addressing himself to the gallery, and not looking at Miss Longmuir. "Now, then, shall we have the flag up?"

There were only two dissentients; one was Flurry, who put his hands in his pockets, and said he wasn't going to destroy his best evening pants; the other was Miss Longmuir, who said that to break an old seal like that was to break luck. She also looked at Andrew in a way that should have gone far to redress the injuries inflicted during dinner. Apparently it did not suffice. Captain Larpent firmly inserted the end of the bar under the edge of the flag. Bernard Shute took hold of the ring.

"All together!" said Andrew.

There was a moment of effort, the flag came up abruptly, and, as abruptly, Bernard sat down in the turf-mould with the flag between his legs. The crowbar slipped forward, and vanished with a hollow-sounding splash down a black chasm; Andrew, thrown off his balance, also slipped forward, and would have followed it, head first, had not Flurry and I caught him.

The chasm was a well, nearly full; the water twinkled at us, impenetrably black; it made me think of the ink in the hollowed palm of a native who had told my fortune, up at Peshawur.

"That was about as near as makes no difference!" said Bernard. "You've cut your cheek, Larpent."

"Have I?" said Andrew vaguely, putting up a rather shaky hand to his face. "I think my head took the edge of the well."

We covered the hole with the old door, and Andrew was taken away to have his wound attended to. It was not a severe wound, but the process was lengthy, and involved the collaboration of all the ladies. It seemed to the three neglected males, waiting for a fourth to play bridge, that this mobilisation of ministering angels was somewhat overdone.

Andrew came down to breakfast next morning with a headache, and said he had slept badly. Had he discovered the source of the Nile in the turf-house the night before, my wife and Miss Longmuir could not have been more adulatory and sympathetic, nor could the projects, based upon the discovery, have been more ambitious. I went forth to my work and to my labour without so much as a dog to wave me farewell; all were in the turf-house, surrounded by visionary force-pumps, bath-rooms, and even by miraged fountains in the garden.

When I drove the car into the yard on my return that afternoon, I was confronted by a long chestnut face with a white blaze, looking at me out of the spare loose-box—the face, in fact, of "the little horse" of whom Flurry had spoken to Andrew. There was also, added to the more familiar heaps of mortar, gravel, and stones, a considerable deposit of black and evil-smelling sludge. It seemed, as was not uncommonly the case, that a good many things had been happening during my absence. The stone floor of the hall was stencilled with an intricate pattern of black paw-marks, and was further decorated with scraps of torn paper; a cold stench pervaded the smoking-room (which was situated above the turf-house); far away, a sound as of a gramophone in the next world indicated that Captain Andrew's *affaire de cœur* was finding an outlet in song.

I followed the sounds to the drawing-room, and found Andrew and Miss Longmuir at the piano, in a harmony obviously world-forgetting, though not likely to be by the world forgot. Philippa was sitting by the oil stove, and was, I hope, deriving some satisfaction from inhaling its fumes, its effect upon the temperature being negligible.

Andrew's song was a Hungarian ditty, truculent and amorous, and very loud; under cover of it my wife told me that he, assisted by Walkin' Aisy and the quarrymen, and attended by Miss Longmuir, had baled out the newly discovered well, and that the quarrymen had exacted whisky to sustain them during the later stages of the process, and that the sludge would be ideal for the roses. They believed the well was filling again beautifully, but they had to leave it because Flurry came over with the horse for Andrew for the paper-chase, and Andrew and Meg went out schooling.

"What paper-chase?" I interpolated coldly.

"Oh, they've got one up for Monday," said Philippa airily. " The children have been tearing up paper all day. I found—rather with horror—that Flurry had given them those old letters out of the turf-house to tear up—I said you and I would ride, of course "—she looked at me with apprehension veiled by defiance, and I said it was thoughtful of her.—" But I want to tell you about old Mrs. Knox," she said, hurrying on. " She told Flurry that the well had never been used since the time of the Famine, when they got up a soup-kitchen here, and the day after they opened the well she said the servants flew in a body out of the house, like wild geese!"

" I don't wonder, if it smelt as it does now," I said. " Was that why they flew?"

" Flurry said he didn't know what lifted them. But Flurry never says he doesn't know unless he *does* know and doesn't want to tell!"

The following day was Saturday, and for the first time for many weeks a Sabbath stillness prevailed on the roof. Walkin' Aisy was absent; no explanation was forthcoming, and I diagnosed a funeral in the neighbourhood. It was on Sunday afternoon that I was roused from my usual meditation—consequent upon Sunday roast beef—by the intelligence that Mrs. William Shanahan wanted to speak to me. Mrs. Shanahan was a fair freckled woman, with a loud voice and a red face and the reputation of ruling Walkin' Aisy with a rod of iron. It appeared that Walkin' Aisy was confined to his bed; that he had had a reel in his head after getting home on Friday, and that whatever work it was that young gentleman gave him to do, he wasn't the better of it.

"And he was as wake in himself and as troubled in his mind as that he couldn't walk to Mass. I told him he should mind the chickens while I'd be out, and when I came in the dog had three of me chickens dead on the floor, and where was himself, only back in the room, and he kneeling there with the two hands up, sayin' his prayers! 'What ails ye?' says I, 'ye old gommoch, that ye'd let the dog kill me chickens?' 'Sure, I was sayin' me prayers,' says he; 'That the Lord mightn't hear your prayers!' says I. God forgive me, I had to say it!"

I recalled her to the question of the chimneys, pointing out that the gable chimney was half down, and could not be left as it was.

To this Mrs. Walkin' Aisy replied at great length that William's father had given him an advice not to go in it, and that the father was dark these scores of years, and it was what he blamed for it was the work he done in Shreelane

House in the time of the Famine. It was after that the sight went bandy with him.

She declined to offer any opinion as to when Walkin' Aisy would return to work, and withdrew, leaving me to consider my position under the Employers' Liability Act in the event of her husband's demise, and to wish, not for the first time, that Andrew (now strolling at his ease with Miss Longmuir, reviewing a course for the paper-chase), had been at Jericho, or any other resort of the superfluous, before he interfered with the tranquil progress of the chimneys towards dissolution.

There were strange lapses at dinner,—delays, omissions, disasters, and Julia the parlourmaid had a trembling hand and a general suggestion of nerve-storm. After dinner it was reported to Philippa that Anthony was not well, and after a prolonged absence she returned with the information that he had had a nightmare, and that there was a rumour in the house that all the servants were going to give warning the following morning. Their reason for this was obscure, but was somehow connected with Mrs. Walkin' Aisy's visit, and the fact that the swing-door leading to the turf-house had opened and shut twice, of its own volition. We did not mention these matters to our guests, and retired to rest in perturbation. I admit that at some time during the night, which was a still one, I heard the turf-house door groan on its hinges, and slam. I went downstairs and found nothing; it was certainly unusual, however, that Bob, the red setter, had abandoned his lair in the smoking-room, and was spending the night on the mat outside my dressing-room door.

Next morning Philippa, considering that a thrust was better than a parry, held a court of enquiry in the lower regions, and, according to her own report, spoke seriously on the grave responsibility incurred by those who frightened other people about nonsense. Julia's version of the proceedings, I heard at a later date. She said that "the Misthress spoke to us lovely, and the Priest couldn't speak better than her. She told us that the divils in hell wasn't worse than us."

Part III

It has been said of Ireland that the inevitable never happens, and that the impossible invariably occurs. When on Monday morning I learned that Flurry was to be one of the hares, and beheld him mounted on his best horse, as covered with bags as a postman on Christmas Day, I recalled the epigram. Another confirmation of the law of the unexpected was the fact that Meg Longmuir, on the "maroon" pony, was his fellow hare, very smart, much elated, and quite unaware that she had been substituted for Sally Knox at the last moment, in order that she might be as a millstone hung round the neck of Flurry. That this arrangement was not what Captain Larpent had desired was sufficiently apparent to the naked eye : why Flurry submitted to it was less obvious.

About a dozen riders had been whipped up to take part in this preposterous affair, and were standing about on the grass in front of Shreelane, cutting up the turf as much as the hardness of the ground would permit, and making as much noise as a pack of hounds at feeding time. The April sun glared hot, the better part of a north-easterly gale was blowing, the horses had over-eaten themselves with the bread of idleness, and were fat and frisky.

" Is he any good ? " said Flurry to me in a low voice, with his eye on Andrew, who was sitting, shrouded in gloom and remoteness, on the chestnut horse.

" Ask Miss Longmuir," I said. " She was schooling with him on Saturday."

" I'll have plenty to do minding her, without asking her questions that she couldn't answer," returned Flurry. He resumed his survey of Andrew. " I wonder will he be able to hold that horse in a snaffle ? He catches hold an odd time."

"Stand by!" said Doctor Hickey, his watch in his hand. "Fifteen seconds more before the hares start!"

"Well, if Larpent goes as big as he talks, he'll do," said Flurry, gathering up his reins.

The ten minutes of grace ebbed slowly away, and preposterous though I still held the affair to be, I do not deny that I was aware of an inward simmering of impatience.

"I'll have the face worn off my watch looking at it if you don't let us start soon!" said Miss Larkie McRory to Hickey.

She was mounted on a long-legged animal that had been summarised by Flurry as "the latter end of a car-horse," and was certainly in need of all the time it could get.

"Don't excite yourself now, or I'll be having to order you a cooling draught!" returned the Doctor, but I perceived that he, in common with everyone else, was edging his horse towards the point of departure.

"Go!"

In the riot of the break-away, I was able to think of nothing but of keeping Daniel from bucking me over his head, but during the hustle at the avenue gates I observed Andrew riding off Bernard, and getting to the front with pale and ferocious determination. The "scent" took us along the road; we followed it over a stony bank and across two fields, at steeplechase pace, and then it ceased. By this time any lingering sense of absurdity had ceased also. We cast ourselves feverishly, like hounds; we galloped great circles; someone found the paper again, and yelled like a maniac. We all yelled in response, a variety of yells, from " Tally Ho " to "Cooee," as, like Bedlam let loose, we rushed to the discoverer. We were up on high land now, and the wind was whirling in our ears, snatching our voices away to infinity, and blowing up the temperatures of horses and riders like a bellows. It had caught away the torn paper and flung it to leeward, into furze brakes, against the sides of the banks, and checks were many, and the horses, convinced that the hounds were somewhere ahead, pulled double. In the bare fields, with their scanty April grass, everything showed up; we were deceived by white stones, by daisies, by dandelion puff-balls, by goose-feathers; most of all we were deceived by country-people, whom, I have no doubt, Flurry had instructed to mislead us.

We had had a long check, consequent on a false trail, when, three fields away, Andrew held up his hat.

" Look at him now, running mute! " giggled

Sally Knox in my ear, as we battered down a road. "He's too cross to shout. He's frantic because he's not the hare, and Meg Longmuir was sent with Flurry! And poor Flurry, who's going such a nice safe line!"

"I suppose we may thank Miss Longmuir for the safe line?" I responded with some difficulty, because Daniel was enjoying himself on the road, according to the idiotic manner of horses.

"No! You may thank the chestnut horse!" ejaculated Flurry Knox's wife, as she hoisted out of the road over a loose wall.

Remembering that Andrew was intended to buy the chestnut horse, the deduction was a simple one. It was also quite clear that, disappointing as it might be, and contrary to the most cherished convention, Andrew was going as big as he talked, and even bigger.

"'Them that's in love is like no one'!" I quoted to Mrs. Flurry, as Captain Larpent, taking the shortest way to a drift of paper on a hillside, charged a tall, furze-tufted fence, and got over with a scramble. We followed, less heroically, by a gap, and ascended the hill, with the torn paper scurrying in front of us in the gusty wind. We had now been going for thirty-five minutes, and were all, horses and riders, something blown; Miss Larkie's car-horse could have been

164

heard down–wind for half a mile, and I would have backed Daniel to out-roar any lion in the den.

Nothing but the checks held us together. Doctor Hickey, and Irving, the District Inspector, were taking the matter seriously, and were riding hard to catch Andrew, for the honour of the country. Bernard Shute and two or three other heavy-weights were afoot, dragging their dripping horses over a bank with an up-hill take off; Miss McRory and the car-horse were making an extremely gradual progress in the rear, and Philippa had pulled back to give her leads, with an unselfishness that was not only futile, but was also a reproach to me and my fellow-men.

We had been going in a big ring, and from the top of the hill we could again see Shreelane, below us among its trees. It was there also that we caught the first sight of the hares, now heading for home and safety. The wind had strengthened to half a gale, and the wild and composite yell with which the hounds viewed their quarry was blown back into their throats. The maroan pony had fulfilled her mission as a handicap; twice we saw Flurry dismount and pull down a gap; once, at a bank, he got behind her and whipped her over like a peg-top. Another field took them to the high road. A puff of white paper fluttered out, and Miss Longmuir looked back and flourished a defiant whip; they turned, and galloped in a cloud of dust along the road for Shreelane.

It was not a nice hill to get down in a hurry, and I should think the chestnut horse dreams of it now, somewhere in the level English Midlands, after he has over-eaten himself on fat English oats. For my part, I remembered a humble but useful path, that links a little group of cottages with the rest of the world.

The paper lay thick on the road in the shelter of the fences; everyone began to ride for a finish, and after a quarter of a mile of pounding in the dust at the heel of the hunt, I considered that Daniel and I had satisfied the demands of honour, and ignobly turned in at the back way to the stable yard, permitting the chase to sweep on to the front gates without me.

In the stable yard I found several objects of interest. The hares were there, dismounted, very hot, and uncaptured; Mrs. Knox was there, seated in her phaeton; there was a cluster of servants at the back door; there were McRorys, leaning on bicycles; there was Cecilia Shute, in her motor, with unknown rank and fashion billowing in motor veils beside her.

All were gazing at a mass of sooty bricks and shattered chimney-pots that lay, scattered wide, in and about the black dredgings of the turf-house well.

" That's the gable chimney," said Flurry coolly ; " it got tired of waiting for Walkin' Aisy. We heard the roar of it as we came in the front gate!" He turned his mail-bag upside down so that its ultimate dregs were blown far and wide. " How did the chestnut horse go with —— ? "

As if in reply, hoofs clattered outside the yard, and the white nose of the chestnut shot into the opening of the yard gate. He plunged past me, with Andrew lying back and tugging at the snaffle. The Shreelane yard was fairly spacious, but I began to think that the thing wasn't as funny as it looked. The horse swerved at Mrs. Knox's phaeton, swerved again as Flurry turned him from his stable door with a flourish of the mail-bag. Andrew wrenched his head straight for the open back gate, and might have got him out without disaster, had not the widespread ruin of the chimney intervened. The chestnut once more tried to swerve, his legs went from under him, and he fell, striking fire from the cobble stones of the yard. Andrew stuck to him to the last instant, but was shot clear, and was flung, head first, into the heap of stones and black mud.

It seemed long, long hours between this catastrophe, and a sufficient subsidence of things in general, for me to be able, without inhumanity, to envisage a whisky and soda. Old Mrs. Knox watched me with approval.

"I'm tired of looking at young men drinking tea," she commented. (It was Mrs. Knox's pleasing idiosyncrasy to look upon me as a young man.) "They were like a pack of curates at a school-feast! Not that I was ever at a school-feast, thank God!" she added, with an abandoned chuckle.

We were sitting in a corner of the dining-room, surrounded by empty cups and crumby plates; tides of tea and of talkers had ebbed and flowed, but Mrs. Knox had sat on—to hear my personal report of Andrew, she said.

"Upon my honour, he escaped very well! A dislocated shoulder is nothing, and the young lady is there to 'tend the wounded Deloraine!'"

She paused, and put her head on one side, as if waiting for the prompter. "How does it go? 'She thought some spirit of the sky had done the bold mosstrooper wrong!'"

She paused again, and looked at me; the evening light shone on her spectacles, and made them impenetrable.

"Now I'm going to give you a piece of advice; 'And I'll not take it!' says Major Yeates, R.M.!"

I protested that I had said nothing of the kind. She prodded me in the knee with a goblin finger.

"*Close that well!* Put on the flagstone, and seal it down again!" She fumbled in her shawls, and pulled out a thin old gold chain. "Here's the seal, the same one that my father sealed it with at the time of the Famine!"

I said that I was ready to do anything that she told me, but it would be interesting to know why.

Mrs. Knox detached the seal from her chain, to which it was knotted by something that I darkly suspected to be a bit of bootlace. It was a cornelian seal, made in the grand manner; massively wrought, the gold smooth from age.

"I daresay you never heard of Major Apollo Riggs? He drove up to this house one fine day in a coach-and-four. Next day the coach-and-four drove away, but Major Apollo Riggs was not in it!"

"He found himself a success at Shreelane?" I suggested.

"Not so much with his host as his hostess!" returned Mrs. Knox portentously.

"A duel?" I asked.

"He was never seen again, my dear!" replied Mrs. Knox. (There are moments, in Ireland, when this term of affection is used not so much affectionately as confidentially.)

At this point the door opened. Mrs. Knox put the goblin finger on her lips, as Philippa, still in her habit, slid into the room.

"The patient and Meg are extremely self-sufficing," she said, dropping into a chair. "His face is turning all colours of the rainbow, and one eye has disappeared, but the other is full of expression and is fixed on Meg!"

"There's not much colour about *you*," I said. "You ought to have a whisky and soda."

"Nonsense!" said Philippa, waving me away; "we've got most of the black stuff out of his hair; even his waistcoat pocket was full of it! And bits of the torn paper had stuck to it, like confetti."

"That suggests a wedding," I observed.

"Quite," said Philippa. "But the absurd thing was that one of the confetti—obviously a bit of those old letters that the children tore up—had the word 'Apollo' on it! It was stuck on to him like a label."

Mrs. Knox clasped her hands, and lay back in her chair.

"I said it was, of course, a tribute to his beauty, but Meg was not at all amused. She thought it was ' *lèse majesté.*' "

"She'll get over that in time," I said, putting the seal in my pocket.

James.

VII

WHEN I FIRST MET DR. HICKEY

THERE was a wonderful chandelier in the hotel dining-room. Fine bronze it was made of, with mermaids, and Tritons, and dolphins flourishing their tails up towards the dingy ceiling-paper, and beaked galleys, on whose prows sat six small lamps, with white china receptacles for paraffin, and smoky brown chimneys. Gone were the brave days when each prow had borne a galaxy of tall wax candles; the chandelier might consider itself lucky in that it had even the paraffin lamps to justify its existence, and that it still hung from a ceiling, instead of sharing the last resting-place of its twin brother, in the bed of the tidal river under the hotel windows.

James, the hotel waiter, knew the family history of the chandelier, as he knew that of most people and things in the county. I commented upon it to a young gentleman with a pointed beard, who sat next to me at dinner, and said that it looked to me like Renaissance. The young gentleman suggested, alternatively, that it looked more like bronze. I did not dispute the point, but I think he found the subject precarious, as he turned to the young lady on his left, and I heard him embark upon a new theme.

"I was half dead with the toothache all day," he observed.

The young lady replied sympathetically that toothache was a fright.

"Well, indeed, that's true," said James, smoothly entering the conversation from behind my chair. "I got my own share of it. Sure there was one time I used to be roaring like a Banshee all night with it."

"Were you so?" said the gentleman, with a wink at me. "That must have been a long time ago, James."

"Well, indeed, it is too, Doctor," replied James meditatively, "going on forty years, I daresay. I went to Dublin, and I went to a great dentist that was in it that time, and he pulled all the teeth I had, and he gave me a new set entirely."

"Oh, my!" said the young lady, "that must have been very expensive."

"It was so," said James, not without pride. "Twenty pounds I gave him."

"That was awful," said the young lady, feelingly; "it was well to be you that had it to spend."

"Well, it wasn't all out so bad," said James;

" sure I only wore them a few times—I wouldn't be bothered with them, and a doctor that was a friend of mine gave me ten pounds for them."

" I suppose they were a fit for a patient of his?" said the doctor.

"They were a bad fit for me, anyway," returned James, glancing over his shoulder at the clattering operations of his two female subordinates, with the eye of the sergeant-major—the eye that always contains a grievance. "I was a footman with the old Lord Garretmore that time. Sure that was where the chandelier came from. A grand house it was, too—big slobs of marble on the tables, and gold legs under them, and ye'd bog to the knees in the carpets. Well, it was the first night after me getting the teeth, there was a gentleman stayed for dinner, and he was to go away by the night train. Forty horses were in the stables, and there wasn't one but was out at grass, and I had to go out beating the bushes for an old mare that was round the house always, herself and her foal, to put her under the side car. 'Prua! Prua!' says I, calling the mare in the dark, and with that the teeth lepped out of my mouth, with respects to you!"

"Oh, fie!" said the mother of the young lady.

"What did you do then, James?" inquired the Doctor.

"I took the white tie off me, and I tied it to the bush that was next me, for a token, and 'twas that way I got them again the next morning, thanks be to God."

Having concluded his story, James started on a perfunctory tour of the table with the wine card. He stopped to pull the turf fire together, and, with a furtive eye at the glass over the chimney-piece, he rearranged the long lock of hair that draped his bald pate. It was dyed, of that peculiar shade of chestnut that disdains subterfuge, and the fact and its suggestions were distressing where an old servant was concerned; so also was the manner in which he hobbled on his heels.

"His walk's full of corns," said the young doctor, eyeing him not without sympathy. "He's a great old character. I believe they keep him here to talk to the tourists."

It is a melancholy fact that in Ireland, in these later days, "characters" have become aware of their position, and palpably live up to their reputation. But James was in a class of his own.

I said didactically, even combatively, that "characters" were free and easy, but that James was easy without being free.

" I'll bet he's not easy in his feet, anyhow ! " said the Doctor brutally. " Have you any more soup there, James ? "

The mother of the young lady, who had hither-to preserved a silence, broken only by the audible assimilation of her soup, here laid down her spoon and said in cryptic disparagement:

" Tin ! "

" Well, I'd say it was the best we had yet," said the Doctor. " I'd undertake to pull a puppy through distemper with it."

" That's the soup she has always for th'assizes," said James. " Grand soup it is, and I declare to ye, she makes it out of egg shells and every old rubbish ! "

The young lady's mother emitted a short laugh, but her empty soup-plate told heavily against her.

The meal wore slowly on. A sea fish, of a genus unknown to me, and amazingly endowed with bones, was consumed in distracted silence.

" I hear you have a fish shop opened in Balli-nagar, Mrs. M'Evoy," remarked the Doctor, taking his last fish bone out of action with pro-fessional adroitness, and addressing the mother of the young lady, " That's very up-to-date. There wasn't one I met from Ballinagar but was bragging of it."

" It was the Hoolahanes that had it," said Mrs. M'Evoy. " It's closed."

" Oh dear, why so ? " said the Doctor. " Why did they do that, I wonder ? "

" They said that morning, noon, and night people were bothering them for fish," returned Mrs. M'Evoy, to whom this triumph of the artistic temperament presented no exceptional feature.

" Unless it might be on a fast day, I'd never ask to taste a bit of fish," remarked James, giving a helping hand to the conversation. " There was a man I knew from this place got his death in Liverpool from a bit of fish. It stuck to the upper gum. ' Bill,' says he to the one that was with him, ' so help me God,' says he, ' I'm dyin',' says he; and sure that's how he met his death ! It was in some grand hotel he was, and he was too shy to give the puff to send out the bit."

" I'd like to send that to the ' B.M.J.','" said the Doctor gravely. " Maybe you could give me the man's name, James ? "

" There was them that could swear to it," said James, depositing a syphon on the table in a determined manner, " but they were before your day, Doctor Hickey."

" How young he is ! " said Miss M'Evoy archly. " Don't be flattering him, James."

"Indeed I'll not flatter him," returned James, "there's plenty doing that."

It was at about this point that a dish containing three roast ducks was placed in front of me. Circumstances had decreed that I sat at the end of the table; it was my task to deal with the ducks, and during the breathless and steamy struggle that ensued, I passed out of the conversation, which, indeed, had resolved itself into a more personal affair between Dr. Hickey and Miss M'Evoy.

It was somewhere in the reposeful period that came with the cheese, that Dr. Hickey ordered a bottle of port, of which he very handsomely invited the ladies and me to partake. He leaned back in his chair.

"Was this in the cellar the time of the flood?" he said, putting down his glass. "I don't mean Noah's flood, James; you mightn't remember that; but the time the river came up in the town here."

"If it was Noah's flood itself," said James, instantly accepting combat, "it couldn't get into *our* cellars. But, faith, it was up in this room you're sitting in, and I had to get up on the table from it, and it ruz to the table, and I had to hang out of the chandelier, and a boat came into the room then and took me out. Sure that was the time that the porpoise came up the river, with the dint of the flood, and she was in it for a week, in front of the hotel."

" In compliment to the visitors, I suppose ? " said the Doctor. " And what happened her, James ? "

" She was in it till a whale came up the river," replied James, with the simplicity of Holy Writ, "and b'Jove he banished her ! "

" It's a wonder you'd let him treat a lady that way, James," said Dr. Hickey.

It was still twilight when we left the dining-room, and strayed to the open hall door, and out into the September evening. In the east a rose-pink moon was rising in lavender haze, and a faint wind blew from it ; the subtle east wind of September, warmed by its journey across the cornfields, turf-scented by the bogs. There was a narrow garden between the hotel and the river, a place where were new and already-neglected flower-beds, and paths heavy with coarse river gravel, and grass that had been cut, not too recently, with a scythe. A thatched summer-house completed the spasmodic effort of the hotel to rise to smartness. The West of Ireland cannot be smart, nor should any right-minded person desire that it should be so.

Dr. Hickey and I sat and smoked on the

parapet wall above the river, while the slated and whitewashed town darkened into mystery. Little lights came slowly out, and behind the town the grey shape of Dreelish mountain lowered in un-compromising abruptness, a brooding presence, felt rather than seen. In the summer-house James was lighting a Chinese lantern, of a somewhat crumpled and rheumatic outline.

"Well, now, that's a great notion!" said Dr. Hickey, with the lethargic and pessi-mistic humour of his type. "That'll be in the prospectus—'Hotel grounds illuminated every night.' I wonder did they buy that at the Jumble Sale after the Fancy Fair in the Town Hall?"

We sat there, and the moon and the round red Chinese lantern looked at each other across the evening, and had a certain resemblance, and I reflected on the fact that an Irishman is always the critic in the stalls, and is also, in spirit, behind the scenes.

"Look at James now," said the Doctor. "He's inviting the ladies out to have coffee in the summer-house. That's very fashionable. I suppose we should go there too."

We sat with Mrs. and Miss M'Evoy in the summer-house, and drank something that was unearthly black in the red light, and was singu-

larly unsuggestive of coffee. The seats were
what is known as "rustic," and had aggressive
knobs in unexpected places; the floor held the
invincible dampness of the West, yet the situation
was not disagreeable. At the other side of the
river men were sitting on a wall, and talking,
quietly, inexhaustibly; now and then a shout of
laughter broke from one of them, like a flame
from a smouldering fire.

"These lads are waiting to go back on the
night mail," said the Doctor; "you wouldn't
think they're up since maybe three this morning
to come in to the fair."

Here a railway whistle made a thin bar of
sound somewhere out under the low moon, that
had now lifted herself clear of the haze. A voice
called from the hill-side:

"Hora-thu! Tommeen! Let yee be coming
on!"

The men tumbled on to the road, and hurried,
heavy-footed, in the direction of the station.

"Sure, they've half an hour yet, the creatures,"
said Mrs. M'Evoy.

"They have, and maybe an hour before they
have the pigs shunted," said James, re-entering
with a plate of biscuits, adorned with pink and
white sugar.

"Ah! what signifies half an hour here or there

on this line!" said Dr. Hickey. "I'm told there was a lady travelling on it last week, and she had a canary in a cage, and the canary got loose and flew out of the window, and by George, the lady pulled the communication cord, and stopped the train!"

"Well, now, she showed her sense," said Mrs. M'Evoy, with an utterance slightly muffled in pink biscuit.

"She and the guard went then trying to catch the canary," continued Dr. Hickey, "and he'd sit till they'd get near him, and then he'd fly on another piece. Everyone that was in the train was hanging out of it, and betting on it, from one carriage to another, and some would back the lady and some would back the bird, and everyone telling them what to do."

"It's a pity *you* weren't in it," said Miss M'Evoy, "they'd have been all right then."

"It was that bare bit of bog near Bohirmeen," pursued Dr. Hickey, without a stagger, "not a tree in it. 'If he have a fly left in him at all,' says a chap out of a Third Smoker, 'ye'll get him in Mike Doogan's bush.' That was the only bush in the country."

"'Twas true for him," said James.

"Well, they got him in the bush," proceeded Dr. Hickey, "singing away for himself; but they had some trouble crossing the drains. I'm told the guard said the lady lepped like a horse!"

"You had it right, all to the singing," commented Mrs. M'Evoy, advancing as it were to the footlights. "I have the little bird upstairs this minute, and she never sang a note yet!"

Mrs. M'Evoy here permitted herself to subside into fat and deep-seated chuckles, and Miss M'Evoy, James, and I gave way suitably to our feelings.

"Well, now, I thought it was a nice idea, the canary to be singing," said Dr. Hickey, emerging from the situation as from a football scrimmage, in which he had retained possession of the ball. "The next time I tell the story, I'll leave that out, and I can say that the lady that lepped like a horse was Mrs. M'Evoy. They'll believe me then."

"Why wouldn't you say the canary was an eagle?" said Miss M'Evoy. "There used to be plenty eagles in these mountains back here."

"Well, indeed, I might too," said Dr. Hickey. "I remember it was somewhere in these parts that an uncle of mine was staying one time, and a man came to the hotel with an eagle to sell to the tourists. My uncle was like Mrs. M'Evoy here, he was very fond of birds; and the man said the eagle'd be a lovely pet. Whatever way it was, he bought it." He paused to light a cigarette, and James pretended to collect the coffee cups.

"He gave the eagle to the Boots to mind for him," resumed the Doctor, "and the Boots put it into an empty bedroom. It wasn't more than seven o'clock next morning when my uncle was wakened up, and the waiter came in. 'There's a man in the kitchen, your honour,' says he, 'and he has a great fighting aigle, and he says he'll fight your honour's aigle in the passage.' They had a grand fight between the two o' them in the spare room, and in the end my uncle's eagle went up the chimney, and the man's eagle went out through the glass in the window. My uncle had a nice bill to pay for all that was broken in the room, and in the end he gave the eagle to the Zoo."

"Faith, he did not!" shouted James suddenly. "He left him stuck in the chimbley! And sure it was I that got him out, and meself that sold him to a gentleman that was going to Ameriky. Sure, I was the waiter!"

Dr. Hickey threw himself back in his rustic chair.

"Holy smoke! This is no place for me," he said; "every story I have is true in spite of me."

Soon afterwards the ladies went to bed, and Dr. Hickey and I smoked on for a time. He explained to me that he was here as "locum" for a friend of his; it wasn't much of a catch, but he was only just after passing for his Medical, and you'd nearly go as locum for a tinker's dog after you had three years' grinding in Dublin put in. This was a God-forsaken sort of a hole, not a hound within fifty miles, nor anyone that would know a hound if they saw one, but the fishing was middling good. From this point the conversation flowed smoothly into channels of sport, and the dual goals of Dr. Hickey's ambition were divulged to me.

"There was a chap I was at school with— Knox his name was—that has a little pack of foxhounds down in the South, and he's as good as promised me I'm to whip in to him if I can get the Skebawn Dispensary that's vacant now, and I might have as good a chance of it as another."

My own ambitions were also, at the moment, dual, being matrimonial, with a Resident Magistracy attached, but I did not feel it necessary to reveal them. I mentioned that I was having a day's fishing here on my way to Donegal to shoot grouse, but did not add that Philippa, to whom I was newly engaged, was implicated in the grouse party, still less that it was my intention to meet her the next afternoon at Carrow Cross Junction, an hour away, and proceed with her to the home of her uncle, an hour or so further on.

"You might have three hours, or maybe four, to wait at Carrow Cross," said Dr. Hickey, as if tracking my thought; "why wouldn't you drive out to the Sports at Carrow Bay? It's only four miles, and there's a Regatta there to-morrow, and when the tide goes out they have races on the sands. I believe there's a trotting-match too, and an exhibition of crochet."

It did not seem to me that I wanted to go to Carrow Bay, but it was not necessary to say so.

Trucks at the station were banging into their neighbours, with much comment from the engine; I thought of Tommeen and his comrades, up since 3 A.M., and still waiting to get home, and it suggested the privileges of those who could go to bed.

It was over a whisky and soda in the heavily reminiscent atmosphere of the smoking-room that Dr. Hickey told me he was going to take the ladies to the Sports, and mentioned that there would be a train at eleven, and a spare seat on the car from Carrow Cross. It required no special effort to see the position that I was to occupy in relation to Mrs. M'Evoy; I followed the diplomatic method of my country; I looked sympathetic, and knew certainly that I should not be there.

I leaned out of my window that night, to look at the river, with the moon on it, hustling over the shallows, and thought of the porpoise, who had been so unchivalrously banished by the whale. I also wondered when the English post got in. I was presently aware of a head projecting from a window just below, and a female voice said, as if in continuance of a conversation :

"We should coax James for the cold duck to take with us."

"That's a good idea," replied the rotund voice of Mrs. M'Evoy; "we'll get nothing out there that a Christian could eat, and there might be that gentleman too." (That gentleman closed one eye.) "Come in now, Ally! There's an east wind coming in that would perish the crows."

The guillotine slam of the sash followed. The river warbled and washed through the stillness; its current was not colder, more clear, than "that gentleman's" resolve that he would not grace the luncheon party at Carrow Bay Sports.

I breakfasted late and in solitude, ministered to by one of the female underlings of James; the voice of James himself, I heard distantly, in war and slaughtering, somewhere behind the scenes.

When I First Met Dr. Hickey

The letter that I wanted had not failed me, and I smoked a very honeyed cigarette over it in the garden afterwards. A glimpse of Dr. Hickey at the hotel door in a palpably new tie, and of Mrs. and Miss M'Evoy in splendour in the hall, broke into my peace. I quietly but unhesitatingly got over the wall of the garden, and withdrew by way of the river bank.

When the 11 o'clock train had left I returned to the halcyon stillness of the hotel; my own train left at 1.30; it was a time favourable, and almost attractive, for letter writing. As I wrote, I heard the voice of James demanding in thunder where was Festus O'Flaherty, and why hadn't he the chickens plucked. A small female voice replied that the Doctor and the ladies had left their lunch after them, and that Festus had run up to the station to try would he overtake them with it, and the thrain was gone.

" And if it was themselves they left after them," retorted James, still in thunder, "what was that to him ? "

To this conundrum no answer was attempted ; I bestowed upon Mrs. M'Evoy some transient compassion, and she and her company departed, hull down, below the horizon of my thoughts.

A few hours afterwards, I trod the solitudes of Carrow Cross Junction, and saw the train that had

187

brought me there bend like a caterpillar round a spur of hill, and disappear. When I looked round again the little bookstall was shuttered up, and the bookstall lady was vanishing down a flight of steps; the porter had entrenched himself in the goods store; the stationmaster was withdrawn from human ken with the completeness only achievable by his kind. I was suspended in space for three hours, and the indifference of my fellow-creatures was unconcealed. A long walk to nowhere and back again was the obvious resource of the destitute.

The town of Carrow Cross lay in a hollow below the station, with the blue turf smoke stagnant above its muddle of slate and thatched roofs; I skirted it, and struck out into the country. I did not find it attractive. Potato fields in September are not looking their best; there were no trees, and loose, crooked walls overran the landscape. The peak of Dreelish mountain was visible, but the dingy green country rose high between me and it, like the cope on the neck of a priest. I walked for an hour; I sat on a wall and read Philippa's letter again, and found, with a shock, that I had only one cigarette left. A fatuous fear of missing the train turned me back in the direction of the station, slightly hungry, and profoundly bored. I came into the town by a convent, and saw the nuns walking flowingly in twos, under chestnut trees; asceticism in its most pictorial aspect, with the orange leaves and the blue September haze, and the black robes and white headgear. I wondered how they managed to go on walking neatly to nowhere and back again with such purpose, and if they felt as jaded as I, and as little enlivened by the environs of Carrow Cross.

The town was an unprepossessing affair of two or three streets, whitewash and thatch squeezed between green and gold pubs, like old country-women among fashionable daughters. Everything was closed; as I looked along the empty street an outside car drawn by a dun pony turned into it at high speed, the pony forging with a double click-clack. As the car swung towards me some one flourished a stick, some one else a red parasol.

"We got a bit tired waiting for the sports," Dr. Hickey said, as he assisted Mrs. M'Evoy to alight at a house labelled Lynch's Railway Hotel, in royal blue; "it seemed that the tide wasn't going out as fast as the Committee expected. It might be another hour or more before the race-course would be above water, and we thought we might as well come on here and get something to eat at the Hotel."

"It has the appearance of being closed," said Mrs. M'Evoy, in a voice thinned by famine.

"That might be a fashion it has in the afternoon, when themselves does be at their dinner," said the car-driver.

The front door was certainly closed, and there was neither knocker nor bell, nothing but a large well-thumbed keyhole. Dr. Hickey hammered with his stick; nothing happened.

"They're gone to the races so," said the car-driver.

In the silence that followed it seemed that I could hear the flagging beat of Mrs. M'Evoy's heart.

"Wait awhile," said Dr. Hickey; "the window isn't bolted!"

The sill was no more than two feet from the ground, the sash yielded to pressure and went up; Dr. Hickey dived in, and we presently heard him assail the front door from inside.

It was locked, and its key had apparently gone to the races. I followed Dr. Hickey by way of the window, so did Miss M'Evoy; we pooled our forces, and drew her mamma after us through the opening of two foot by three, steadily, as the great god Pan drew the pith from the reed.

We found ourselves in a small sitting-room, almost filled by a table; there was a mature smell of cabbage, but there was nothing else to suggest the presence of food. We proceeded to the nether regions, which were like a chapter in a modern realistic novel, and found a sickly kitchen fire, the horrid remains of the Lynch family breakfast, an empty larder, and some of the home attire of the race-goers, lying, as the tree lies, where it fell.

" There's a sort of a butcher in the town," said Dr. Hickey, when the search-parties had converged on each other, empty-handed, "maybe we could cook something——"

" If it was even a bit of salt pork—" said Mrs. M'Evoy, seizing the poker and attacking the sleepy fire.

" Let you get some water, and I'll wash the plates," said Miss M'Evoy to Dr. Hickey.

I looked at my watch, saw that I had still an hour and a half to play with, and departed to look for the butcher.

Neither by sign-board nor by shop front did the Carrow Cross butcher reveal himself. I was finally investigating a side street, where the houses were one-storeyed, and thatched, and wholly unpromising, when a heavy running step, that might have been a horse's, thundered behind me, and a cumbrous pale woman, with the face of a fugitive, plunged past me, and burst

in at a cottage door like a mighty blast of wind.
A little girl, in tears, thudded barefooted after
her. The big woman turned in the doorway,
and shrieked to me.

"Thim's madmen, from th' Asylum! Come
inside from them, for God's sake!"

I looked behind me up the street, and saw a
small, decorous party of men, flanked by a couple
of stalwart keepers in uniform. One of the men,
a white-faced being in seedy black, headed them,
playing an imaginary fiddle on his left arm, and
smiling secretly to himself. Whether the lady
had invited me to her house as a protector, or
as a refugee, I did not know: she herself had
vanished, but through the still open door I saw,
miraculously, a fragment or two of meat, hanging in the interior. I had apparently chanced
upon the home of the Carrow Cross butcher.

A greasy counter and a chopping-block put
the matter beyond doubt; I beat upon an inner
door: a wail of terror responded, and then a
muffled voice:

"Come in under the bed to me, Chrissie,
before they'd ketch ye!"

There was nothing for it but to take from a
hook a grey and white fragment that looked like
bacon, place half-a-crown on the counter, and
depart swiftly.

"I gave a few of the Asylum patients leave to go to the Sports," said Dr. Hickey, a little later, when we were seated between the large bare table and the wall of the little sitting-room, with slices of fried pork weltering on our plates. "I saw the fellow waltzing down the street. Ah! he's fairly harmless, and they've a couple o' keepers with them anyway."

"The only pity was that you left the half-crown," said Mrs. M'Evoy; "a shilling was too much for it."

Mrs. M'Evoy was considerably flushed, and had an effective black smear on her forehead, but her voice had recovered its timbre. There was a tin of biscuits on the table, there was a war-worn brown teapot, and some bottles of porter; it was now four hours since I had eaten anything; in spite of the cold and clear resolve of the night before, I was feeding, grossly yet enjoyably, with Dr. Hickey and his friends.

"This is a Temperance Hotel for the past year," remarked Dr. Hickey, delicately knocking off the head of a porter bottle with the sitting-room poker. "That's why it was upstairs I found the porter. I suppose they took the corkscrew to the Sports with them."

"How did they lose the license at all?" said

Mrs. M'Evoy; "I thought there wasn't a house in Carrow Cross but had one."

"It was taken from them over some little mistake about selling potheen," replied Dr. Hickey, courteously applying the broken neck of the bottle to Mrs. M'Evoy's tumbler. "The police came to search the house, and old Lynch, that was in bed upstairs, heard them, and threw a two-gallon jar of potheen out of the top back window, to break it. The unlucky thing was that there was a goose in the yard, and it was on the goose it fell."

"The creature!" said Miss M'Evoy, "was she killed?"

"Killed to the bone, as they say," replied the Doctor; "but the trouble was, that on account of falling on the goose the jar wasn't broken, so the bobbies got the potheen."

"Supposing they summons you now for the porter!" said Mrs. M'Evoy, facetiously, casting her eye through the open window into the bare sunshiny street.

"They'll have summonses enough at Carrow Bay to keep them out of mischief," returned Dr. Hickey. "It's a pity now, Major, you didn't patronise the Sports. They might have put you on judging the cakes with Mrs. M'Evoy."

"Why then, the one they put on with me was

the man they had judging the vegetables," said Mrs. M'Evoy, after a comfortable pull at the contraband porter. " 'That's a fine weighty cake,' says me lad, weighing a sponge-cake on his hand. "We'll give that one the prize."

"I wish you brought it here with you," said her daughter, "as weighty as it was."

"They put *me* judging the row-boats," said Dr. Hickey, "but after the third race I had to give up, and put five stitches in one of the men that was in the mark-boat."

I said that the mark-boat ought to have been a fairly safe place.

"Safe !" said Dr. Hickey. " It was the hottest corner in the course. I thought they were sunk twice, but they might have been all right if they hadn't out-oars and joined in the race on the second round. They got in first, as it happened, and it was in the course of the protest that I had to put in the stitches. It was a good day's sport, as far as it went."

"Ah, there's no life in a Regatta without a band," said Miss M'Evoy languidly, with her elbows on the table and her cup in her hand. "Now Ringsend Regatta's sweet !"

"I'm afraid Miss M'Evoy didn't enjoy herself to-day," said Dr. Hickey. "Of course she's used to so much attention in Dublin——"

"It's kind of you to say that," said Miss M'Evoy; "I'm sure you're quite an authority on Dublin young ladies."

"Is it me?" said Dr. Hickey; "I'd be afraid to say Boo to a goose. But I've a brother that could tell you all about them. He's not as shy as I am."

"He must be a great help and comfort to you," returned Miss M'Evoy.

"He's very romantic," said Dr. Hickey, "and poetical. He was greatly struck with two young ladies he met at the Ringsend Regatta last month. He mistook their address, someway, and when he couldn't find them, what did he do but put a poem in the papers—the Agony Column, y'know——"

"We'd like to hear that," said Mrs. M'Evoy, putting her knife into the salt with unhurried dexterity.

"I forget it all, only the last verse," said Dr. Hickey, "it went this way:

'You are indeed a charming creature,
Perfect alike in form and feature,
I love you and none other.
Oh, Letitia—Here's your Mother!'"

As Dr. Hickey, his eyes modestly on his plate, concluded the ode, I certainly intercepted a peculiar glance between the ladies.

" I call that very impident," said Mrs. M'Evoy, winking at me.

" It was worth paying a good deal to put that in print!" commented Miss M'Evoy unkindly. "But that was a lovely Regatta," she continued, "and the music and the fireworks were grand, but the society's very mixed. Do you remember, M'ma, what happened to Mary and me that evening, the time we missed you in the dark?"

"Indeed'n I do," said Mrs. M'Evoy, her eyes still communing with her daughter's, "and I remember telling you it was the last evening I'd let you out of my sight."

"It was a gentleman that picked up my umbrella," began Miss M'Evoy artlessly.

Dr. Hickey dropped his knife on the floor, and took some time to pick it up.

"And he passed the remark to me that it was a nice evening," went on Miss M'Evoy. "'It is,' said I. Now, M'ma, why wouldn't I give him a civil answer?"

"That's according to taste," said Mrs. M'Evoy.

"Well indeed I didn't fancy his looks at all. It was pitch dark only for the fireworks, but I thought he had a nasty kind of a foreign look, and a little pointed beard on him too. If you saw the roll of his eye when the green fire fell out of the rockets you'd think of Mephistopheles——"

" There's no doubt Mephistopheles was one of Shakespeare's grandest creations," said Dr. Hickey hurriedly. His eyes besought my aid. It struck me that this literary digression was an attempt to change the conversation.

Miss M'Evoy resumed her narrative.

" ' That's a pretty flower you have in your button-hole,' said he. ' It is,' said I."

" You didn't tell him a great deal he didn't know," said her mother.

" ' Maybe you might give it to me ? ' said he. ' Maybe I might not ! ' said I. ' And where do you live ? ' said he. ' Percy Place,' says Mary, before you could wink. Anyone would have to believe her. ' Upon my soul,' said he, ' I'll have the pleasure of calling upon you. Might I ask what your name is ? ' ' O'Rooney,' says Mary, ' and this is my cousin, Miss Letitia Gollagher.' Well, when Mary said ' Gollagher,' I *burst !* "

Miss M'Evoy here put down her cup, and to some slight extent repeated the operation.

" I suppose the foreign gentleman told you his own name then ? " said Dr. Hickey, whose complexion had warmed up remarkably.

" He did not," said Miss M'Evoy ; " but perhaps that was because he wasn't asked, and it was then M'ma came up. I can tell you he didn't wait to be introduced ! "

" I have a sister-in-law living in Percy Place," said Mrs. M'Evoy, passing her handkerchief over her brow, and addressing no one in particular, " and it was some day last month she was telling me of a young man that was knocking at all the doors down the street, and she thought he was a Collector of some sort. He came to her house too, and he told the girl he was looking for some ladies of the name of Gollagher or O'Rooney."

She paused, and regarded Dr. Hickey.

"I wonder did he find them?" asked Dr. Hickey, who was obviously being forced on to the ropes.

" I thought *you* might be able to tell us that!" said Mrs. M'Evoy, delivering her knock-out blow with the suddenness that belongs to the highest walks of the art.

Miss M'Evoy, with equal suddenness, uttered a long and strident yell, and lay back in her place, grasping my arm as she did so, in what I am convinced was wholly unconscious sympathy. She and I were side by side, facing the window, and through the window, which, as I have mentioned, was wide open, I was aware of a new element in the situation.

It was a figure in blue in the street outside ; a soft and familiar blue, and it bore a parasol of the same colour. The figure was at a standstill ; and **very** blue, the burning blue of tropical heavens, were the eyes that met mine beneath the canopy of the parasol. Even before my own had time to blink I foreknew that never, in time or in eternity, should I be able to make Philippa accept thoroughly my explanation.

Philippa's explanation was extremely brief, and was addressed rather to the empty street of Carrow Cross than to me, as I crawled by her side. There had been, she said, half an hour to wait, and as I was not at the station—the blue eyes met mine for a steely moment—she had gone for a little walk. She had met some horrid drunken men, and turned into another street to avoid them, and then——

A brimming silence followed. We turned up the road that led to the station.

"There are those men again!" exclaimed Philippa, coming a little nearer to me.

In front of us, deviously ascending the long slope, was the Asylum party; the keepers, exceedingly drunk, being assisted to the station by the Lunatics.

VIII

THE BOSOM OF THE McRORYS

SINCE the day when fate had shipwrecked us at the end of the Temple Braney shrubbery, and flung us, dripping, into the bosoms of the McRorys, we had been the victims of an indissoluble friendship with the family. This fulfilled itself in many ways.

Gratitude, what is known as Common Gratitude (which is merely a hollow compliance with the voice of conscience), impelled us to lunch Mr. and Mrs. McRory, heavily and elaborately (but without any one to meet them); to invite the whole family to a lawn-tennis party (and the whole family came); and, at other people's tennis parties, to fawn upon them (when it was no longer possible to elude them). It was a despicable position, and had I at all foreseen, when the picnic sank at Temple Braney pier, that the result would have been dinner-parties, I should unhesitatingly have left Philippa to drown.

The intimacies imposed by Common Gratitude had, under the healing hand of time, become less acute, and might, indeed, have ceased to affect

us, had not fate again intervened, and cemented
the family friendship in the most public way
possible. There befell a Harvest Festival in
Skebawn Church, with a Bishop, and an Anthem,
and a special collection. To it the McRorys, for-
saking their own place of worship, came in
power, and my wife, very superfluously, indicated to Mrs. McRory a seat in our pew. The
pew is a front one, and Mrs. McRory became at
once a figure-head to the rest of the congregation
—a buxom figure-head, upholstered tightly in
royal blue satin, that paled the ineffectual fires
of the pulpit dahlias, and shouted in a terrible
major chord with the sunflowers in the east
window. She creaked mysteriously and rhyth-
mically with every breath ; a large gold butterfly,
poised on an invisible spring, quivered and
glittered above her bonnet. It was while waiting
for the service to begin that Philippa was inspired
to whisper to Mrs McRory some information,
quite immaterial, connected with the hymns.
The next moment I perceived that Mrs. McRory's
butterfly had fixed its antennæ into some adjunct
of my wife's hat that was at once diaphanous
and sinewy, with the result that the heads of
the two ladies were locked together. A silent
struggle ensued ; the butterfly's grappling-irons
held, so also did the hat-trimming, and Philippa

and Mrs. McRory remained brow to brow in what seemed to be a prolonged embrace. At this point Philippa showed signs of collapse ; she said that Mrs. McRory's nose, glowing like a ruby within two inches of her own, made her hysterical. I affected unconsciousness, while my soul thirsted for an axe with which to decapitate one or both of the combatants, and subsequently to run amok among the congregation, now, as the poet says, "abashlessly abandoned to delight." The butterfly's vitals slowly uncoiled, and were drawn out into a single yet indomitable strand of gold wire ; the Bishop was imminent, when a female McRory in the pew behind (known to the Fancy as "Larkie") intervened with what were, I believe, a pair of manicure scissors, and the incident closed.

It was clear that our blood-brotherhood with the McRorys was foreordained and predestined. We evaded two invitations to dinner, but a third was inescapable, even though an alarming intimacy was foreshadowed by the request that we should come "in a very quiet way."

"Do they expect us to creep in in tennis shoes ?" I demanded.

"I think it only means a black tie," said Philippa, with the idea that she was soothing me.

"If I have to go to a McRory Free-and-Easy, I shall not act as such," I returned, slamming myself into my dressing-room, and dragging forth ceremonial attire.

As, with a docility that I was far from feeling, I followed my wife into the drawing-room at Temple Braney, and surveyed the semicircle of McRorys and unknown notabilities (summarised as "Friends from Dublin") that silently awaited us, I felt that neither freedom nor ease would be my lot. But few things in life are quite as bad as one expects them to be—always excepting sea-sickness. In its dreary circuit of the room, my eye met that of my old friend Miss Bobby Bennett, of the Curranhilty Hunt, niece of its Master, and consultant and referee in all its affairs. My friendship with Miss Bennett was of an ideal nature ; when we met, which was seldom, we were delighted to see one another ; in the intervals we forgot one another with, I felt sure, an equal completeness. Her social orbit was incalculable; she resembled a fox of whom I heard an earth-stopper say that you "couldn't tell any certain place where he wouldn't puck out." Whether it was at Punchestown, or at a Skebawn Parish tea, or judging cakes and crochet at an Agricultural Show, wherever she appeared it was with the same air of being on top of the situation and of extracting the utmost from it.

To me befell the onerous task of taking the Lady of the House in to dinner, but upon my other hand sat Miss Bennett (squired by a Friend from Dublin of apparently negligible quality), and before I had recovered from the soup—a hell-broth of liquid mustard that called itself mulligatawny—I found that to concentrate upon her was no more than was expected of me by both ladies. Mrs. McRory's energies were indeed fully engrossed by the marshalling of a drove of heated females, who hurried stertorously and spasmodically round the table, driven as leaves before the wind by fierce signals from their trainer. Opposite to me sat that daughter of the house whose manicure scissors had terminated the painful episode of the butterfly. I had always maintained that she was the prettiest of the McRorys, and it was evident that Irving, the new District Inspector of R.I.C., who sat beside her, shared my opinion. He was a serious, lanky young man, and at such moments as he found himself deprived of Miss McRory's exclusive attention, he accepted no alternative, and devoted himself austerely to his food.

Miss Bennett's intention was, I presently discovered, to hunt with Flurry Knox's hounds on the following day : she had brought over a horse, and it became clear to me that her secondary intention was to return without it.

"Larkie McRory's going to take up hunting," she said in her low swift voice. "The new D.I. hunts, you know."

Miss Bennett's astute grey eyes rested upon the young lady in question, and returned to me laden with inference.

"He's got a horse from a farmer for her to ride to-morrow—goodness knows what sort of a brute it is!—I hope she won't break her neck. She's the best of the lot. If the old man had sense he'd buy my mare for her—he's full of money—and I'd let her go cheap, too, as I have a young one coming on."

It is worthy of mention that I have never known Miss Bennett's stable composed of anything save old ones to go cheap and young ones coming on. I asked her what she would give me if I didn't tell Mr. McRory that her mare was touched in the wind.

"I'll give you in charge for defamation of character," replied Miss Bennett, with speed comparable only to the dart of an ant-eater's tongue. "Anything else you'd like to know? But look at Larkie now, I ask of you! Quick!"

I did as desired, and was fortunate enough

to see Miss McRory in the act of putting a spoonful of salt in Mr. Irving's champagne, what time he was engaged in repulsing one of Mrs. McRory's band of flaming ministers, who, with head averted in consultation with a collaborator, was continuously offering him melted butter, regardless of the fact that he had, at the moment, nothing in front of him but the tablecloth.

"There's Miss Larkie's Dublin manners for you," said Miss Bennett, and passed on to other themes.

I should say theme, because, speaking broadly, Miss Bennett had but one, and all roads sooner or later led to it. During the slow progress of the meal I was brought up to date in the inner gossip of the Curranhilty country. I learned that Mrs. Albert Dougherty had taken to riding astride because she thought it was smart, and it was nothing but the grab she got of the noseband that saved her from coming off every time she came down a drop. I asked for that Mr. Tomsy Flood whose career had twice, at vital points, been intersected by me.

"Ah, poor Tomsy! He took to this, y'know," Miss Bennett slightly jerked her little finger, "and he wouldn't ride a donkey over a sod of turf. They sent him out to South Africa, to an ostrich farm, and when the people found he

couldn't ride they put him to bed with a setting
of ostrich eggs to keep them warm, and he did
that grand, till some one gave him a bottle of
whisky, and he got rather lively and broke all
the eggs. They say it's a lay-preacher he's
going to be now!"

Across a dish of potatoes, thrust at me for the
fourth time, I told Miss Bennett that it was all
her fault, and that she had been very unkind to
Tomsy Flood. Miss Bennett gave me a look
that showed me what she still could do if she
liked, and replied that she supposed I was
sorry that she hadn't gone to South Africa
with him.

"I suppose we'll all be going there soon," she
went on. "Uncle says if Home Rule comes there
won't be a fox or a Protestant left in Ireland in
ten years' time; and he said, what's more, that if
he had to choose it mightn't be the Protestants
he'd keep! But that was because the Dissent-
ing Minister's wife sent in a claim of five pounds
to the Fowl Fund, and said she'd put down poison
if she didn't get it."

Not thus did Philippa and old McRory, at
their end of the table, fleet the time away. Old
McRory, as far as I could judge, spoke not at all,
but played tunes with his fingers on the tablecloth, or preoccupied himself with what seemed

to be an endeavour to plait his beard into a point. On my wife's other hand was an unknown gentleman, with rosy cheeks, a raven moustache, and a bald head, who was kind enough to solace her isolation with facetious stories, garnished with free and varied gestures with his knife, suggestive of sword-practice, all concluding alike in convulsive tenor laughter. I was aware, not unpleasantly, that Philippa was bearing the brunt of the McRory bean-feast.

When at length my wife's release was earned, and the ladies had rustled from the room in her wake, with all the conscious majesty of the Mantle Department, I attempted some conversation with my host, but found that it was more considerate to leave him to devour unmolested the crystallised fruits and chocolates that were not, I felt quite sure, provided by Mrs. McRory for the Master of the House. I retired upon the D.I., my opinion of whom had risen since I saw him swallow his salted champagne without a change of countenance. That he addressed me as "Sir" was painful, but at about my age these shocks have to be expected, and are in the same category as lumbago, and what my dentist delicately alludes to as " dentures."

The young District Inspector of Irish Constabulary has wisdom beyond his years: we talked profoundly of the state of the country until the small voice of old McRory interrupted us.

"Major," it said, "if you have enough drink taken we might join the ladies."

Most of the other gallants had already preceded us, and as I crossed the hall I heard the measured pounding of a waltz on the piano: it created an impulse, almost as uncontrollable as that of Spurius Lartius and Herminius, to dart back to the dining-room.

"That's the way with them every night," said old McRory dispassionately. "They mightn't go to bed now at all."

Old McRory had a shadowy and imperceptible quality that is not unusual in small fathers of large families; it always struck me that he understood very thoroughly the privileges of the neglected, and pursued an unnoticed, peaceful, and observant path of his own in the background. I watched him creep away in his furtive, stupefied manner, like a partly-chloroformed ferret. "'Oh, well is thee, thou art asleep!'—or soon will be," I said to myself, as I turned my back on him and faced the music.

I was immediately gratified by the spectacle of Philippa, clasped to the heart of the gentleman who had been kind to her at dinner, and moving with him in slow and crab-like sidlings round the carpet. Her eyes met mine with passionate appeal; they reminded me of those of her own fox-terrier, Minx, when compelled to waltz with my younger son.

The furniture and the elder ladies had been piled up in corners, and the dancing element had been reinforced by a gang of lesser McRorys and their congeners, beings who had not been deemed worthy of a place at the high table. Immured behind the upright piano sat Mrs. McRory, thumping out the time-honoured " Blue Danube " with the plodding rhythm of the omnibus horse. I furtively looked at my watch; we had dined at 7.30, and it was now but a quarter to ten o'clock. Not for half an hour could we in decency withdraw, and, finding myself at the moment beside Miss Larkie McRory, it seemed to me that I could do no less than invite her to take the carpet with me.

I am aware that my dancing is that of ten years ago, which places it in the same scrap-heap class as a battleship of that date, but Miss McRory told me that she preferred it, and that it exactly suited her step. It would be as easy to describe the way of a bird in the air as to define Miss McRory's step; scrap-heap or no, it made me feel that I walked the carpet like a thing of life. We were occasionally wrecked upon reefs of huddled furniture, and we sustained a collision or two of first-rate magnitude : after these episodes my partner imperceptibly steered me to a corner, in which I leaned heavily against whatever was most stable, and tried to ignore the fact that the floor was rocking and the walls were waving, and that it was at least two years since I had exceeded in this way.

It was in one of these intervals that Miss McRory told me that she was going hunting next day, and that he—her long hazel-grey eyes indicated Mr. Irving, now slowly and showily moving a partner about the room—had got a horse for her to ride, and she had never hunted before. She hoped to goodness she wouldn't fall off, and (here she dealt me the fraction of a glance) she hoped I'd pick her up now and again. I said that the two wishes were incompatible, to which she replied that she didn't know what incompatible meant ; and I told her to ask Mr. Irving whether he had found that salt and champagne were compatible.

" I thought you only wore that old eyeglass for show," replied Miss McRory softly, and again looked up at me from under her upcurled Irish eyelashes ; " it was out of spite he drank it ! A girl did that to my brother Curly at a dance, and he poured it down her back."

"I think Mr. Irving treated you better than you deserved," I replied paternally, adventuring once more into the tide of dancers.

When, some five minutes afterwards, I resigned my partner to Irving D.I., I felt that honour had been satisfied, and that it was now possible to leave the revel. But in this I found that I had reckoned, not so much without my host, as without my fellow-guest. Philippa, to my just indignation, had blossomed into the success of the evening. Having disposed of the kind-hearted gentleman (with the pink cheeks and the black moustache), she was immediately claimed by Mr. De Lacey McRory, the eldest son of the house, and with him exhibited a proficiency in the latest variant of the waltz that she had hitherto concealed from me. The music, like the unseen orchestra of a merry-go-round, was practically continuous. Scuffles took place at intervals behind the upright piano, during which music-books fell heavily upon the keys, and one gathered that a change of artist was taking place, but the fundamental banging of the bass was maintained, and the dancing ceased not. The efforts of the musicians were presently reinforced by a young lady in blue, who supplied a shrill and gibbering *obligato* upon a beribboned mandoline, and even, at some passionate moments, added her voice to the *ensemble*.

"Will this go on much longer?" I asked of Miss Bennett, with whom I had withdrawn to the asylum of a bow window.

"D'ye mean Miss Cooney O'Rattigan and her mandoline?" replied Miss Bennett. "I can tell you it was twice worse this afternoon when she was singing Italian to it. I never stayed here before, and please goodness I never will again; the wardrobe in my room is crammed with Mrs. McRory's summer clothes, and the chest of drawers is full of apples! Ah, but after all," went on Miss Bennett largely, "what can you expect from a cob but a kick? Didn't Tomsy Flood find a collection of empty soda-water bottles in his bed the time he stayed here for the wedding, when you found him stitched up in the feather bed!"

I said that the soda-water bottles had probably prepared him for the ostrich eggs, and Miss Bennett asked me if it were true that I had once found a nest of young mice in the foot of my bed at Aussolas, because that was the story she had heard. I was able to assure her that, on the contrary, it had been kittens, and passing from these pleasing reminiscences I asked her to come forth and smoke a cigarette in the hall with me, as a preliminary to a farther advance in the direction of the motor. I have a sincere regard for

Miss Cooney O'Rattigan.

Miss Bennett, but her dancing is a serious matter, with a Cromwellian quality in it, suggestive of jack boots and the march of great events.

The cigarettes were consolatory, and the two basket-chairs by the fire in the back-hall were sufficiently comfortable ; but the prospect of home burned like a beacon before me. The clock struck eleven.

"They're only beginning now!" said Miss Bennett, interpreting without resentment my glance at it. "Last night it was near one o'clock in the morning when they had high tea, and then they took to singing songs, and playing 'Are you there, Mike?' and cock-fighting."

I rose hastily, and began to search for my overcoat and cap, prepared to plunge into the frosty night, when Miss Bennett offered to show me a short way through the house to the stable-yard, where I had left the car.

"I slipped out that way after dinner," she said, picking up a fur-lined cloak and wrapping it about her. "I wanted to make sure the mare had a second rug on her this cold night."

I followed Miss Bennett through a wheezy swing-door ; a flagged passage stretched like a tunnel before us, lighted by a solitary candle planted in its own grease in a window. A long battle-line of bicycles occupied one side of the passage; there were doors, padlocked and cob-webbed, on the other. A ragged baize door at the end of the tunnel opened into darkness that smelt of rat-holes, and was patched by a square or two of moonlight.

"This is a sort of a lobby," said Miss Bennett. "Mind! There's a mangle there—and there are oars on the floor somewhere——"

As she spoke I was aware of a distant hum-ming noise, like bees in a chimney.

"That sounds uncommonly like a motor," I said.

"That's only the boiler," replied Miss Bennett; "we're at the back of the kitchen here."

She advanced with confidence, and flung open a door. A most startling vista was revealed, of a lighted room with several beds in it. Children's faces, swelled and scarlet, loomed at us from the pillows, and an old woman, with bare feet and a shawl over her head, stood transfixed, with a kettle in one hand and a tumbler in the other.

Miss Bennett swiftly closed the door upon the vision.

"My gracious heavens!" she whispered, "what on earth children are those? I'm sure it's mumps they have, whoever they are. And how secret the McRorys kept it!—and did you see it was punch the old woman was giving them?"

"We might have asked her the way to the yard," I said, inwardly resolving to tell Philippa it was scarlatina; "and she might have given us a light."

"It was this door I should have tried," said my guide, opening another with considerable circumspection.

Sounds of hilarity immediately travelled to us along a passage; I followed Miss Bennett, feeling much as if I were being led by a detective into Chinatown, San Francisco. A square of light in the wall indicated one of those inner windows that are supposed to give light mutually to room and passage, and are, as a matter of fact, an architect's confession of defeat. Farther on a door was open, and screams of laughter and singing proceeded from it. I admit, without hesitation, that we looked in at the window, and thus obtained a full and sufficient view of the *vie intime* of the Temple Braney kitchen. A fat female, obviously the cook, was seated in the midst of a remarkably lively crowd of fellow-retainers and camp-followers, thumping with massive knuckles on a frying-pan, as though it were a banjo, and squalling to it something in an unknown tongue.

"She's taking off Miss Cooney O'Rattigan!" hissed Miss Bennett, in ecstasy. "She's singing Italian, by way of! And look at those two brats of boys, Vincent and Harold, that should have been in their beds two hours ago!"

Masters Vincent and Harold McRory were having the time of their lives. One of them, seated on the table, was shovelling tipsy-cake into his ample mouth with a kitchen spoon; the other was smoking a cigarette, and capering to the squalls of the cook.

As noiselessly as two bats Miss Bennett and I flitted past the open door, but a silence fell with a unanimity that would have done credit to any orchestra.

"They saw us," said Miss Bennett, scudding on, "but we'll not tell on them—the creatures!"

An icy draught apprised us of an open door, and through it we escaped at length from the nightmare purlieus of the house into the yard, an immense quadrangle, where moonlight and black shadows opposed one another in a silence that was as severe as they. Temple Braney House and its yard dated from what may be called the Stone Age in Ireland, about the middle of the eighteenth century, when money was plenty and labour cheap, and the Barons of Temple Braney, now existent only in guide-books, built, as they lived, on the generous scale.

We crossed the yard to the coach-house in which I had left my motor: its tall arched doorway was like the mouth of a cave, and I struck a match. It illuminated a mowing-machine, a motor-bicycle, and a flying cat. But not my car. The first moment of bewilderment was closed by the burning of my fingers by the match.

"Are you sure it was here you left it?" said Miss Bennett, with a fatuity of which I had not believed her capable.

The presence of a lady was no doubt a salutary restraint, but as I went forth into the yard again, I felt as though the things I had to leave unsaid would break out all over me like prickly heat.

"It's the medical student one," said Miss Bennett with certainty, "the one that owns the motor-bike."

The yard and the moonlight did not receive this statement with a more profound silence than I.

"I'm sure he won't do it any harm," she went on, making the elementary mistake of applying superficial salves to a wound whose depths she was incapable of estimating. "He's very good about machinery—maybe it's only round to the front door he took it."

As Miss Bennett offered these consolations I saw two small figures creep from the shadows of the house. Their white collars shone in the moonlight, and, recognising them as the youngest members of the inveterate clan of McRory, I hailed them in a roar that revealed very effectively the extent of my indignation. It did not surprise me that the pair, in response to this, darted out of the yard gate with the speed of a pair of minnows in a stream.

I pursued, not with any hope of overtaking them, but because they were the only clue available, and in my wake, over the frosty ground, in her satin shoes, followed that sound sportswoman, Miss Bennett.

The route from the stable-yard to the front of Temple Braney House is a long and circuitous one, that skirts a plantation of evergreens. At the first bend the moonlight displayed the track of a tyre in the grass; at the next bend, where the edge was higher, a similar economy of curve had been effected, and that the incident had been of a fairly momentous nature was suggested by the circumstance that the tail lamp was lying in the middle of the drive. It was as I picked it up that I heard a familiar humming in the vicinity of the hall door.

" He didn't go so far, after all," said Miss Bennett, somewhat blown, but holding her own, in spite of the satin shoes.

I turned the last corner at a high rate of speed, and saw the dignified Georgian façade of the house, pale and placid in the moonlight ; through the open hall door a shaft of yellow light fell on the ground. The car was nowhere to be seen, yet somewhere, close at hand, the engine throbbed and drummed to me,—a *cri de cœur*, as I felt it, calling to me through the accursed jingle of the piano that proceeded from the open door.

" Where the devil——? " I began.

Even as I spoke I descried the car. It was engaged, apparently, in forcing its way into the shrubbery that screened one end of the house. The bonnet was buried in a holly bush, the engine was working, slowly but industriously. The lamps were not lighted, and there was no one in it.

" Those two imps made good use of their legs, never fear them ! " puffed Miss Bennett ; " the 'cuteness of them—cutting away to warn the brother ! "

" What's this confounded thing ? " I said fiercely, snatching at something that was caught in the handle of the brake.

Miss Bennett snatched it in her turn, and held it up in the moonlight, while I stilled the fever of the engine.

" Dublin for ever ! " she exclaimed. " What is

It but the streamers of Miss Cooney's mandoline! There's the spoils of war for you! And it's all the spoils you'll get—the whole pack of them's hid in the house by now!"

From an unlighted window over the hall door a voice added itself to the conversation.

"God help the house that holds them!" it said, addressing the universe.

The window was closed.

"That's old McRory!" said Miss Bennett in a horrified whisper.

Again I thought of Chinatown, sleepless, incalculable, with its infinite capacity for sheltering the criminal.

"—But, darling," said Philippa, some quarter of an hour later, as we proceeded down the avenue in the vaulted darkness of the beech-trees (and I at once realised that she had undertaken the case for the defence), "you've no reason to suppose that they took the car any farther than the hall door."

"It is the last time that it will be taken to *that* hall door," I replied, going dead slow, with my head over the side of the car, listening to unfamiliar sounds in its interior—sounds that did not suggest health. "I should like to know how many of your young friends went on the trip——"

"My dear boy," said Philippa pityingly, "I ask you if it is likely that there would have been more than two, when one of them was the lady with the mandoline! And," she proceeded with cat-like sweetness, "I did not perceive that you took a party with you when you retired to the hall with your old friend Miss Bennett, and left me to cope single-handed with the mob for about an hour!"

"Whether there were two or twenty-two of them in the car," I said, treating this red herring with suitable contempt, "I've done with your McRorys."

I was, very appropriately, in the act of passing through the Temple Braney entrance gates as I made this pronouncement, and it was the climax of many outrages that the steering-gear, shaken by heaven knows what impacts and brutalities, should suddenly have played me false. The car swerved in her course—fortunately a slow one—and laid her bonnet impulsively against the Temple Braney gate pillar, as against a loved one's shoulder.

As we regained our composure, two tall forms appeared in the light of the head lamps, and one of them held up his hand. I recognised a police patrol.

"That's the car right enough," said one of

them. He advanced to my side. " I want your name, please. I summons you for furious driving on the high road, without lights, a while ago, and refusing to stop when called on to do so. Go round and take the number, M'Caffery."

When, a few days later, the story flowed over and ran about the country, some things that were both new and interesting came to my ears.

Flurry Knox said that Bobby Bennett had sold me her old mare by moonlight in the Temple Braney yard, and it was a great credit to old McRory's champagne.

Mrs. Knox, of Aussolas, was told that I had taken Mrs. McRory for a run in the car at one o'clock in the morning, and on hearing it said " De gustibus non est disputandum."

Some one, unknown, repeated this to Mrs. McRory, and told her that it meant " You cannot touch pitch without being disgusted."

Mrs. Cadogan, my cook, reported to Philippa that the boy who drove the bread-cart said that it was what the people on the roads were saying that the Major was to be fined ten pounds ; to which Mrs. Cadogan had replied that it was a pity the Major ever stood in Temple Braney, but she supposed that was laid out for him by the Lord.

IX

PUT DOWN ONE AND CARRY TWO

The promise of that still and moonlit December night, wherein we had bean-feasted with the McRorys, was shamelessly broken.

The weather next morning was a welter of wind and mist, with rain flung in at intervals. The golden fox on the stable weathercock was not at peace for a moment, facing all the southern points of the compass as if they were hounds that held it at bay. For my part, I do not know why people go out hunting on such days, unless it be for the reason that many people go to church, to set an example to others.

Philippa said she went because she had done her hair for riding before she could see out of the window—a fiction beneath the notice of any intelligent husband. I went because I had told my new groom, Wilson (an English disciplinarian), that I was going, and I was therefore caught in the cogs of the inexorable wheel of stable routine. I also went because I nourished a faint hope that I might be able to place before the general public, and especially before Flurry Knox, an authentic

first version of the McRory episode. More-
over, I had a headache; but this I was not
going to mention, knowing that the sun never
sets upon the jests consecrated to after-dinner
headaches.

As we rode away from Shreelane, and felt the
thick small rain in our faces, and saw the spray
blown off the puddles by the wind, and heard the
sea-gulls, five miles inland, squealing in the mist
overhead, I said that it was preposterous to think
of hunting at Lonen Hill in such weather, and
that I was going home. Philippa said that we
might as well go on to the meet, to exercise the
horses, and that we could then come straight
home. (I have a sister who has said that I am a
lath painted to look like iron, and that Philippa is
iron painted to look like a lath.)

The meet was in shelter, the generous shelter
of Lonen Hill, which interposed itself between us
and the weather. There is just space for the
road, between the shore of Lough Lonen and the
southern face of the hill, that runs precipitously
up into the sky for some six hundred feet, dark
with fir-trees, and heather, and furze, fortified
with rock—a place renowned as a fastness for
foxes and woodcock (whose fancies as to desir-
able winter residences generally coincide). One
would have thought that only a pack of monkeys

could deal with such a covert, but hounds went through it, and so did beaters—or said they did.

We found the hounds waiting in an old quarry under the side of the hill, and, a little farther on, a very small and select company of waterproofs was huddled under the branches of a fir-tree that hung over the road. As we neared them I recognised Miss Bennett's firm and capable back: she was riding the black mare that she had come over to "pass on" to old McRory. It was Philippa who pointed out that she was accompanied by Miss Larkie McRory, seated on a stout and shaggy animal, whose grey hindquarters were draped by the folds of its rider's voluminous black macintosh, in a manner that recalled the historic statue of the Iron Duke. Farther on, Mrs. Flurry and her mother, the redoubtable Lady Knox, were getting out of a motor and getting themselves on to their horses.

"There's room under the umbrella for Mrs. Yeates!" called out Miss Bennett hospitably, "but the Major must find one for himself, and a very big one, too!"

"We could make room for him here," said Miss Larkie McRory, "if he liked to come."

I maintained, I hope, an imperturbable demeanour, and passed on.

"Who is that?" said Lady Knox, approaching me, on her large and competent iron grey.

I informed her, briefly, and without prejudice.

"Oh, one of that crew," said Lady Knox, without further comment.

Lady Knox is not noted for receptive sympathy, yet this simple statement indicated so pleasingly our oneness of soul in the matter of the McRorys, that I was on the verge of flinging overboard the gentlemanlike scruples proper to a guest, and giving her the full details of last night's revel. At this moment, however, her son-in-law came forth from the quarry with his hounds, and his coadjutors, Dr. Hickey and Michael, and moved past us.

"Yeates!" he called out, "I'd be obliged to you if you'd take that point up on the hill, on the down-wind side, where he often breaks." He looked at me with a serious, friendly face. "He won't break *down*, you know—it's only motors do that."

This witticism, concocted, no doubt, in the seclusion of the quarry, called for no reply on my part—(or, to be accurate, no suitable reply presented itself). There was an undoubted titter among the waterproofs; I moved away upon my mission at a dignified trot: a trot is seldom dignified, but Daniel has dignity enough for himself and his rider.

Daniel stands sixteen hands two inches in his stockings, of which he wears one white one, the rest of his enormous body being of that unlovely bluish-dun colour to which a dark bay horse turns when clipped. His best friend could not deny that he "made a noise"; his worst enemy was fain to admit that he was glad to hear it in front of him at a nasty place. Some one said that he was like a Settled Religious Faith, and no lesser simile conveys the restful certainty imparted by him. It was annoying, no doubt, to hear people say, after I had accomplished feats of considerable valour, that that horse couldn't make a mistake, and a baby could ride him; but these were mere chastenings, negligible to the possessor of a Settled Religious Faith.

I trotted on through the rain, up a steep road seamed with watercourses, with Lonen Hill towering on my left, and a lesser hill on my right. Looking back, I saw Flurry dismount, give his horse to a boy, and clamber on to the wall of the road: he dropped into the wood, and the hounds swarmed over after him, looking like midgets beside the tremendous citadel that they were to attack. Hickey and Michael, equally dwarfed by the immensities of the position, were already betaking themselves through the mist to their allotted outposts in space. Five-and-twenty couple of hounds would have been little enough for that great hill-side ; Flurry had fifteen, and with them he began his tough struggle through the covert, a solitary spot of red among pine-stems, and heather, and rocks, cheering his fifteen couple with horn and voice, while he climbed up and up by devious ways, seemingly as marvellously endowed with wind as the day itself. I cantered on till, at the point where the wood ended, it became my melancholy duty to leave the road and enter upon the assault of the hill. I turned in at a gap beside the guardian thorn-bush of a holy well, on whose branches votive rags fluttered in the wind, and addressed Daniel to his task of carrying thirteen stone up an incline approximating to a rise of one in three.

A path with the angles of a flash of lightning indicated the views of the local cow as to the best method of dealing with the situation. Daniel and I accepted this, as we had done more than once before, and we laboured upwards, parallel with the covert, while the wind, heavy with mist, came down to meet us, and shoved against us like a living thing. We gained at length a shelf on the hill-side, and halting there in the shelter of a furzy hummock, I applied myself to my job.

From the shelf I commanded a long stretch of the boundary wall of the wood, including a certain gap which was always worthy of special attention, and for a quarter of an hour I bent a zealous and travelling gaze upon the wall, with the concentration of a professor of a Higher Thought Society.

As is not unusual in such cases, nothing happened. At rare intervals a hint of the cry of hounds was carried in the wind, evanescent as a whiff from a summer garden. Once or twice it seemed to swing towards me, and at such moments the concentration of my eyeglass upon the gap was of such intensity that had the fox appeared I am confident that he would instantly have fallen into a hypnotic trance. As time wore on I arrived at the stage of obsession, when the music of the hounds and the touches of the horn seemed to be in everything, the wind, the streams, the tree branches, and I could almost have sworn hounds were away and running hard, until some vagrant voice in the wood would dispel the mirage of sound. This was followed by the reactionary period of pessimism, when I seemed to myself merely an imbecile, sitting in heavy rain, staring at a stone wall. Half an hour, or more, passed.

" I'm going out of this," I said to myself defiantly ; " there's reason in the roasting of eggs."

It seemed, however, my duty to go up rather

than down, and I coerced Daniel into the bed
of a stream, as offering the best going available.
It led me into a cleft between the hill-side and the
wall of the covert, which latter was, like a thing
in a fairy tale, changing very gradually from a
wall into a bank. I ascended the cleft, and
presently found that it, too, was changing its
nature, and becoming a flight of stairs. Daniel
clattered slowly and carefully up them, basing his
feet, like Sir Bedivere, on "juts of slippery crag
that rang sharp-smitten with the dint of arméd
heels."

We had reached the top in safety when I
heard a thin and wavering squeal behind me,
and looking back saw Miss Larkie McRory
ascending the rocky staircase on the grey cob,
at a speed that had obviously, and legitimately,
drawn forth the squeal.

"Oh, gracious! The brute! I can't stop
him!" she cried as she rushed upon me.

The grey cob here bumped into Daniel's massive stern, rebounded, and subsided, for the excellent reason that no other course was open to
it. Miss McRory's reins were clutched in a
looped confusion, that summoned from some
corner of my brain a memory of the Sultan's
cipher on the Order of the Medjidie: her hat
was hanging down her back, and there was a

picturesqueness about her hair that promised disaster later on. Her hazel eyes shone, and her complexion glowed like a rose in rain.

" Mr. Irving's fit to be tied!" she continued. " His horse jumped about like a mad thing when he saw those awful steps——!"

Sounds of conflict and clattering came from below. I splashed onwards in the trough between the hill and the fence, and had emerged into a comparatively open space with my closely attendant McRory, when the impassioned face of Mr. Irving's Meath mare shot into view at the top of the steps. The water in the trough was apparently for her the limit of what should or could be endured. She made a crooked spring at the hill-side, slipped, and, recognising the bank as the one civilised feature in a barbarous country, bounced sideways on to the top of it, pivoted there, and sat down backwards into a thicket of young ash and hazel trees. A succession of short yells from Miss McRory acclaimed each phase of the incident; Mr. Irving's face, as he settled down amongst the branches, was as a book where men might read strange matters, not of an improving nature.

It was probably the reception accorded to the bay mare by the branches and briars in which she had seated herself that caused her to return to the top of the bank in a kangaroo-bound, as active as it was unexpected. Horses can do these things when they choose, but they seldom choose. From the top of the bank she dropped into the trough, and joined us, with her nerves still in a state of acute indignation, and less of her rider in the saddle than is conventional, but a dinge in his pot-hat appeared to be the extent of the damage. Miss McRory's eye travelled from it to me, but she abstained from comment. It was the eye of a villain and a conspirator. I had by no means forgotten the injuries inflicted on me by her brothers, nor did I forget that Flurry had said that there wasn't one of the family but was as clever as the devil and four times as unscrupulous. Yet, taken in conjunction with the genuineness of her complexion, and with the fact that Irving was probably twenty years my junior, "I couldn't"—as the song says—"help smiling at McRory O'More" (behind the back of young Mr. Irving, D.I.).

It transpired that Irving, from some point of vantage below, shared, it would appear, with Miss McRory, had seen the hounds running out of the top of the wood, and had elected to follow me. He did not know where any one was, had not heard a sound of the horn, and gave it as his opinion that Flurry was dead, and that trying to hunt in this country was simply farcical. He bellowed these things at me in his consequential voice as we struggled up the hill against the immense weight of wind, in all the fuss, anxiety, and uncertainty out of which the joys of hunting are born. It was as we topped the ultimate ridge that, through the deafening declamations of the wind, I heard, faint as a bar of fairy music, distant harmonies as of hounds running.

The wind blew a hole in the mist, and we had a bird's-eye view of a few pale-green fields far below: across one of them some pigmy forms were moving; they passed over a dark line that represented a fence, and proceeded into the heart of a cloud.

"That's about the limit," shouted Irving, dragging at his mare's mouth, as she swerved from a hole in the track. "It's only in this God-forsaken country that a fox'd go away in the teeth of a storm like this!"

To justify to Mr. Irving the disregard of the Lonen Hill foxes for the laws of the game was not my affair. It seemed to me that in piloting him and Miss McRory I was doing rather more than humanity had any right to expect. I have descended Lonen Hill on various occasions, none of them agreeable, but never before with an avalanche travelling hard on my heels—a composite avalanche that slid, and rushed, and dropped its hind-legs over the edge at bad corners, and was throughout vocal with squeals, exclamations, inquiries as to facts of which Providence could alone be cognisant, and thunderous with objurgations. The hill-side merged at length into upland pasture, strange little fields, composed partly of velvet patches, like putting-greens, predominantly of nightmare bunkers of rocks and furze. We rushed downwards through these, at a pace much accelerated by the prevalence of cattle gaps; the bay mare, with her head in the air, zigzagging in bounds as incalculable as those of a grasshopper; the grey cob, taking sole charge of Miss McRory, tobogganing with her hind feet, propping with her fore, and tempering her enthusiasm with profound understanding of the matter. Finally, a telegraph-post loomed through the fog upon us, and a gate discovered itself, through which we banged in a bunch on to the high road. A cottage faced us, with a couple of women and an old man standing outside it.

To them we put the usual question, with the usual vehemence (always suggestive of the King's Troopers in romance, hotly demanding information about a flying rebel).

"I didn't see a fox this long while," replied

the old man deliberately, "but there was a few jocks went west the road a while ago."

The King's Troopers, not specially enlightened, turned their steeds and went in pursuit of the jocks. A stone gap, flung in ruins among black hoof-marks, soon gave a more precise indication, and we left the road, with profound dubiety on my part as to where we were going and how we were going to get there. The first fence decided the matter for Irving, D.I. It was a bank on which slices of slatey stone had been laid, much as in Germany slabs of cold sausage are laid upon bread. The Meath mare looked at it but once, and fled from it at a tangent; the grey pony, without looking at it, followed her. Daniel selected an interval between the slabs, and took me over without comment. Filled by a radiant hope that I had shaken off both my companions, I was advancing in the line of the hoof-tracks, when once more I heard behind me on the wind cries as of a storm-driven sea-gull, and the grey cob came up under my stirrup, like a runaway steam pinnace laying itself beside a man-o'-war. Miss McRory was still in the saddle, but minus reins and stirrup; the wind had again removed her hat, which was following her at full stretch of its string, like a kite. Had it not been for her cries I should have said, judging by her face, that she was thoroughly enjoying herself.

Having achieved Daniel's society the cob pulled up, and her rider, not without assistance from me, restored her hat, reins, and stirrup to their proper spheres. I looked back, and saw Irving's mare, still on the farther side of the fence, her nose pointing to the sky, as if invoking the protection of heaven, and I knew that for better for worse Miss McRory was mine until we reached the high road. No doubt the thing was to be: as one of our own poets has sung of Emer and Cuchulain, "all who read my name in Erin's story would find its loving letters linked with" those of McRory. The paraphrase even rhymed —another finger-mark of Fate. Yet it was hard that, out of all the possible, and doubtless eager, squires of the hunting-field I should have been chosen.

The hoof-tracks bent through a long succession of open gaps to a farmyard, and there were swallowed in the mire of a lane. I worked the lane out for every inch it was worth, with the misty rain pricking my face as it were with needles, and the intention to go home at the earliest possible opportunity perfecting itself in my heart. But the lane, instead of conducting us to the high road, melted disastrously into a turf bog. I pulled up, and the long steady booming of the sea upon the rocks made a deep undertone to the wind. There was no voice of hound or horn, and I was on the point of returning to the farmhouse when the mist, in its stagey, purposeful way, again lifted, and laid bare the sky-line of a low hill on our left. A riderless horse was limping very slowly along it, led by something that seemed no higher than a toadstool. Obviously we were on the line of the hunt, and obviously, also, it was my duty to enquire into the matter of the horse. I turned aside over a low bank, hotly followed by the grey cob, and the wail to which I was now becoming inured. As Miss McRory arrived abruptly at my side, she cried that she would have been off that time only for the grab she got of his hair. (By which I believe she meant the mare's mane.)

Fortune favoured us with broken-down fences; we overtook the horse, and found it was Flurry Knox's brown mare, hobbling meekly in tow of a very small boy. In one of her hind fetlocks there was a clean, sharp cut that might have been done with a knife.

In answer to my questions the small boy pointed ahead. I polished my eyeglass, and, with eyes narrowed against the wind, looked into the south-west, and there saw, unexpectedly, even awfully near, the Atlantic Ocean, dingy and angry, with a long line, as of battle-smoke, marking its assault upon the cliffs. Between the cliffs and the hill on which we were standing a dark plateau, striped with pale grey walls, stretched away into the mist.

"There's the huntsman for ye," squeaked the little boy, who looked about six years old.

I descried at a distance of perhaps a quarter of a mile a figure in a red coat, on foot, in the act of surmounting one of the walls, accompanied by a hovering flock of country boys.

"The dogs is out before him," pursued the little boy at the full pitch of his lungs. "I seen the fox, too. I'll go bail he has himself housed in the Coosheen Grohogue by now."

"Gracious!" said Miss McRory.

I said he probably had a simpler telegraphic address, and that, no matter where he was, it was now my duty to overtake Mr. Knox and offer him my horse; "and you," I added, "had better get this little boy to show you the way to the road."

Miss McRory replied confidently that she'd sooner stay with me.

I said, as well as I remember, that her preference was highly flattering, but that she might live to regret it.

Miss McRory answered that she wished I wouldn't be spying at her through that old glass of mine ; she knew well enough she was a show, and her hair was coming down, and she'd as soon trust herself to the cat as to that little urchin.

As I made my way downwards over the knife-edged ridges of rock and along their intervening boggy furrows, I should myself have been grateful for the guidance of the cat. Even the grey cob accepted the matter as serious, and kept the brake hard on, accomplishing the last horrid incident of the descent—a leap from the slant of the hill on to the summit of a heathery bank— without frivolity, even with anxiety. We had now arrived at the plateau above the cliffs— a place of brown, low-growing ling, complicated by boggy runnels, and heavily sprinkled with round stones. The mist was blowing in thicker than ever, Flurry and his retinue were lost as though they had never been, and the near thunder of the breakers, combined with the wind, made an impenetrable din round me and Miss McRory.

After perhaps a mile, in the course of which I got off several times to pull down loose walls for the benefit of my companion, I discovered the rudiments of a lane, which gradually developed into a narrow but indubitable road. The rain had gone down the back of my neck and into my boots: I determined that if Flurry had to finish the run on all-fours, I would stick to the lane until it took me to a road. What it took me to was, as might have been foreseen in any County Cork bohireen, a pole jammed across it from wall to wall and reinforced by furze-bushes—not a very high pole, but not one easy to remove. I pulled up and looked dubiously from it to Miss McRory.

"D'ye dare me?" she said.

"I bet you sixpence you take a toss if you do," I replied firmly, preparing to dismount.

"Done with you!" said Miss McRory, suddenly smiting the grey cob with a venomous little cutting whip (one that probably dated from the sixties, and had for a handle an ivory grey-hound's head with a plaited silver collar round its neck).

I have seldom seen a pole better and more liberally dealt with, as far as the grey cob's share of the transaction went, and seldom, indeed, have I seen a rider sail more freely from a saddle than Miss McRory sailed. She alighted on her hands and knees, and the cob, with the sting of the whip still enlivening her movements, galloped on up the lane and was lost in the mist.

"Well, you won your sixpence," said Miss

McRory dauntlessly, as I joined her. " I suppose you're delighted."

I assured her with entire sincerity that I was very much the reverse, and proceeded at high speed in pursuit of the cob. The result of this excursion—a fairly prolonged one—was the discovery that the lane led into a road, and that it was impossible to decide in which direction the fugitive had gone. I returned in profound gloom to my young lady, and found her rubbing herself down with a bunch of heather.

" So you couldn't ketch her!" she called out as I approached. "What'll we do now?" She was evidently highly amused. " I'll tell the Peeler it was your fault. You dared me!"

My reply need not be recorded: I only know it was by no means up to the standard to which Miss McRory was accustomed.

I took what seemed to be the only possible course, and established her seated sideways on my saddle, with her foot—and it is but fair to say, a very small foot—in the leather instead of the stirrup, and her right hand knotted in Daniel's mane. I held the off stirrup, and splashed beside her in the ruts and mud. The mist was thicker than ever, the wind was pushing it in from the sea in great masses, and Miss McRory and I progressed onward in a magic circle of some twenty yards in diameter, occupied only by herself and me, with Daniel thrown in as chaperon.

On arriving at the road I relied on the wind for guidance, and turning to the right, let it blow us in what was, I trusted, our course. It was by this time past three o'clock, we were at least nine or ten miles from home, and one of my boots had begun to rub my heel. There was nothing for it but to keep on as we were going, until we met something, or some one, or died.

It is worthy of record that in these afflicting circumstances Miss Larkie McRory showed a staying power, attained, probably, in the long and hungry bicycle picnics of her tribe, that was altogether commendable. Not for an instant did she fail to maintain in me the belief that she found me one of the most agreeable people she had ever met, a little older, perhaps, than Irving, D.I., but on that very account the more to be confided in. It was not until the pangs of hunger recalled to me the existence of my sandwiches that I discovered she had no food with her, nor, as far as could be gathered, had she had any breakfast.

"Sure they were all snoring asleep when I started. I just got a cup o' tea in the kitchen——"

This, I suppose, was a point at which I might suitably have said something incisive about the feats of her brethren on the previous night, but with deplorable weakness I merely offered her my sandwiches. Miss McRory replied that she'd fall off in a minute if she were to let go the mane, and why wouldn't I eat them myself? I said if there were any shelter left in Ireland I would wait till I got there, and we could then decide who should eat them.

Æons of mist and solitude ensued. I must have walked for an hour or more, without meeting anyone except one old woman, who could only speak Irish, and I had begun to feel as if my spur were inside my boot instead of outside, when I became aware of something familiar about the look of the fences. It was not, however, until I felt shelter rising blessedly about us, and saw the thorn bush with the rags hanging from it, that I realised that our luck had turned, and we had blundered our way back to the holy well under the side of Lonen Hill. The well was like a tiny dripping cave, about as big as a beehive, with a few inches of water in it; a great boulder stood guard over it, and above it stooped the ancient and twisted thorn bush. It seemed indicated as a place of rest, none the less that my heel was by this time considerably galled by my boot.

Miss McRory glissaded from my saddle into

my arms, and was assisted by me to deposit herself on a flat stone beside the well, stiff, wet, but still undefeated. We shared my sandwiches, we drank whisky mixed with the water of the holy well, and Miss McRory dried her face with her handkerchief, and her complexion looked better than ever. Daniel, slowly and deliberately, ate the rags off the thorn bush. I have been at many picnics that I have enjoyed less.

By the time we had got to the gingerbread biscuits I had discovered that Mr. Irving thought she had talked too much to me after dinner last night, and that it was a wonder to her how men could be so cross about nothing. I said I was sorry she called it nothing, at which she looked up at me and down again at the gingerbread, and did not reply. After this I felt emboldened to ask her why she had been called so inappropriate a name as " Larkie."

Miss McRory agreed that it was indeed a silly old name, and that it was a friend of one of her brothers, a Mr. Mulcahy, who had said that she and her sisters were " 'Lorky little gurls with lorge dork eyes.' He had that way of speaking," she added, " because he thought it was grand, and he always kept his watch at English time. He said he ran over to London so often it wasn't worth while to change it."

She herself had never been out of Ireland, and she supposed she'd never get the chance.

I said that when she married Mr. Mulcahy she could keep her watch at Irish time, so as to equalise things.

Miss McRory suggested that I should give her a watch as a wedding present, and that, English or Irish time, it would be all hours of the night before we were home.

I realised with a slight shock that the position had indeed become inverted when one of the House of McRory had to remind me, after about four hours in her undiluted society, of the flight of time. It was now past four, which was bad enough, and a still greater shock awaited me in the discovery that I was dead lame, the interval of repose having been fatal to my damaged heel.

I have always asserted, and shall continue to do so to my dying day, that the way out of the difficulty was suggested by Miss McRory. I mounted Daniel, Miss McRory ascended the boulder by the holy well, announcing that she was as stiff as fifty crutches, and that once she got up she'd be there for life. The thing was done somehow, thanks to the incomparable forbearance of Daniel, and with Miss McRory seated behind me on his broad back, and her arms clasped round my waist, I once more, and very cautiously, took the road.

Daniel continued to conduct himself like a gentleman, but considering how precarious was the position of Miss McRory, it was unnerving to feel her shaken by silent and secret laughter.

"You'll fall off," I warned her.

She replied by a further paroxysm, and asked me what size I took in stays—she supposed about forty inches.

Dusk was now an accomplished fact: thickened with fog and rain, it was even turning to darkness as we descended the long hill. But, humanly speaking, the end was in sight. There was, I knew, a public-house a couple of miles farther on, where a car might be hired, and there I proposed to bid a long farewell to Miss Larkie McRory, and to send her home by herself, to have rheumatic fever, as I assured her.

We moved on and on, at a careful foot-pace: we were out in the wind again, and it was very cold. It was also quite dark. Silence fell upon us, and, after a time, the sustained pressure of Miss McRory's hat-brim against my shoulder suggested that it was the silence of exhaustion, if not of sleep. I thought of her with compassion. I believe I formulated her to myself as a poor little girl, and found myself asserting with defiance to imaginary detractors that no one could say she hadn't pluck, and that, in spite of her family, she really had a soul to be saved.

Again we found ourselves in shelter, and a greater darkness in the darkness told that we were in the lee of a wooded hill. I knew where I was now, and I said to Miss McRory that the pub was just round the corner, and she replied at once that that was where they always were, in Dublin anyway. She also said she thought she heard horses' hoofs coming up behind us. I pushed on.

We turned the corner, and were immediately struck blind by the twin glare of the lamps of a motor, that lay motionless, as in ambush, at the side of the road. Even the equanimity of Daniel was shattered ; he swung to one side, he drifted like a blown leaf, and Miss McRory clung to me like a knapsack. As we curveted in the full glare of the limelight, I was aware of a figure in a pot-hat and a vast fur coat standing near the motor. Even as I recognised Lady Knox three or four muddy hounds trailed wearily into the glare, and a voice behind me shouted, " 'Ware horse ! "

Flurry came on into the light : there was just room in me for a sub-conscious recognition of the fact that he was riding the missing grey cob, and that this was a typical thing, and one that might have been expected.

At the hunt dinner that took place soon afterwards some one sang a song, one that I have ceased to find amusing. The first verse runs as follows :

> " Throttin' to the Fair,
>   Me and Moll Moloney,
> Sittin', I declare,
>   On a single pony——"

By a singular coincidence, the faces of all those present turned towards me.

X

THE COMTE DE PRALINES

"I HAD forgotten how nice London is!" purred Philippa, as we moved beautifully across the threshold of Bill Cunningham's club, and were conducted to the lift with a tender deference that was no more than was due to our best clothes.

The Ladies' Tea-room at Bill's club was a pleasant place, looking forth, high above the noise, upon trees that were yellow in the hazy October afternoon. In a very agreeable bow-window were Lady Derryclare and the tea-table, and with her were her son, and a small and ornamental young man, who was introduced to us as Mr. Simpson-Hodges.

"Front name John, known to a large circle of admirers as 'Mossoo,'" supplemented Bill, whose hands were so clean that I found it difficult to recognise him.

"So called because of the incredible circumstance that he can speak French, in spite of the best Public School education," said Lady Derryclare. "When I think of the money that has been wasted on you! You good for nothing creature!"

"It's more his looks," pursued Bill, "his dark foreign beauty——

"These humorists!" said Mr. Simpson-Hodges indulgently, showing a set of white teeth under a diminutive black moustache. "Please, Lady Derryclare, let's talk of something pleasant."

"Ask him about the chickens you made him get from the Chicken Farmers for the dance his regiment gave," said Bill to his mother.

"Oh, that was rather a bad business," said Mr. Simpson-Hodges apologetically, with an eye on Philippa, who, in a new hat, was looking about five-and-twenty. "I'm sure no one wants to hear about it."

"Mossoo ran the supper and he ordered three brace," said Bill, "but they never turned up till the week after the show! The postman was viewed coming up to the Mess towing something after him on a long painter. The painter was superfluous. The chickens would have followed him at a trot if he had been kind to them. They kept them for the drag, I believe. Didn't you, Mossoo? He's one of the Whips, you know."

"They'd have been quite useful," admitted Mr. Simpson-Hodges.

"How interesting to be a Whip!" said Philippa, looking at him with egregious respect.

"Rather too interesting, sometimes," replied

Simpson-Hodges, expanding to the glance in a way not unfamiliar to me. "Last time we were out the fellow with the drag started from the cross-roads where we were going to meet, and was asinine enough to take it a bit down the road before he went into the country, and, as it happened, we were bringing the hounds up to the meet by that particular road. They simply put down their heads and ran it heel for all they were worth! The First Whip and I galloped our best, but we couldn't get to their heads, and we all charged into the middle of the meet full-cry!"

"Oh! I wish I had been there!" said Philippa ardently.

"We wished we were anywhere else," replied Mr. Simpson-Hodges; "the Brigadier was there, and everybody. We heard all about it afterwards, I can tell you!"

"That ought to have happened in Mr. Knox's country, Major Yeates!" said Lady Derryclare, whose interest in fox-hunting was more sympathetic than technical.

"We don't run drags, Lady Derryclare," I said reproachfully, but Lady Derryclare had already entered upon another topic.

Simpson-Hodges, however, did not end there.

A week afterwards Philippa and I crept home, third class, with full trunks and empty pockets, sustained only by the aphorism, evolved by my wife, that economies, and not extravagances, are what one really regrets. It was approaching the end of November before we next heard of Simpson-Hodges. The Derryclares had come down for their first woodcock shoot, and Bill swooped over one morning in the big Daimler and whirled us back with him over the forty intervening miles of bog and mountain, to shoot, and to dance on the carpet after dinner, and to act charades; to further, in short, the various devices for exercising and disciplining a house party. Mr. John Simpson-Hodges was there, no less ornamental than in London, and as useful as he was ornamental. He shot well, he danced beautifully, and he made of the part of a French Count in a charade so surprising a work of art that people said—as is the habit of people—that he ought to be making a hundred a week on the stage.

Before we left the Derryclares Philippa told me that she had arranged with "those boys"—by which she referred to Mr. Cunningham and the French Count—to come over next week and have a hunt with Flurry Knox's hounds. Something whispered to me that there was more in this than met the eye, but as they were to provide their own mounts the position was unassailable, and I contented myself with telling her that a predilection for the society of the young was one of the surest signs of old age.

It was not till we were all seated at breakfast on the morning of the meet (which was to be at Castle Knox), that it was suggested, with all the spontaneity of a happy thought, by Bill, that "Mossoo" should be introduced to the members of the Hunt as a Frenchman who was unable to speak English.

"Call him the Comte de Pralines," said Philippa, with suspicious promptitude.

"You can call him Napoleon Buonaparte if you like," I said defiantly, "*I* shall stay at home!"

"All the Curranhilty people will be there," said Philippa softly.

The thought of introducing the Comte de Pralines to Miss Bobbie Bennett was certainly attractive.

"I refuse to introduce him to Lady Knox," I said with determination, and knew that I had yielded.

A meet at Castle Knox always brought out a crowd ; there were generally foxes, and always luncheon, and there was a touch of the G.O.C. about Lady Knox that added a pleasing edge of anxiety, and raised the meet to something of the nature of a full-dress parade. I held to my point about Lady Knox, and did nothing more compromising than tremble in the background, while Bill Cunningham presented the Comte de Pralines to the lady of the house, supplementing the presentation with the statements that this was his first visit to Ireland, and that he spoke no English.

The Comte de Pralines, in the newest of pink coats, and the whitest of breeches, and the most glittering of boots and spurs, stood on the step below Lady Knox, with the bridle of his hireling over his arm, and his shining silk hat in his hand. Still with his hat in his hand, and looking, as Miss Larkie McRory whispered to me, "as pretty as a Christmas card," the Count rippled forth a stream of mellifluous French, commenting upon the beauty of the day, of the place, of the scene.

Lady Knox's face deepened to so apoplectic a crimson, and her eyes became so fixed that I, watching the scene apprehensively, doubted if it were not my duty to rush at her and cut open her hunting-stock. When the Count ceased, having, as far as I could gather, enquired as to when she had last been to Auteuil, and if she had ever hunted in France, Lady Knox paused, and said very slowly :

"Er—*j'espère que nous aurons un bon jour aujourdhui.*" Then, rapidly, to me, "Take your friend in for a drink, Major Yeates."

My heart bled for her, and also quaked for myself, but I was into it now, up to my chin.

During the next ten minutes Bill Cunningham, feebly abetted by me, played the game remorselessly, sparing neither age nor sex. In the hall, amidst the sloe-gins and the whiskies and sodas (to which the Count, for a foreigner, took remarkably kindly), introductions slipped between cup and lip, poisoning the former and paralysing the latter. The victims took it variously; some sought refuge in bright smiles and large foreign gestures; some, in complete mental overthrow, replied in broken English to Mossoo's sugared periods; all were alike in one point, they moved as swiftly as might be, and as far as possible, out of the immediate neighbourhood of the Comte de Pralines. Philippa, who, without any solid attainment, can put up a very good bluff in French, joined spasmodically in these encounters, alternately goading Mossoo to fresh outrages, and backing out when the situation became too acute. I found her, affecting to put her sandwiches into the case on her saddle, and giving way to her feelings, with her face pressed against her mare's shoulder.

"I introduced him to Bobbie Bennett," she said brokenly; "and he asked her if she spoke French. She looked at me as if she were drowning, and said, '*Seulement très petit*'!"

I said, repressively, that Lady Knox could see her, and that people would think, firstly, that she was crying, and secondly, that she was mad.

"But I *am* mad, darling!" replied my wife, turning a streaming face to me.

I informed her of my contempt for her, and, removing myself from her vicinity, collected myself for the introduction of the Count to Flurry Knox and Dr. Hickey. By this time most of the Field were mounted, and the Comte de Pralines bent to his horse's mane as he uncovered with grave courtesy on his presentation to the Master and the First Whip, and proceeded to express the profundity of his gratification at meeting an Irish Master of Hounds. The objects of the attention were palpably discomposed by it; Flurry put a finger to his cap, with a look at me expressive of No Surrender; Dr. Hickey, in unconscious imitation of the Count, bowed low, but forgot about his cap.

"He has no English, I'm told," said Flurry, eyeing the Count suspiciously.

I stopped myself on the verge of bowing assent, so infectious was the grace of the Pralines manner.

Miss Larkie McRory.

"Is he come to buy horses for the German Army?" went on Flurry. (It need hardly be said that this occurred before the War.)

I explained that he was French.

"You wouldn't know what these foreigners might be up to," returned Mr. Knox, quite unconvinced. "I'm going on now——"

He too moved expeditiously out of the danger zone.

The Field straggled down the avenue, and progressed over tracts of tussocky grass in the wake of the hounds, towards the plantation that was the first draw. The Keeper was outside the wood, with the assurance that there was a score of foxes in it, and that they had the country ate.

"Maybe they'll eat the hounds, so," said Flurry. "Let you all stay outside. You can be talking French now for a bit——"

I looked round to see who were availing themselves of this permission. The Count had by this time been introduced to Miss Larkie McRory; Philippa was apparently acting as interpreter, and Miss McRory was showing no disposition to close the interview. The Field had withdrawn, and had formed itself into a committee-meeting on the Count.

It was warm and sunny in the shelter of the wood. Although the time was November there were still green leaves on some of the trees; it was a steamy day after a wet night, and I thought to myself that if the hounds *did* run— Here came a challenge from the wood, answered multitudinously, and the next minute they were driving through the laurels towards the entrance gates, with a cry that stimulated even the many-wintered Daniel to capers quite unbefitting his time of life, or mine. The Castle Knox demesne is a large one, and being surrounded by a pro-hibitively high and coped wall, it is easier to find a fox there than to get away with one. Mighty galloping on the avenues followed, with inter-ludes in the big demesne fields, where every gate had been considerately left open, and in which every horse with any pretensions to *savoir faire* stiffened his neck, and put up his back, and pulled. The hounds, a choir invisible, carried their music on through the plantations, with whimpering, scurrying pauses, with strophe and anti-strophe of soprano and bass. Sometimes the cry bore away to the demesne wall, and some one would shout "They're away!" and the question of the Front Gate versus the Western Gate would divide us like a sword. Twice, in the undergrowth, above the sunk fence that separated us from the wood, the quick, com-posed face of the fox showed itself; at last, when things were getting too hot in the covert, he sprang like a cat over the ditch, and flitted across the park with that gliding gait that dissimulates its own speed, while I and my fellows offered a painful example of the discordance of the human voice when compared with that of the hound, and five or six couple pitched themselves out of the wood and stretched away over the grass.

It was fortunate for the Comte de Pralines that his entirely British view-holloa was projected for the most part into my ear (the drum of which it nearly split) and was merged in the general enthusiasm as we let ourselves go.

"For God's sake, Major Yeates!" said Michael, the Second Whip, thundering up beside me as we neared the covert on the further side of the park, "come into the wood with me and turn them hounds! Mr. Flurry's back on another fox with the body of the pack, and he's very near his curse!"

I followed Michael into the covert, and was myself followed by a section of the Field, who might, with great advantage, have remained outside. In the twinkling of an eye Michael was absorbed into the depths of the wood ; so also were the six couple, but not so my retinue, who pursued me like sleuth-hounds, as I traversed the covert at such speed as the narrow rides permitted. I made at length the negative discovery that it contained nothing save myself and my followers, a select party, consisting of the Comte de Pralines, Miss McRory, Miss Bobbie Bennett, Lady Knox's coachman on a three-year-old, and a little boy in knickerbockers, on a midget pony with the bearing of a war-horse and a soul to match. We had come to a baffled pause at the cross-ways, when faint and far away, an indisputable holloa was borne to us.

"They've gone out the West Gate," said the coachman, from among the tree-trunks into which he had considerately manœuvred the kicking end of the three-year-old. "It must be they ran him straight out into the country——"

We made for the West Gate, reached it without sight or sound of Flurry or anyone else, and, on the farm road outside it, pulled up to listen.

The holloa was repeated; half a mile ahead a gesticulating figure signalled to us to come on. I wish to put it on record that I said I could not hear the hounds. The Comte de Pralines (excitable, like all Frenchmen) spurred his hireling at the opposite bank, saying, as he shot past me:

"It's no damned use humbugging here any longer!"

As I turned Daniel to follow him, my eyes

met those of Miss Larkie McRory, alight with infernal intelligence; they challenged, but at the same time they offered confederacy. I jumped into the field after the Count; Miss McRory followed.

"I'll tell Lady Knox on you!" she murmured, as she pounded beside me on the long-legged spectre, who, it may be remembered, had been described as "the latther end of a car-horse."

The holloa had come to us from the side of a smooth green hill, and between us and it was a shallow valley, neatly fenced with banks that did credit to Sir Valentine Knox's farming. The horses were fresh, the valley smiled in the conventional way, and spread sleek pastures before us; we took the down grade at a cheerful pace, and the banks a shade faster than was orthodox, and the coachman's three-year-old made up in enthusiasm what he lacked in skill, and the pony, who from the first was running away, got over everything by methods known only to itself. The Comte de Pralines held an undeviating line for the spot whence the holloa had proceeded; when we reached it there was no one to be seen, but there was another holloa further on. The pursuit of this took us on to a road, and here the Castle Knox coachman, who had scouted on ahead, yelled something to the effect that he saw a rider out before him, accompanying the statement by an application of the spurs to the dripping but undaunted three-year-old. A stretching gallop up the road ensued, headed by the little boy and the coachman, who had both secured a commanding lead. The pace held for about a hundred yards, when the road bent sharply to the left, more sharply indeed than was anticipated by the leaders, who, as their mounts skidded as it were on one wheel round the corner, sailed from their saddles with singular unanimity and landed in the ditch. At the same moment the rider we had been following came into view; he was a priest, in immaculate black coat and top-hat, seated on a tall chestnut horse, and proceeding at a tranquil footpace on his own affairs.

He had seen the fox, he admitted (I am inclined to think he had headed him), and he had heard a man shouting, but no hounds had come his way. He was entirely sympathetic, and, warm as I was at the moment, a chill apprehension warned me that we might presently need sympathy.

"It's my belief," said Miss Bennett, voicing that which I had not put into words, "we've been riding after the fox, and the hounds didn't leave the covert at all!"

An elaborate French oath from the Count fell, theatrical as a drop-scene, on the close of the first act. Miss Larkie McRory looked at him admiringly, and allowed just the last rays of her glance to include me.

It was when we had retraced our steps to the bend of the road that we had a full view of the Castle Knox coverts, crowning in gold and brown those pleasant green slopes, easy as the descent to Avernus, down which we had galloped with such generous ardour some fifteen minutes ago. Outside the West Gate, through which we had emerged from the demesne, were three motionless figures in scarlet; Lady Knox and her grey horse were also recognisable; a few hounds were straying undecidedly in the first of the grass fields that we had traversed.

A note of the horn leaped to us across the valley, an angry and peremptory note. One of the scarlet figures started at a canter and turned the hounds. Another and longer blast followed. As if in obedience to its summoning, the coachman's three-year-old came ramping, riderless, down the road; he passed us with his head high in air and his flashing eye fixed upon the distant group, and, with a long shrill neigh, put his tail over his back and directed his flight for his owner and her grey horse.

"God help poor Tierney!" said Miss Bennett, in a stricken voice, "and ourselves too! I believe they saw us all the time, and we galloping away on the line of the fox!"

"I'm going home," I said. "Will you kindly make my apologies to the Master?"

"I'll kindly do no such thing," replied Miss Bennett. "I'll let Flurry Knox cool off a bit before I meet him again, and that won't be this side of Christmas, if *I* can help it! Good-bye, dear friends!"

She turned her mare, and set her face for her own country.

There now remained only the Count, Miss McRory, and myself, and to remove ourselves from the field of vision of the party at the gate was our first care. We had, no doubt, been thoroughly identified, nevertheless the immediate sensation of getting a furzy hill between us and Flurry was akin to that of escaping from the rays of a burning-glass. In shelter we paused and surveyed each other.

The Comte de Pralines, with his shiny hat very much on the back of his head, put down his reins, shoved his crop under his knee, and got out his cigarette case.

"Well," he began philosophically, striking a match, "our luck ain't in——!"

He broke off, the match went out, and a lively glow suffused his unsheltered countenance.

"*Vous voyez mon cher*—" he resumed, very rapidly. "*J'ai appris quelques petits mots——*"

"What a lovely English accent he has!" interrupted Miss McRory rapturously; "it's a lot nicer than his French one. To look at him you'd never think he was so clever. It's a pity he wouldn't try to pick up a little more."

"Now, that's hitting a man when he's down," said the Comte de Pralines. "I want some one to be kind to me. I've had a poor day of it; no one would talk to me. I stampeded them wherever I went."

"I didn't notice Miss McRory stampeding to any great extent," I said.

"Wait awhile!" rejoined Miss McRory. "Maybe the stampeding will be going the other way when you and he meet Lady Knox!"

"I shan't wait an instant," said the Comte de Pralines, "you and Major Yeates will explain."

The horses had been moving on, and the covert was again in sight, about a quarter of a mile away on our left. There was nothing to be seen, but hounds were hunting again in the demesne; their cry drove on through the woods inside the grey demesne wall; they were hunting in a body, and they were hunting hard.

At each moment the cry was becoming more remote, but it was still travelling on inside the wall. The fear of Flurry fell from us as a garment, and the only question that presented itself was whether to return to the West Gate or to hold on outside. It was a long-accepted theory at Castle Knox that the demesne wall was not negotiable, and that the foxes always used the gates, like Christians; bearing this in mind, I counselled the Front Gate and the outside of the wall. A couple of lanes favoured us; we presently found ourselves in a series of marshy fields, moving along abreast of the invisible hounds in the wood. They were in the thickest and least accessible part of it, and Flurry's voice and horn came faintly as from a distance.

I explained that it was impossible to ride that part of the wood, but that, if they held on as they were going, the Front Gate would make it all right for us, and of course Flurry would——

"Oh! look, look, look!" shrieked Miss McRory, snatching at my arm and pointing with her whip.

A short way ahead of us a huge elm tree had fallen upon the wall; the greenish-yellow leaves still clinging to its branches showed that the catastrophe was recent. It had broken down the wall to within five or six feet of the ground, and was reclining in the breach that it had made, with its branches sprawling in the field. I followed the line of Miss Larkie's whip, and was just in time to see a fox float like a red leaf from one of these to the ground, and glide straight across our front. He passed out of sight over a bank, and the Count stood up in his stirrups, put his finger in his ear, and screamed in a way that must have been heard in the next county. I contributed a not in-effective bellow, and Miss McRory decorated the occasion with long thin squeals.

The hounds, inside the wall, answered in an agony that was only allayed by the discovery that the trunk of the tree formed as handy a bridge for them as for the fox. They came dropping like ripe fruit through the branches, and, under our rejoicing eyes, swarmed to the fox's line, and flung on, in the fullest of full-cry, over the bank on which we had last seen him. I have not failed to assure Flurry Knox that anything less suggestive of " sneaking away with the hounds " than the manner of our departure could hardly be conceived, but Mr. Knox has not withdrawn the phrase.

It may be conceded that Flurry had grounds for annoyance. Had I had the fox in one hand and the Ordnance Map in the other, I could hardly have improved on the course steered by our pilot. Up hill for a bit, when the horses were fresh, with gradients just steep enough to temper Daniel's well-sustained tug of war, yet not so steep as to make a three-foot bank look like a house, or to guarantee a big knee at each "stone gap." Then high and dry country, with sheep huddled in defensive positions in the corners of the fields, and grass like a series of putting-greens, minus the holes, and fat, comely banks, and thin walls, from which the small round stones rattled harmlessly as Miss McRory's car-horse swept through them. Down into a long valley, with little sky-blue lakes, set in yellow sedge; and there was a helpful bog road there, that nicked nicely with the bending line of the hounds through the accompanying bog, and allayed a spasm of acute anxiety as to whether we should ever get near them again. Then upwards once more, deviously, through rougher going, with patches of low-growing furze sprouting from blackened tracts where the hill-side had been set on fire, with the hounds coming to their noses among brakes of briars and bracken; finally, in the wind and sun of the hill-top, a well-timed check.

We looked back for the first time, half in fear that we might find Flurry hot on our track, half in hope that he and his horn were coming to our help; but neither in the green country nor in the brown valley was there any sign or sound of him. There was nothing to be seen but a couple of men standing on a fence to watch us, nothing to be heard except cur dogs vociferating at every cottage.

" Fifteen couple on," said the Count professionally. " How many does Knox usually have out ? "

" All he's got," I said, mopping my brow.

" I don't see the two that have no hair on their backs," said Miss McRory, whose eyes, much enhanced by the radiant carmine of her cheeks, beamed at us through wisps and loops of hair. " I know them, they're always scratching, the poor things ! "

That Miss McRory and her steed kept, as they did, their place in what is known to history as the Great Castle Knox Run, is a matter that I do not pretend to explain. Some antiquarian has unearthed the fact that the car-horse had three strains of breeding, and had twice been second in a Point-to-Point; but I maintain that credit must be ascribed to Miss Larkie, about whom there is something inevitable; some street-boy quality of being in the movement.

We were now on a heathery table-land, with patches of splashy, rushy ground, from which the snipe flickered out as the hounds cast themselves through it. Presently, on the top of a hard, peaty bank, a hound spoke, hesitatingly, yet hopefully, and plunged down on the other side; the pack crowded over, and drove on through the heather. Daniel changed feet on a mat of ling with a large stone in it, and therefrom ramped carefully out over a deep cut in the peat, unforeseen, and masked by tufts of heather. The hireling of the Comte de Pralines had, up to this, done his work blamelessly, if without originality; he had an anxiousness to oblige that had been matured during a dread winter when he had been the joint property of three subalterns, but he reserved to himself a determination to drop economically off his banks, and boggy slits were not in his list of possibilities.

How the matter occurred I do not know, but, when I looked round, his head alone was visible, and the Count was standing on his in the heather. Miss McRory's car-horse, who had pulled up in the act of following the Count, with a suddenness acquired, no doubt, in the shafts of a Cork covered-car, was viewing the scene with horror from the summit of the bank. The hounds were by this time clear of the heather, and were beginning to run hard ; it was not until I was on the further side of the next bank that I cast another fleeting look back ; this time the Count was standing on his feet, but the hireling was still engulfed, and Miss McRory was still on the wrong side of the slit. After that I forgot them, wholly and heartlessly, as is invariable in such cases.

As a matter of fact, I had no attention to spare for anyone but myself, even though we went, for the first twenty minutes or so, as on rubber tyres, through bland dairy farms wherein the sweet influences of the dairy-cow had induced gaps in every fence, and gates into every road. The scent, mercifully for Daniel, was not quite what it had been ; the fox had run through cattle, and also through goats (a small and odorous party, on whose behalf, indeed, some slight intervention on my part was required), and it was here, when crossing a road, that a donkey and her foal, moved by some mysterious attraction akin to love at first sight, attached themselves to me. Undeterred by the fact that the mother's foreleg was fettered to her hind, the pair sped from field to field in my wake ; at the checks, which just then were frequent, they brayed enthusiastically. I thought to elude them at a steep drop into a road, but they toboganned down it without an effort; when they overtook me the fetter-chain was broken, and clanked from the mother's hind-leg as if she were a family ghost.

There came at length a moment, outside a farm-house, when it seemed as if the fox had beaten us. Here, on the farther side of Castle Knox, I was well out of my own country, and what the fox's point might be was represented by the letter X. Nevertheless it was here that I lifted the hounds and brought off the cast of a life-time; I am inclined to think that he had lain down under a hayrick and was warned of our approach by the voices of my attendant jackasses; my cast was probably not much more of a fluke than such inspirations usually are, but the luck was with me. Old Playboy, sole relic of my deputy Mastership, lifted his white head and endorsed my suggestion with a single bass note; Rally, Philippa's prize puppy, uttered a soprano cadenza, and the pack suddenly slid away over the pasture fields, with the smoothness and una-nimity of the *Petits Chevaux* over their green cloth.

It was now becoming for Daniel and me some-thing of an effort to keep our proud and lonely

place in or about the next field to the hounds.
The fields were coming smaller, the gaps fewer;
Daniel had no intention of chucking it, but he
gave me to understand that he meant to take the
hills on the second speed. And, unfortunately,
the hills were coming. The hounds, by this time
three fences ahead, flung over a bank on the up-
grade, a bank that would give pause for reflection
at the beginning of a run. I tried back, scrambled
into a lane, followed it up the hill, with the cry of
the hounds coming fainter each minute, dragged
a cart wheel and a furze bush out of a gap with
my crop, found myself in a boggy patch of turnips,
surrounded by towering fuchsia hedges, and
realised that the pack had passed in music out of
sight.

I stood still and looked at my watch. It was
already an hour and twenty minutes from the
word "Go!" and the hounds were not only gone
but were still going. A man who has lost hounds
inevitably follows the line of least resistance. I
retired from the turnip field, and abandoned
myself to the lane, which seemed not disinclined
to follow the direction in which the hounds had
been heading. Since the hayrick episode they
had been running right-handed, and the lane bent
right-handed over the end of the hill, and presently deposited me on a road. It was one of

the moments when the greatness of the world
is borne in upon the wayfarer. There was a
spacious view from the hill-side ; three parishes,
at least, offered themselves for my selection, and I
surveyed them, solitary and remote as the evening star, and with no more reason than it for
favouring one more than another. A harrowing,
and, by this time, but too familiar cry, broke on
my ear, an undulating cry as of a thing that
galloped as it roared. My admirers were still
on my trail ; I gave Daniel a touch of the spurs
and trotted on to the right.

No human being was visible, but some way
ahead there was a slated house at a cross-roads ;
there, at all events, I could get my bearings.
There were porter-barrels outside it, and from
some distance I heard two voices, male and female,
engaged in loud and ferocious argument ; I had
no difficulty in diagnosing a public-house. When
Daniel and I darkened the doorway the shouting
ceased abruptly, and I saw a farmer, in his Sunday
clothes, making an unsteady retreat through a
door at the back of the shop. The other disput-
ant, a large, middle-aged woman, remained entrenched behind the counter, and regarded me
with a tranquil and commanding eye. She informed me, as from a pulpit, that I was six miles
from Castle Knox, and with dignity, as though

leaving a pulpit, she moved from behind the counter, and advanced to the door to indicate my road. I asked her if she had seen anything of the hounds.

"There was one of your dogs looked in the door to me a while ago," she replied, " but he got a couple of boxes from the cat that have kittens; I d'no what way he went. Indeed I was bothered at the time with that poor man that came in to thank me for the compliment I paid him in going to his sister's funeral."

I said that he certainly seemed to feel it very much. At which she looked hard at me and said that he was on his way to a wedding, and that it might be he had a drop taken to rise his heart. "He was after getting a half a crown from a gentleman—a huntsman like yourself," she added, "that was striving to get his horse out of a ditch."

"Was there a lady with him?" I asked.

"There was, faith! And the two o' them legged it away then through the country, and they galloping like the deer!"

So, in all love, we parted; before I reached the next turning renewed sounds of battle told me that the compliment was still being pressed home.

My road, bending ever to the right, strolled through an untidy nondescript country, with little

bits of bog, and little lumps of hill, and little rags
of fields. I had jogged a mile or so when I saw
a hound, a few fields away to my right, poking
along on what appeared to be a line; he flopped
into a boggy ditch, and scrambled from it on to
a fence. He stood there undecidedly, like any
human being, reviewing the situation, and then I
saw his head and stern go up. The next moment
I also heard what he had heard, a faint and far-
away note of the horn. It came again, a long
and questing call.

The road was flat and fairly straight; far away
upon it something was moving gradually into my
scope of vision, something with specks of red in
it. It advanced upon me, firmly, and at a smart
pace; heading it, like the ram of a battleship,
was Mr. Knox. With him, "of all his halls had
nursed," remained only the two hounds with the
hairless backs, the two who, according to Miss
McRory, were always scratching. Behind him
was a small and unsmiling selection from those
who, like him, had lost the hunt. Lady Knox
headed them; my wife and Bill brought up the
rear. The hound whom I had seen in the bog
had preceded me, and was now joining himself to
his two comrades, putting the best face he could
upon it, with a frowning brow and his hackles up.
The comrades, in their official position of sole

representatives of the pack, received him with orthodox sternness, and though unable, for obvious reasons, to put their hackles up, the bald places on their backs were of an intimidating pink.

My own reception followed the same lines.

"Where are the hounds?" barked Flurry, in the awful tones of a parent addressing a governess who, through gross neglect, has mislaid her charges.

Before I had had time to make up my mind whether to be truculent or pacific, there was a shout away on our left. At some little distance up a by-road, a man was standing on a furze-plumed bank, beckoning to us with a driving-whip. Flurry stood in his stirrups, and held up his cap. The man yelled information that was wholly unintelligible, but the driving-whip indicated a point beyond him, and Flurry's brown mare jumped from a standstill to a gallop, and swung into the by-road.

The little band of followers swung after him. When Lady Knox was well ahead, I followed, and found myself battering between high banks behind Philippa and Bill Cunningham.

"Where's Mossoo?" my wife said breathlessly, as Daniel's head drew level with her sandwich case. "We met the man who pulled him out of the ditch—up in the hills there——"

"Yes, by Jove!" said Bill, "Flurry asked him if it was a Frenchman, and the chap said, 'French or German, he had curses as good as yourself!' I told Flurry it must have been you!"

"I don't mind Flurry, it's Lady Knox——" began Philippa.

Here we all came to a violent full-stop. Flurry's advance had been arrested by a covered-car and horse drawn across the road; the horse was eating grass, the driver, with the reins in his hand, was standing with his back to us on the top of the bank from which he had hailed us, howling plaudits, as if he were watching a race. There were distant shouts, and barking dogs, and bellowing cattle, and blended with them was the unmistakable baying of hounds.

I daresay that what Flurry said to the driver did him good—did Flurry good, I mean. The car lurched to one side, and, as we squeezed past it, we saw between its black curtains a vision of a scarlet-faced bride, embedded in female relatives; two outside cars, driverless, and loaded with wedding guests, were drawn up a little farther on. Flurry, still exploding like a shell, thundered on down the lane; the high bank ended at a gateway, he turned in, and as we crushed in after him we were greeted by a long and piercing "Who-whoop!"

We were in a straggling field with furzy patches in it. At the farther end of it was a crowd of country people on horses and on foot, obviously more wedding-guests; back of all, on a road below, was a white-washed chapel, and near it, still on the chestnut horse, was the priest who had headed the morning fox. Close to one of the clumps of furze the Comte de Pralines was standing, knee-deep in baying hounds, holding the body of the fox high above his head, and uttering scream upon scream of the most orthodox quality. He flung the fox to the hounds, the onlookers cheered, Miss McRory, seated on the car-horse, waved the brush above her head, and squealed at the top of her voice something that sounded like "Yoicks!" Her hair was floating freely down her back; a young countryman, in such sacrificial attire as suggested the bridegroom, was running across the field with her hat in his hand.

Flurry pulled up in silence; so did we. We were all quite outside the picture, and we knew it.

"Oh, the finest hunt ever you see!" cried the bridegroom as he passed us; "it was Father Dwyer seen him shnaking into the furze, the villyan!"

"Worry, worry, worry! Tear him and eat him, old fellows!" shouted the Comte de Pralines. "Give the hounds room, can't you, you chaps! I suppose you never saw them break up a fox before!" This to the wedding guests, who had crowded in, horse and foot, on top of the scuffling, growling pack.

Flurry turned an iron face upon me. His eye was no bigger than a pin's head.

"I suppose it's from Larkie McRory he got the English?" he said; "he learnt it quick."

"The McRorys don't speak English!" said Lady Knox, in a voice like a north-east wind.

"*Seulement très petit!*" Philippa murmured brazenly.

Whether Lady Knox heard her or not, I am unable to say. Her face was averted from me, and remained as inflexible as a profile on a coin —a Roman coin, for choice.

The faculty of not knowing when you are beaten is one that has, I think, been lauded beyond its deserving. Napoleon the Great has condemned manœuvring before a fixed position, and Lady Knox was clearly a fixed position. Accepting these tenets, I began an unostentatious retirement, in which I was joined by Philippa. We were nearing safety and the gate of the field, when a yearning, choking wail came to us from the lane.

"The Bride?" queried my wife hysterically.

It was repeated; in the same instant my

admirers, the jackasses, *mère et fils*, advanced upon the scene at a delirious gallop, and, sobbing with the ecstasy of reunion, resumed their attendance upon Daniel.

For a moment the attention of the field, including even that of the Roman coin, was diverted from the Comte de Pralines, and was concentrated upon our retreat.

XI

THE SHOOTING OF SHINROE

Mr. Joseph Francis M'Cabe rose stiffly from his basket chair, picked up the cushion on which he had been seated, looked at it with animosity, hit it hard with his fist, and, flinging it into the chair, replaced himself upon it, with the single word:

"Flog!"

I was aware that he referred to the flock with which the cushions in the lounge of Reardon's Hotel were stuffed.

"They have this hotel destroyed altogether with their improvements," went on Mr. M'Cabe between puffs, as he lit his pipe. "God be with the time this was the old smoking-room, before they knocked it and the hall into one and spoilt the two of them! There were fine solid chairs in it that time, that you'd sleep in as good as your bed, but as for these wicker affairs, I declare the wind 'd whistle through them the same as a crow's nest." He paused, and brought his heel down heavily on the top of the fire. "And look at that for a grate! A Well-grate they call it,— *I'd* say, 'Leave Well alone!' Thirty years I'm

284

coming to Sessions here, and putting up in this house, and in place of old Tim telling me me own room was ready for me, there's a whipper-snapper of a snapdragon in a glass box in the hall, asking me me name in broken English" (it may be mentioned that this happened before the War), " and ' Had I a Cook's ticket?' and down-facing me that I must leave my key in what he called the ' Bew-ro.' "

I said I knew of a lady who always took a Cook's ticket when she went abroad, because when she got to Paris there would be an Englishman on the platform to meet her, or at all events a broken Englishman.

Mr. M'Cabe softened to a temporary smile, but held on to his grievance with the tenacity of his profession. (I don't think I have mentioned that he is a Solicitor, of a type now, unfortunately, becoming obsolete.) He had a long grey face, and a short grey moustache; he dyed his hair, and his age was known to no man.

"There was one of Cook's tourists sat next me at breakfast," he resumed, "and he asked me was I ever in Ireland before, and how long was I in it. ' Wan day,' says I ! "

" Did he believe you?" I asked.

" He did," replied Mr. M'Cabe, with something that approached compassion.

I have always found old M'Cabe a mitigating circumstance of Sessions at Owenford, both in Court and out of it. He was a sportsman of the ingrained variety that grows wild in Ireland, and in any of the horse-coping cases that occasionally refresh the innermost soul of Munster, it would be safe to assume that Mr. M'Cabe's special gifts had ensured his being retained, generally on the shady side. He fished when occasion served, he shot whether it did or not. He did not exactly keep horses, but he always knew some one who was prepared to "pass on" a thoroughly useful animal, with some infirmity so insignificant that until you tried to dispose of him you did not realise that he was yours, until his final passing-on to the next world. He had certain shooting privileges in the mountains behind the town of Owenford (bestowed, so he said, by a grateful client), and it had often been suggested by him that he and I should anticipate some November Sessions by a day, and spend it "on the hill." We were now in the act of carrying out the project.

"Ah, these English," M'Cabe began again, mixing himself a glass of whisky and water, "they'd believe anything so long as it wasn't the truth. Talking politics these lads were, and by the time they had their ham and eggs swallowed they had the whole country arranged. 'And

look,' says they—they were anglers, God help
us!—'look at all the money that's going to
waste for want of preserving the rivers!' 'I
beg your pardon,' says I, 'there's water-bailiffs
on the most of the rivers. I was defending a
man not long since, that was cot by the water-
bailiff poaching salmon on the Owen. 'And
what proof have you?' says I to the water-bailiff.
'How do you know it was a salmon at all?' 'Is
it how would I know?' says the bailiff, 'didn't I
gaff the fish for him meself!'"

"What did your anglers say to that?" I
enquired.

"Well, they didn't quite go so far as to tell me
I was a liar," said Mr. M'Cabe tranquilly. "Ah,
telling such as them the truth is wasting what
isn't plenty! Then they'll meet some fellow that
lies like a tooth-drawer, and they'll write to the
English *Times* on the head of him!" He
stretched forth a long and bony hand for the
tumbler of whisky and water. "And talking of
tooth-drawers," he went on, "there's a dentist
comes here once a fortnight, Jeffers his name is,
and a great sportsman too. I was with him to-
day"—he passed his hand consciously over his
mouth, and the difference that I had dimly felt
in his appearance suddenly, and in all senses of
the word, flashed upon me—"and he was telling

me how one time, in the summer that's past, he'd been out all night, fishing in the Owen. He was going home before the dawn, and he jumped down off a bank on to what he took to be a white stone—and he aimed for the stone, mind you, because he thought the ground was wet—and what was it but a man's face!" M'Cabe paused to receive my comment. "What did he do, is it? Ran off for his life, roaring out, 'There's a first-rate dentist in Owenford!' The fellow was lying asleep there, and he having bundles of spurge with him to poison the river! He had taken drink, I suppose."

"Was he a water-bailiff too?" said I. "I hope the conservators of the river stood him a set of teeth."

"If they did," said M'Cabe, with an unexpected burst of feeling, "I pity him!" He rose to his feet, and put his tumbler down on the chimney-piece. "Well, we should get away early in the morning, and it's no harm for me to go to bed."

He yawned—a large yawn that ended abruptly with a metallic click. His eyes met mine, full of unspoken things; we parted in a silence that seemed to have been artificially imposed upon Mr. M'Cabe.

The wind boomed intermittently in my chimney during the night, and a far and heavy growling told of the dissatisfaction of the sea. Yet the morning was not unfavourable. There was a broken mist, with shimmers of sun in it, and the carman said it would be a thing of nothing, and would go out with the tide. The Boots, a relic of the old *régime*, was pessimistic, and mentioned that there were two stars squez up agin the moon last night, and he would have no dependence on the day. M'Cabe offered no opinion, being occupied in bestowing in a species of dog-box beneath the well of the car a young red setter, kindly lent by his friend the dentist. The setter, who had formed at sight an unfavourable opinion of the dog-box, had resolved himself into an invertebrate mass of jelly and lead, and was with difficulty straightened out and rammed home into it.

"Have we all now?" said M'Cabe, slamming the door in the dog's face. "Take care we're not like me uncle, old Tom Duffy, that was going shooting, and was the whole morning slapping his pockets and saying, 'Me powder! me shot! me caps! me wads!' and when he got to the bog, 'O tare an' ouns!' says he, 'I forgot the gun!'"

There are still moments when I can find some special and not-otherwise-to-be-attained flavour in driving on an outside car; a sense of personal achievement in sitting, by some method of instinctive suction, the lurches and swoops peculiar to these vehicles. Reardon's had given us its roomiest car and its best horse, a yellow mare, with a long back and a slinging trot, and a mouth of iron.

"Where did Mr. Reardon get the mare, Jerry?" asked M'Cabe, as we zigzagged in successive hairbreadths through the streets of Owenford.

"D-Dublin, sir," replied the driver, who, with both fists extended in front of him and both heels planted against his narrow footboard, seemed to find utterance difficult.

"She's a goer!" said M'Cabe.

"She is—she killed two men," said Jerry, in two jerks.

"That's a great credit to her. What way did she do it?"

"P-pulled the lungs out o' them!" ejaculated Jerry, turning the last corner and giving the mare a shade more of her head, as a tribute, perhaps, to her prowess.

She swung us for some six miles along the ruts of the coast road at the same unflinching pace, after which, turning inland and uphill, we began the climb of four miles into the mountains. It was about eleven o'clock when we pulled up beside a long and reedy pool, high up in the heather; the road went on, illimitably it seemed, and was lost, with its attendant telegraph posts, in cloud.

" Away with ye now, Jerry," said M'Cabe; " we'll shoot our way home."

He opened the back of the dog-box, and summoned its occupant. The summons was disregarded. Far back in the box two sparks of light and a dead silence indicated the presence of the dog.

" How snug you are in there!" said M'Cabe; " here, Jerry, pull him out for us. What the deuce is this his name is? Jeffers told me yesterday, and it's gone from me."

" I d'no would he bite me?" said Jerry, taking a cautious observation and giving voice to the feelings of the party. " Here, poor fellow! Here, good lad!"

The good lad remained immovable. The lure of a sandwich produced no better result.

" We can't be losing our day with the brute this way," said M'Cabe. " Tip up the car. He'll come out then, and no thanks to him."

As the shafts rose heavenwards, the law of gravitation proved too many for the setter, and he slowly slid to earth.

" If I only knew your dam name we'd be all right now," said M'Cabe.

The carman dropped the shafts on to the mare, and drove on up the pass, with one side of the car turned up and himself on the other. The yellow mare had, it seemed, only begun her day's work. A prophetic instinct, of the reliable kind that is strictly founded on fact, warned me that we might live to regret her departure.

The dentist's setter had, at sight of the guns, realised that things were better than he had expected, and now preceded us along the edge of the lake with every appearance of enthusiasm. He quartered the ground with professional zeal, he splashed through the sedge, and rattled through thickets of dry reeds, and set successively a heron, a water-hen, and something, unseen, that I believe to have been a water-rat. After each of these efforts he rushed in upon his quarry, and we called him by all the gun-dog names we had ever heard of, from Don to Grouse, from Carlo to Shot, coupled with objurgations on a rising scale. With none of them did we so much as vibrate a chord in his bosom. He was a large dog, with a blunt stupid face, and a faculty for excitement about nothing that impelled him to bound back to us as often as possible, to gaze in our eyes in brilliant enquiry, and to pant and prance before us with all the fatuity of youth. Had he been able to speak, he would have asked idiotic questions, of that special breed that exact from their victim a reply of equal imbecility.

The lake and its environs, for the first time in M'Cabe's experience, yielded nothing; we struck up on to the mountain side, following the course of an angry stream that came racing down from the heights. We worked up through ling and furze, and skirted flocks of pale stones that lay in the heather like petrified sheep, and the dog, ranging deliriously, set water-wagtails and anything else that could fly; I believe he would have set a blue-bottle, and I said so to M'Cabe.

"Ah, give him time; he'll settle down," said M'Cabe, who had a thankfulness for small mercies born of a vast experience of makeshifts; "he might fill the bag for us yet."

We laboured along the flank of the mountain, climbing in and out of small ravines, jumping or wading streams, sloshing through yellow sedgery bog; always with the brown heather running up to the misty skyline, and always with the same atrocious luck. Once a small pack of grouse got up, very wild, and leagues out of range, thanks to the far-reaching activities of the dog, and once a hermit woodcock exploded out of a clump of furze, and sailed away down the slope, followed by four charges of shot and the red setter, in equally innocuous pursuit. And this, up to luncheon time, was the sum of the morning's sport.

We ate our sandwiches on a high ridge, under the lee of a tumbled pile of boulders, that looked as if they had been about to hurl themselves into the valley, and had thought better of it at the last moment. Between the looming, elephant-grey mountains the mist yielded glimpses of the far greenness of the sea, the only green thing in sight in this world of grey and brown. The dog sat opposite to me, and willed me to share my food with him. His steady eyes were charged with the implication that I was a glutton; personally I abhorred him, yet I found it impossible to give him less than twenty-five per cent. of my sandwiches.

"I wonder did Jeffers take him for a bad debt," said M'Cabe reflectively, as he lit his pipe.

I said I should rather take my chance with the bad debt.

"He might have treated me better," M'Cabe grumbled on, "seeing that I paid him seven pound ten the day before yesterday, let alone that it was me that was the first to put him up to this—this bit of Shinroe Mountain that never was what you might call strictly preserved.

When he came here first he didn't as much as know what cartridges he'd want for it. 'Six and eight,' says I, 'that's a lawyer's fee, so if you think of me you'll not forget it!' And now, if ye please," went on Mr. Jeffers' preceptor in sport, "he's shooting the whole country and selling all he gets! And he wouldn't as much as ask me to go with him; and the excuse he gives, he wouldn't like to have an old hand like me connyshooring his shots! How modest he is!'

I taunted M'Cabe with having been weak enough thus to cede his rights, and M'Cabe, who was not at all amused, said that after all it wasn't so much Jeffers that did the harm, but an infernal English Syndicate that had taken the Shinroe shooting this season, and paid old Purcell that owned it ten times what it was worth.

"It might be as good for us to get off their ground now," continued M'Cabe, rising slowly to his feet, "and try the Lackagreina Valley. The stream below is their bounds."

This, I hasten to say, was the first I had heard of the Syndicate, and I thought it tactless of M'Cabe to have mentioned it, even though the wrong that we had done them was purely technical. I said to him that I thought the sooner we got off their ground the better, and we descended the hill and crossed the stream, and

M'Cabe said that he could always shoot this next stretch of country when he liked. With this assurance, we turned our backs on the sea and struck inland, tramping for an hour or more through country whose entire barrenness could only be explained on the hypothesis that it has been turned inside out to dry. So far it had failed to achieve even this result.

The weather got thicker, and the sport, if possible, thinner; I had long since lost what bearings I possessed, but M'Cabe said he knew of a nice patch of scrub in the next valley that always held a cock. The next valley came at last, not without considerable effort, but no patch of scrub was apparent. Some small black and grey cattle stood and looked at us, and a young bull showed an inclination to stalk the dog; it seemed the only sport the valley was likely to afford. M'Cabe looked round him, and looked at his watch, and looked at the sky, which did not seem to be more than a yard above our heads, and said without emotion:

"Did ye think of telling the lad in the glass box in the hall that we might want some dinner kept hot for us? I d'no from Adam where we've got to!"

There was a cattle track along the side of the valley which might, though not necessarily, lead somewhere. We pursued it, and found that it led, in the first instance, to some blackfaced mountain sheep. A cheerful interlude followed, in which the red setter hunted the sheep, and we hunted the setter, and what M'Cabe said about the dentist in the intervals of the chase was more appropriate to the occasion than to these pages.

When justice had been satiated, and the last echo of the last yell of the dog had trembled into silence among the hills, we resumed the cattle-track, which had become a shade more reliable, and, as we proceeded, began to give an im-. pression that it might lead somewhere. The day was dying in threatening stillness. Lethargic layers of mist bulged low, like the roof of a marquee, and cloaked every outline that could yield us information. The dog, unchastened by recent events, and full of an idiot optimism, continued to range the hillside.

" I suppose I'll never get the chance to tell Jeffers my opinion of that tom-fool," said M'Cabe, following with an eye of steel the perambulations of the dog ; " the best barrister that ever wore a wig couldn't argue with a dentist ! He has his fist half way down your throat before you can open your mouth ; and in any case he'll tell me we couldn't expect any dog would work for us when we forgot his name. What's the brute at now?"

The brute was high above us on the hillside, setting a solitary furze bush with convincing determination, and casting backward looks to see if he were being supported.

"It might be a hare," said M'Cabe, cocking his gun, with a revival of hope that was almost pathetic, and ascending towards the furze bush.

I neither quickened my pace nor deviated from the cattle track, but I may admit that I did so far yield to the theory of the hare as to slip a cartridge into my gun.

M'Cabe put his gun to his shoulder, lowered it abruptly, and walked up to the furze bush. He stooped and picked up something.

"He's not such a fool after all!" he called out; "ye said he'd set a blue-bottle, and b' Jove ye weren't far out!"

He held up a black object that was neither bird nor beast.

I took the cartridge out of my gun as unobtrusively as possible, and M'Cabe and the dog rejoined me with the product of the day's sport. It was a flat-sided bottle, high shouldered, with a short neck; M'Cabe extracted the cork and took a sniff.

"Mountain dew no less!" (Mr. M'Cabe ad-

hered faithfully to the stock phrases of his youth.)
"This never paid the King a shilling! Give me
the cup off your flask, Major, till we see what
sort it is."

It was pretty rank, and even that seasoned
vessel, old M'Cabe, admitted that it might be
drinkable in another couple of years, but hardly
in less; yet as it ran, a rivulet of fire, through
my system, it seemed to me that even the water
in my boots became less chill.

"In the public interest we're bound to remove
it," said M'Cabe, putting the bottle into his game
bag; "any man that drank enough of that 'd rob
a church! Well, anyway, we're not the only
people travelling this path," he continued; "whoever put his afternoon tea to hide there will
choose a less fashionable promenade next time.
But indeed the poor man couldn't be blamed for
not knowing such a universal genius of a dog
was coming this way! Didn't I tell you he'd fill
the bag for us!"

He extracted from his pockets a pair of knitted
gloves, and put them on; it was equivalent to
putting up the shutters.

It was shortly after this that we regained touch
with civilisation. Above the profile of a hill a
telegraph post suddenly showed itself against the
grey of the misty twilight. We made as bee-like

a line for it as the nature of the ground permitted, and found ourselves on a narrow road, at a point where it was in the act of making a hairpin turn before plunging into a valley.

"The Beacon Bay road, begad!" said M'Cabe; "I didn't think we were so far out of our way. Let me see now, which way is this we'd best go."

He stood still and looked round him, taking his bearings; in the solitude the telegraph posts hummed to each other, full of information and entirely reticent.

The position was worse than I thought. By descending into the valley we should, a couple or three miles farther on, strike the coast road about six miles from home; by ascending the hill and walking four miles, we should arrive at the station of Coppeen Road, and, with luck, there intercept the evening train for Owenford.

"And that's the best of our play, but we'll have to step out," concluded M'Cabe, shortening the strap of his game-bag, and settling it on his back.

"If I were you," I said, "I'd chuck that stuff away. Apart from anything else, it's about half a ton extra to carry."

"There's many a thing, Major, that you might do that I might not do," returned M'Cabe with solemnity, "and in the contrairy sense the statement is equally valid."

He faced the hill with humped shoulders, and fell with no more words into his poacher's stride, and I followed him with the best imitation of it that I could put up after at least six hours of heavy going. M'Cabe is fifteen years older than I am, and I hope that when I am his age I shall have more consideration than he for those who are younger than myself.

It was now nearly half-past five o'clock, and by the time we had covered a mile of puddles and broken stones it was too dark to see which was which. I felt considerable dubiety about catching the train at Coppeen Road, all the more that it was a flag station, demanding an extra five minutes in hand. Probably the engine-driver had long since abandoned any expectation of passengers at Coppeen Road, and, if he even noticed the signal, would treat it as a practical joke. It was after another quarter of an hour's trudge that a distant sound entered into the silence that had fallen upon M'Cabe and me, an intermittent grating of wheels upon patches of broken stone, a steady hammer of hoofs.

M'Cabe halted.

" That car's bound to be going to Owenford," he said ; " I wonder could they give us a lift."

A single light (the economical habit of the South of Ireland) began to split the foggy darkness.

"Begad, that's like the go of Reardon's mare!" said M'Cabe, as the light swung down upon us.

We held the road like highwaymen, we called upon the unseen driver to stop, and he answered to the name of Jerry. This is not a proof of identity in a province where every third man is dignified by the name of Jeremiah, but as the car pulled up it was Reardon's yellow mare on which the lamplight fell, and we knew that the fates had relented.

We should certainly not catch the train at Coppeen Road, Jerry assured us; "she had," he said, "a fashion of running early on Monday nights, and in any case if you'd want to catch that thrain, you should make like an amber-bush for her."

We agreed that it was too late for the preparation of an ambush.

"If the Sergeant had no objections," continued Jerry, progressing smoothly towards the tip that would finally be his, "it would be no trouble at all to oblige the gentlemen. Sure it's the big car I have, and it's often I took six, yes, and seven on it, going to the races."

I was now aware of two helmeted presences on the car, and a decorous voice said that the gentlemen were welcome to a side of the car if they liked.

"Is that Sergeant Leonard?" asked M'Cabe, who knew every policeman in the country. "Well, Sergeant, you've a knack of being on the spot when you're wanted!"

"And sometimes when he's not!" said I.

There was a third and unhelmeted presence on the car, and something of stillness and aloofness in it had led me to diagnose a prisoner.

The suggested dispositions were accomplished. The two policemen and the prisoner wedged themselves on one side of the car, M'Cabe and I mounted the other, and put the dog on the cushion of the well behind us (his late quarters in the dog-box being occupied by half a mountain sheep, destined for the hotel larder). The yellow mare went gallantly up to her collar, regardless of her augmented load; M'Cabe and the Sergeant leaned to each other across the back of the car, and fell into profound and low-toned converse; I smoked, and the dog, propping his wet back against mine, made friends with the prisoner. It may be the Irish blood in me that is responsible for the illicit sympathy with a prisoner that sometimes incommodes me; I certainly bestowed some of it upon the captive, sandwiched between two stalwarts of the R.I.C., and learning that the strong arm of the Law was a trifle compared with the rest of its person.

"What sport had you, Major?" enquired Jerry, as we slackened speed at a hill.

I was sitting at the top of the car, under his elbow, and he probably thought that I was feeling neglected during the heart-to-heart confidences of M'Cabe and the Sergeant.

"Not a feather," I replied.

"Sure the birds couldn't be in it this weather," said Jerry considerately; he had in his time condoled with many sportsmen. "I'm after talking to a man in Coppeen Road station, that was carrying the game bag for them gentlemen that has Mr. Purcell's shooting on Shinroe Mountain, and what had the four o' them after the day— only one jack-snipe!"

"They went one better than we did," I said, but, as was intended, I felt cheered—"what day were they there?"

"To-day, sure!" answered Jerry, with faint surprise, "and they hadn't their luncheon hardly ate when they met one on the mountain that told them he seen two fellas walking it, with guns and a dog, no more than an hour before them. 'That'll do!' says they, and they turned about and back with them to Coppeen Road to tell the police."

"Did they see the fellows?" I asked lightly, after a panic-stricken pause.

" They did not. Sure they said if they seen them, they'd shoot them like rooks," replied Jerry, "and they would too. It's what the man was saying if they cot them lads to-day they'd have left them in the way they'd be given up by both doctor and priest! Oh, they're fierce altogether ! "

I received this information in a silence that was filled to bursting with the desire to strangle M'Cabe.

Jerry leaned over my shoulder, and lowered his voice.

" They were saying in Coppeen Road that there was a gentleman that came on a mothor-bike this morning early, and he had Shinroe shot out by ten o'clock, and on with him then up the country ; and it isn't the first time he was in it. It's a pity those gentlemen couldn't ketch *him ! They'd* mothor-bike him ! "

It was apparent that the poaching of the motor-bicycle upon the legitimate preserves of carmen was responsible for this remarkable sympathy with the law ; I, at all events, had it to my credit that I had not gone poaching on a motor-bicycle.

Just here M'Cabe emerged from the heart-to-heart, and nudged me in the ribs with a confederate elbow. I did not respond, being in no mood for confederacy, certainly not with M'Cabe.

" The Sergeant is after telling me this prisoner

he has here is prosecuted at the instance of that
Syndicate I was telling you about," he whispered
hoarsely in my ear, "for hunting Shinroe with
greyhounds. He was cited to appear last week,
and he didn't turn up; he'll be before you to-
morrow. I hope the Bench will have a fellow-
feeling for a fellow-creature!"

The whisper ended in the wheezy cough that
was Mr. M'Cabe's equivalent for a laugh. It was
very close to my ear, and it had somewhere in
it the metallic click that I had noticed before.

I grunted forbiddingly, and turned my back
upon M'Cabe, as far as it is possible to do so on
an outside car, and we hammered on through the
darkness. Once the solitary lamp illumined the
prolonged countenance of a donkey, and once or
twice we came upon a party of sheep lying on
the road; they melted into the night at the
minatory whistle that is dedicated to sheep, and
on each of these occasions the dentist's dog was
shaken by strong shudders, and made a convulsive attempt to spring from the car in pursuit.
We were making good travelling on a long
down-grade, a smell of sea-weed was in the mist,
and a salt taste was on my lips. It was very
cold; I had no overcoat, my boots had plumbed
the depths of many bogholes, and I found myself shivering like the dog.

It was at this point that I felt M'Cabe fumbling at his game-bag, that lay between us on the seat. By dint of a sympathy that I would have died rather than betray, I divined that he was going to tap that fount of contraband fire that he owed to the dentist's dog. It was, apparently, a matter of some difficulty; I felt him groping and tugging at the straps.

I said to myself, waveringly: "Old blackguard! I won't touch it if he offers it to me."

M'Cabe went on fumbling:

"Damn these woolly gloves! I can't do a hand's turn with them."

In the dark I could not see what followed, but I felt him raise his arm. There was a jerk, followed by a howl.

"Hold on!" roared M'Cabe, with a new and strange utterance, "Thtop the horth! I've dropped me teeth!"

The driver did his best, but with the push of the hill behind her the mare took some stopping.

"Oh, murder! oh, murder!" wailed M'Cabe, lisping thickly, "I pulled them out o' me head with the glove, trying to get it off!" He scrambled off the car. "Give me the lamp! Me lovely new teeth——"

I detached the lamp from its socket with all speed, and handed it to M'Cabe, who hurried back on our tracks. From motives of delicacy I remained on the car, as did also the rest of the party. A minute or two passed in awed silence, while the patch of light went to and fro on the dark road. It seemed an intrusion to offer assistance, and an uncertainty as to whether to allude to the loss as "them," or "it," made enquiries a difficulty.

"For goodneth'ake have none o' ye any matcheth, that ye couldn't come and help me?" demanded the voice of M'Cabe, in indignation blurred pathetically by his gosling-like lisp.

I went to his assistance, and refrained with an effort from suggesting the employment of that all-accomplished setter, the dentist's dog, in the search; it was not the moment for pleasantry. Not yet.

We crept along, bent double, like gorillas; the long strips of broken stones yielded nothing, the long puddles between them were examined in vain.

"What the dooth will I do to-morrow?" raged M'Cabe, pawing in the heather at the road's edge. "How can I plead when I haven't a blathted tooth in me head?"

"I'll give you half a crown this minute, M'Cabe," said I brutally, "if you'll say 'Sessions'!"

Here the Sergeant joined us, striking matches

as he came. He worked his way into the sphere of the car-lamp, he was most painstaking and sympathetic, and his oblique allusions to the object of the search were a miracle of tact.

"I see something white beyond you, Mr. M'Cabe,'" he said respectfully, "might that be them?"

M'Cabe swung the lamp as indicated.

"No, it might not. It's a pebble," he replied, with pardonable irascibility.

Silence followed, and we worked our way up the hill.

"What's that, sir?" ventured the Sergeant, with some excitement, stopping again and pointing. "I think I see the gleam of the gold!"

"Ah, nonthenth, man! They're vulcanite!" snapped M'Cabe, more irascibly than ever.

The word nonsense was a disastrous effort, and I withdrew into the darkness to enjoy it.

"What colour might vulcanite be, sir?" murmured a voice beside me.

Jerry had joined the search-party; he lighted, as he spoke, an inch of candle. On hearing my explanation he remarked that it was a bad chance, and at the same instant the inch of candle slipped from his fingers and fell into a puddle.

"Divil mend ye for a candle! Have ye a match, sir? I haven't a one left!"

As it happened, I had no matches, my only means of making a light being a patent tinder-box.

"Have you a match there?" I called out to the invisible occupants of the car, which was about fifteen or twenty yards away, advancing towards it as I spoke. The constable politely jumped off and came to meet me.

As he was in the act of handing me his match-box, the car drove away down the hill.

I state the fact with the bald simplicity that is appropriate to great disaster. To be exact, the yellow mare sprang from inaction into a gallop, as if she had been stung by a wasp, and had a start of at least fifty yards before either the carman or the constable could get under weigh. The carman, uttering shrill and menacing whistles, led the chase, the constable, though badly hampered by his greatcoat, was a good second, and the Sergeant, making the best of a bad start, followed them into the night.

The yellow mare's head was for home, and her load was on its own legs on the road behind her; hysterical yelps from the dentist's dog indicated that he also was on his own legs, and was, in all human probability, jumping at the mare's nose. As the rapturous beat of her hoofs died away on the down-grade, I recalled the assertion that she had pulled the lungs out of two men, and it seemed to me that the prisoner had caught the psychological moment on the hop.

"They'll not ketch him," said M'Cabe, with the flat calm of a broken man, "not to-night anyway. Nor for a week maybe. He'll take to the mountains."

The silence of the hills closed in upon us, and we were left in our original position, plus the lamp of the car, and minus our guns, the dentist's dog, and M'Cabe's teeth.

Far, far away, from the direction of Coppeen Road, that sinister outpost, where evil rumours were launched, and the night trains were waylaid by the amber-bushes, a steady tapping sound advanced towards us. Over the crest of the hill, a quarter of a mile away, a blazing and many-pointed star sprang into being, and bore down upon us. "A motor-bike!" ejaculated M'Cabe. "Take the light and thtop him—he wouldn't know what I wath thaying—if he ran over them they're done for! For the love o' Merthy tell him to keep the left thide of the road!"

I took the lamp, and ran towards the bicyclist, waving it as I ran. The star, now a moon of acetylene ferocity, slackened speed, and a voice behind it said:

"What's up?"

I stated the case with telegraphic brevity, and the motor-bicycle slid slowly past me. Its rider had a gun slung across his back, my lamp revealed a crammed game-bag on the carrier behind him.

"Sorry I can't assist you," he called back to me, keeping carefully at the left-hand side of the road, "but I have an appointment." Then, as an afterthought, "There's a first-rate dentist in Owenford!"

The red eye of the tail light glowed a farewell and passed on, like all the rest, into the night.

I rejoined M'Cabe.

He clutched my arm, and shook it.

"That wath Jefferth! *Jefferth*, I tell ye! The dirty poacher! And hith bag full of our birdth!"

It was not till the lamp went out, which it did some ten minutes afterwards, that I drew M'Cabe from the scene of his loss, gently, as one deals with the bereaved, and faced with him the six-mile walk to Owenford.

Michael J. Abberton
J.S. Abbott
J.B. Abbott
P.M. Adamson
I.R. Scott Aiton
Edward Allen
J.A. Allen
O.J.R. Allen
D.W. Allen
P.H.B. Allsop
J.R. Allt
P.T.K. Anderson
Cecily Anderson
D.G. Andrew
Miss Diane Andrews
Graham P. Andrews
N.C. Ansdell
C.J. Armstrong
Lt. Col. R.M. Arnold
Mrs M. Atkinson

Lt. Col. A.E.
  Bagwell-Purefoy
D.F. Bailey
Col. & Mrs. Glenn O.
  Baker
Commander C.E.
  Baker OBE RN
David C.F. Baker
Mrs. R.W.S. Baker
W.J. Baker
H.A.S. Bancroft
A. Banfield MH
G.C. Banks
John Barker
A.R. Barnes
R.A. Barnett
Sir David Barran
F.J. Barratt

H.L. Barrett
A.G.S. Barstow
H.R. Barton
D.S. Bass
Paul Bass
B.H. Bateman
P.B. Bates
Anwer Bati
Mrs. E.M. Bazley
Hon. Mrs. M.H.
  Beaumont
A.F.L. Beeston
Diana Lady Beith
Nicholas John
  Belcher
Mrs. Margaret Bell
R.A. Bendall
F.G. Bendell
Mrs. Janet L. Bennett
J.C. Benson
Mrs. M.D. Berger
G.F.M. de Bethune
M. Ide Betts
Major K.R. Mck
  Biggs
R.J. Bird
Mrs. A.L. Birt
Dr. Bernard Black
W.T. Blackband
Peter Blacklock
E.C. Blake
The Rev. Michael
  Bland
A.H. Boddy
M.J.A. Bond
D. Boot
Miss Mary J.E.
  Bower
James T. Bowie

John Bowker
John G. Bowler
Mrs. M. Bown
Lt. Col. D.H. Boydell
R.P. Brett
D.C. Bright
Frank Brightman
G.C.V. Brittain
Miss J. Brodie Hoare
Capt. C.A.J. Bromley
  Gardner
D. Brown B V SC
  MRCVS
N.B. Buckland
Dr. C. Bullock- Davies
John S. Burgess
John D.C. Burridge
Philip Burrows
Dr. J.D.K. Burton
L.D. Burton
Dermot S.L. Butler
K.F. Butler
M.J. Butterfield
Brendan Byrne

A.J. Cairns
Mrs. A.J.C.
  Campbell
L.R. Campfield
R.J. Canning
The Rev. W.R.D.
  Capstick
J.A. Caslaw
The Rev. George
  Cassidy
Mrs. E.L. Catto
Lord Charles Cecil
Mrs. K.G.F.
  Chavasse

Mrs B. Chetwynd-
 Stapylton
J.R. Clack
H. Clarkson
Jane Cockburn
J.W.G. Cocke
Miss U. Codrington
Robert Coggins
C.J. Collingwood
Ken Collins
Edwin Collins
Prof. Carl B. Cone
M.L. Congdon
J.C. Conner
W.H. Cooper
John Cope MP
M.D. Corke
M.H. Couchman
P. Roylance Court
S.R. Craddock
H.P. Craig
Miss G.E. Cresswell
M.G. Cripps
R.N.R. Cross
J.P.O. Crowe
C.C. Cumming
Major G.J.P.
 Cummins
S.B. Cunningham
G. Cuttle

T.L.A. Daintith
R.D. Dalraine
M.S. Dalziel CBE
Michael R. Dampier
John H. Daniels
B.J. Davidson
Dr. M.L.R. Davies
R.W. Howard Davies
Mrs. J.A. Davis
Elizabeth Janet
 Dawkes

Mrs. H.L.R. Day
Martyn J. Dearden
Lt. Col. C.G.
 Delforce DSO TD
Rowland P. Dell
Simon Dell
Peter W. Dennes
John Devaux
G. Dickinson
Nigel Dobbins
J.F. Doble
Dr. William Dodd
Mrs. B.H. Donald
Flt. Lt. R.C.T.
 Dorsett
W.B. Draper
Mrs. G. Lloyd
 Drummond
R.H. Dudley
Mrs. J. Duxberry

R.C. Edgell
N.P. Edgell
Dr. W.L.
 Edmundson
E.F. Edwards
Major F.M. Edwards
P.S.A. Edwards
Mrs B. Ellington
Miss S.D. Elmes
James Emmet
Mrs. S. Esmond
M.G. Esther
L.J.C. Evans
Commander
 Raymond Evans
 RN
Mrs Evelyn

Cdr. H. Falcon-
 Steward
J.C. Fareham

T.C. Farmbrough
Major A. Farrant
J.E. Farrer
Lt. Col. R.I. Feild
 MC
K.P. Fennell
Dr. J.B. Ferguson
M.A. Ferrier
Mrs. Maralyn Ferrier
R.A.J. Finn
J.S. Fisher
Mrs. L.U. Fisher
M.E. Fitzgerald-Hart
Mrs. Elizabeth
 Florey
P.R. Forrester
Dr. C.A. Foster
Mrs. D.J. Foster
K.M. Fox
Major R.P. Fox
Miss M.M. Fraser-
 Roberts
Mrs. D.P. Freeman
Mrs. R. Fremantle
Lt. Col. S.J. Furness

Leslie G. Gallop
James J. Gammons
Oliver Gardener
R.R.G. Gardner
W.J. Garnham
Professor J.C.A.
 Gaskin
Dr. Hugh Gibbs
Mrs. R.I. Gilchrist
His Hon. Judge S.S.
 Gill
H.R. Gillespie
Richard Gilman MD
 FACS
G.N. Gingell
Nicholas Gingell

Anthony Goddard
John Godley
Captain W.E.B. Godsal RN
C.A. Gold
Mrs. H.B. Goldsmid
J.G. Goldsworth
T.S.H. Gooch
R.H. Good
Paul Goodlet
J.S. Gordon
Major J.B. Gordon-Duff
T.F. Gostling
Mrs. J.R. Gough
G.B. Graham
His Hon. Judge G.J. Graham
David Granger
B.T. Gray
Mrs. J.M. Greenwell
Robin E. Greenwood
Mrs. Pamela Greenwood
Mrs. V.J.H. Grieve
G.S. Griffiths
Mrs. G. Grimshaw
Miss J.A. Groom
John D. Grossart
Freda Grounds
A.D. Gunner
P.L. Guy MH

Mrs. P.R. Hadfield
Mrs. B. Halford
A.D.A.S. Hall
Mrs. A.B. Hall
Wing/Co. N.G. Halliday
J.A.L. Hamilton
The Hon. Mrs. E.A. Hamilton

R.M. Hannam
J.I. Hardwick
G.M. Hardy
Lady Hardy-Roberts
M.B. Harman
Capt. J.W.F. Harriman
Edwin Harrison
Dr. Nicholas Hart
D. Harverson OBE
Christine Harvey
T.D. Harvey
Mrs. P.C.E. Haswell
Joseph Hawes
C.H. Hay
Major Charles Hay
Derek Hayes
I.S. Haynes MFH
Mrs. A.M. Hayward
John Heald
John E. Heath
David Hebb
John Hefford
Mrs. A.M. Hesketh
Dr. R. Hewlett
E.C. Hicks
David C. Hicks
C.J. Highton
Miss Sophie Hill
J.R. Hinchliffe
C.F. Hingston
Mrs. S.G. Hoare
Captain E.M.B. Hoare RN (ret'd)
J.A. Hock
T. Hodson
J.S. Hollins-Gibson
K.M. Holmes
Rupert Mansfield Holmes
Mrs. M. Holt

Mr. & Mrs. R.W.J. Hopkins
G.W. Hopkinson
H.L. Hoppe
Capt. M.A. Houghton
D.C.A. Howden
Mrs. H. Howe
Miss Wendy Howes
John Vivian Hughes
P.B. Hunter
James Hunter Blair
T.F. Hutchinson
Mrs. B.L. Huttenbach
Maj. I.F. Hyne

A.F. Iliffe
Nigel Ince
Mrs. A.W. Ingham
G.W. Iredell
Miss Margery Isemonger

Mrs. J.M. Jachim
Mrs. C. Jacoby
Geoffrey W. Jarman
D.C. Jarrett
D.M. Jarvis
David Jeffcoat
Mrs. P.A. Jerram
D.E. Johnston
H. Thomson Jones

Mrs. E.C.W. Kaye
Michael Leo Keane
Dr. A.J.I. Kelynack
F.C. Kent
Derek R.E. Kent
David Kenward
Dr. D.F. Kerr
Mrs. Timothy King
Peter B. King

E.S. King
J.B. Kirkaldy
Dr. Mary Ellen Kitler
Col. J.D. Kitson
Mrs. Laraine M. Knowles
Martin Kochanski

L.P.F. L'Estrange OBE
Miss Helena Lacey
Mrs. Christine Lambert
Arvin Law
J.R. Lawder
Mrs. Mary G. Lawton
Clare Le Vay
Mrs. J. Leach
M.S. Ledger MOH
Guy Liddle
George Linfoot
C.S. Lippell
Robin J. Lipscombe
Sir Gilbert Longden
Roger Losa
H.C. Lowcock
P.M. Luttman-Johnson
Peter Lynn

His Hon. Judge G. Macdonald
A.M. Macewan
Lt. Col. C.H.T. Macfetridge
A.J. Mack
The Rev. Hugh Mackay
J.H.M. Mackenzie
Capt. M.J. Mackinlay Macleod

J.G.H. Mackrell
I.F. Maclean
K.M. Macleod DSC
J.J. Macnamara
Stephen Mahony
R.D. Mann
C.D. Mann
Mrs. Ann Mansel
Miss M.H. Markham
William G. Martin
Dr. D. Martyn-Johns
Peter I. Maslen
R.J. Mason & P.J. Mason B.Ed. (Hon.)
S.C.W. Mason
Spencer G. Maurice
John McCaig
W. McCloughan
Peter O. McDougall
Dr. Ewen McEwen
B.T. McGeough
D.J. McGlynn
Mrs. Sheila McKinley
M.A. Meacham
W.J.B. Meakin
C.J. Mears
J.H. Mendoza
A.P. Millen
C.H. Millin
A.L.W. Minns
A.J. Minter
Kenneth A. Moore
Peter Moore
Mrs. J.D. Moore
G.E. Morris
G.G. Mosley
D.R. Mourton
Miss Anne Muir
Mrs. A.M. Mumford

Mrs. S.J. Nash
Mrs. P.M. Neighbour
D.E.A. Neville
Basil Newall
C.S.W. Newbury
Mrs. M. Newcomb
D. Newell
Brian Newton
M.T. Nicholson
J.D. Nicol
M.G. Norcock

Edward O'Doherty
Roseanne O'Reilly
Neville Oates
Michael W. Osborn
Mrs. M.E. Osborn
Mrs. V. Oswald
C.D. Outred
Mrs. G.J. Owen

Mrs. S. Paine
G.H. Paris
E.B. Park
H.M. Parker
Mrs. P.H. Parker
Mrs. C.H. Parlby
M.L. Patterson
R.J.G. Payne
Jonathan R.H. Pearson
R.S.L. Penn
Mrs. Daphne Perrett
D.J. Peters JP MA
H.M. Peters
Mrs. V.M. Pettifer
Miss R.T. Phelps
Dr. A.J.B. Phillips MB BS
J.A. Pickston
David S. Pinney
Dr. B.G. Pirie

C.M. Plumbe
Dr. Vincent Powell-
  Smith
R.J. Pratt
Dr. H. Preston-
  Thomas
A.T. Prince
R.F.D. Pritchard
Anthony Pye

Dr. T.J. Quaite

D.K.L. Rae
Brig. E. Rait-Kerr
Miss K. Randall
J.H. Ratcliff
Major J.C. Ratcliffe
Miss Eirwen Read
P.F. Rednall
M.M. Reeve
J.G. Reid
Trevor Richards
Andrew W.G.
  Rickett
Michael Riviere
Mrs. J. Roberts
A.W. Robinson
T.J. Roberts
Mrs. Dorothy
  Pomeroy Robinson
B.E. Robinson
Mrs. Laurence Rook
J.M. Rose
D.R. Rosevear
John Rowley
Maurice Russell MC
J.F. Rutherford
Mrs. Neil Rutherford

Robert Sawers
Philipp Schoeller
J.C. Sedgwick

S.M. Selka
J.A. Seymour-Jones
  FRCS
M.M. Shannon
M.E. Sharp
Mrs. R. Shaw
Frank Sheardown
M.F. Sheardown
John Shearman
A.J. Shears
Lt. Col. F.W.L.
  Shepard
Mrs. F.R. Short
E.G. Silvester
C.A.G. Simkins
Mr. & Mrs. A.C.
  Simmons
D.L. Sinnott
Norman P. Skerrett
Douglas A. Sloan
  MFH
J. Smallwood
F.J.R. Smith
John L.E. Smith
N.L.H. Smith
Mrs. P.A. Smith
Mrs. Maureen Smyth
M.F. Somerville
I.P.G. Southward
Sir John Sparrow
Mrs. A.M. Speakman
Major B.L. Speegle
Simon Stacey
Mrs. M.D. Stacy-
  Marks
Miss Lesley Stark
E.W. Stearn
Mrs. S.R. Stebbing
David Steeds
B.G. Steff
Brigadier J.W.
  Stephens

Charles Walter
  Stewart
J.S.R. Storer
Mrs. J.R. Strange
J.H. Stratton
Mrs. T.J. Stubbs
P.A. Surtees
Mrs. D. Sutherland
Dr. R.N.P. Sutton
S.J. Swabey
Susan Swantek
M.C. Swift
Lt. Col. G. Symonds
A. Symonds

G. Thompson
Ray Thompson
Miss D.G. Thomson
David Thorpe
Eric A. Tidy
E.H. Tindall
Major J.V. Titley
  RAMC
Bruce Todd
Maj. Gen. D.A.H.
  Toler
H.W. Townsend
J.J. Trapp
Mrs. P.M. Trei
A.F. Tremeer
Mrs. Jennifer M.
  Trippier
Mrs. J. Tritton
R.M. Trounson
J.G.L. Trump
F.M. Turner
Mrs. R.L. Turner
Mrs. J.M. Turner
William J. Twibill

R.J. Unwin

D.B. Vale
William Von Raab

Michael Wace
T. Wainwright
Harry Wakelin
Mrs. F.J. Wakem
J.H. Walker
Major M.P. Walker
Colonel V.G. Wallace
H.B. Waller
A.T. Warwick CEng MIEE
H.A. Waterson
David W. Wates MFH
P.A.C. Wauchope

Mrs. H.D. Webb
W.R.B. Webb
Martin Webster
Mrs. W.B. Van N. Wedd
Miss Josephine K.M.A. Welch
B. Welton
B.C. Whitaker
Noel Whitcomb
Edmund H. White
Ralph White
A.P. Whitehead
Mrs. B. Wickham
J.G.S. Wilkinson
Dorian Williams
John Williams
C.N. Wilmot-Smith

Steven N. Wilshire
Miss Ann E. Wilson
John Winch
K.R. Wing
Harry Wolton QC
Douglas J. Wood
Mrs. Michael Woodhead
J.G. Woodrow
J.H.G. Woollcombe
Mrs. G.A. Worsley
W.D. Wright
C.P. Wykeham-Martin
Rhydain Wynn-Williams
A.G. Yates
Ian Yeaman

OTHER PUBLICATIONS OF
THE R.S. SURTEES SOCIETY

SOME EXPERIENCES
and
FURTHER EXPERIENCES OF AN IRISH R.M.

by E. Œ. Somerville and Martin Ross

Some Experiences and *Further Experiences* each contain twelve episodes in which Major Sinclair Yeates recounts, with sober dignity, humour and tolerance, his social, sporting and professional discomfitures as a Resident Magistrate in South-West Ireland at the turn of the century. The rhetoric and deceit of the natives provide the wit and drama. Circumstances make Major Yeates a connoisseur of whole-hearted insincerity.

The R.S. Surtees Society's editions of *Some Experiences* and *Further Experiences* are as nearly as practicable facsimiles of the first editions, of 1899 and 1908 respectively. They include the black and white illustrations by **Miss Somerville** from the first editions (30 in *Some Experiences* and 35 in *Further Experiences*).

Price **£7.95,** in each case, packing and postage included.

SET OF THREE

The price for a set of all three Irish R.M. novels—*Some Experiences, Further Experiences* and *In Mr Knox's Country*—is **£21.**

Instructions for ordering are on page 323.

R.S. SURTEES

Mr. Sponge's Sporting Tour. Facsimile of 1853 edition. 13 full-page coloured plates and 90 engravings by **John Leech.** Introduction by **Auberon Waugh.**

Mr. Facey Romford's Hounds, 24 coloured plates by **Leech** and **"Phiz".** 50 engravings. Introduction by **Enoch Powell.**

"Ask Mamma". Facsimile of 1858 edition. 13 coloured plates and 70 engravings by **Leech.** Introduction by **Rebecca West.**

Handley Cross; or, Mr. Jorrocks' Hunt. Facsimile of 1854 edition. 17 coloured plates and 100 engravings by **Leech.** Introduction by **Raymond Carr.**

Jorrocks' Jaunts and Jollities. Facsimile of 1874 edition. 31 coloured plates by **Henry Alken, "Phiz"** and **W. Heath.** Introduction by **Michael Wharton** ("Peter Simple").

Hillingdon Hall, or **The Cockney Squire.** Facsimile of 1888 edition. 13 coloured plates by **Wildrake, W. Heath** and **Jellicoe.** Introduction by **Robert Blake.**

Price £14.95 in each case, including packing and postage. Separate sets of coloured plates are £5 in each case, including packing and postage.

The Horseman's Manual: being a treatise on Soundness, the Law of Warranty and generally on the Laws relating to Horses. Surtees' first book, published in 1831. Hugh Davidson has published a numbered facsimile edition of 600 copies, of which 98 remain. **Price £10.50,** packing and postage included.

Further R.S. Surtees novels. After *Plain or Ringlets?*, to be available at the end of March 1986, (see advertisement at the beginning of this book), it is the intention of the Society to publish **Hawbuck Grange.** With its republication the Society will have republished all eight of R.S. Surtees' completed novels.

CAPTAIN GRONOW

Gronow's *"Anecdotes of the Camp, the Court and the Clubs at the Close of the Last War with France"* and *"Recollections and Anecdotes"* are combined in a single volume (The Reminiscences of Captain Gronow).

The Society's edition is based on the limited edition of 1889 and contains 17 full-page colour plates, including Joseph Grego's remarkable aquatints of etchings from original and contemporary sources. Sets of these plates are available separately.

Price **£14.95,** packing and postage included.

For the second volume of Gronow see the advertisement at the beginning of this book.

Ordering

Send your order to **the Hon. Mrs. Robert Pomeroy, R.S. Surtees Society, Rockfield House, Nunney, nr. Frome, Somerset.** Please show your requirement, name and address clearly. Your order should be accompanied by a cheque for the appropriate amount, made payable to the R.S. Surtees Society. If you are ordering more than one item, it would be helpful if you would include a note showing how the sum on your cheque is made up.

J. A. ALLEN & CO. (THE HORSEMAN'S BOOKSHOP) LTD.

1 LOWER GROSVENOR PLACE, LONDON, SW1

(Adjacent to Royal Mews, Buckingham Palace).

**For Over Half a Century we have
Specialised in Books Old & Modern
On Hunting and all Equine and
Equestrian Sports**

Catalogues Issued

Telephone 834/5606 (3 lines)